The Saga of the Brothers Mountain

Michael W. Mountain

ISBN: 978-0-6159-5390-8 (sc)
ISBN: 978-1-4834-1309-9 (e)

Edited by: Julie Barrett

Front and back cover artwork: LaVonne Mountain

Lulu Publishing Services rev. date: 5/23/2014

CONTENTS

DEDICATION

I AM DEDICATING MY BOOK, *THE Saga of the Brothers Mountain*, to all the Mountain family members who had the courage to leave the tyranny of Ireland under British rule for the freedom and opportunities in America. Their perils were many, but they overcame the insurmountable odds and survived. Without their initiatives we would not be here today.

In addition, to my parents Rose and William John Mountain and my grandfather William Louis Mountain.

Introduction

Brief History of County Cork Ireland and the of Barron of Imokilly 1700-1850

In approximately 1695, a series of penal laws were passed by the Irish Parliament (members were Protestants only), for the express purpose of to trying to rid all of Ireland of Catholicism by forcing Catholics to convert to Protestantism. The laws banned Catholics from the following: owning a gun, being a professional (except medical), being involved in politics, owning land, attaining an education (except for that in the Protestant faith), and owning a horse over a value of five pounds.

The laws were so harsh that many the Irish folk converted to Protestantism, as it was the only way to escape the penalties that were incurred by those who broke the penal laws. In 1728 more laws were passed, which included a ban on Catholics from voting. A law was also introduced that held that if a man would convert to Protestantism he would be given his Catholic father's estate, even before that father's death. This obviously produced many hostile feelings and feuds within Irish families.

Catholics were not by themselves the only group to be discriminated against. In 1704, a law was passed which banned Presbyterians from being on town councils and holding other official political positions. Presbyterian ministers were even banned from conducting wedding ceremonies.

Most Irish landlords were Protestants, simply because the laws forbade Catholics from owning land. The Irish peasants themselves, who were both Protestant and Catholic, ate potatoes almost exclusively, since the land was scarce and potatoes were an intensive crop.

Many thousands of Irish decided to cut their losses and set sail on immigration ships to the Americas. This is the origin of about half of what are now referred to as Irish Americans. Hundreds of Irish died on the ships, which were so overcrowded that they became known as "the coffin ships." By 1851 the population of Ireland had fallen 25% to 6 million and the emigration continued till around 1900, by which time only 4,500,000 Irishmen remained in Ireland.

The Barron Imokilly (Irish: Ui Mhic Coille) is located in southern Ireland in the County of Cork. Imokilly is one of the baronies of Ireland and a historical geographical unit of land. Its chief town is Youghal. It is one of 24 baronies in the County of Cork with the township of Killeagh being one of them. Baronies were created for administrative purposes after the Norman invasion as subdivisions of counties. While they have been administratively obsolete since 1898, they continue to be used in land registrations and for specific occasions, such as in planning permissions.

The barony in Imokilly is pretty compact in form and consists of two limestone vales separated by a range of brownstone hills with a corresponding range being placed between the southern valley and the ocean. The direction both of high and low land is from the East to the West.

The family surname of Mountain from Southwest County Cork Ireland appears to have been descended from a branch of the McCarthy family. The McCarthy family adopted the nickname of "Mountain" to distinguish themselves from the many branches of McCarthy families in that area. During these times, there were "The Mountain McCarthys," "The River McCarthys," and "The Hill McCarthys." To make the differential easier, the name McCarthy was eliminated, thus the surnames of Mountain, River, and Hill were established.

My fictionalized tale of the Mountain family begins in the Barron of Imokilly, in the surrounding area of the Township of Killeagh, in County Cork Ireland. The story continues as the family, like many other Irish families before them, travels to America to find religious and personal freedom.

CHAPTER I

Mountain Family of Killeagh Ireland

ON DECEMBER 30, 1818, IN THE Barron of Imokilly, outside the Township of Killeagh, in County Cork Ireland, a woman named Mary Mountain went into hard labor with her third son. Mary's mother-in-law Margaret, a trained midwife, was called to help deliver the child. Margaret was well-versed in the perils of childbirth, having assisted in many births over the years.

Margaret determined immediately that Mary was in trouble. The baby was turned, so instead of coming out head first, he was set to try and come out feet or butt first, commonly called breech. Mary moaned in pain and was sweating profusely in their cold and damp little mud hut. Margaret felt they must leave Mary alone for the time being to allow the child to try and turn naturally. If the child did not turn soon, Margaret would attempt to turn the baby by gently rubbing Mary's abdomen until he turned. In any case it was going to be very painful and very risky for both mother and child.

Mary lay in quiet agony for over two days. She would not scream as Margaret had encouraged her to do, as she was determined not to show her family the extreme pain she was in or her fear. On January 1, 1819, William Mountain entered the world kicking and fighting, just as his mother was figuratively doing facing death. William had turned in the womb with the help of his grandmother Margaret, but the internal damage to Mary was done. Margaret carried little William to the living room where his father James and grandfather Edmund were waiting.

Margaret handed William to his grandfather and told her son to go and comfort his wife. As he passed by, she grabbed James's arm.

"Mary is bleeding to death and I can't stop it," she told him. "It will be a blessing if she goes soon, to rid her of her pain. Your Mary saw her little William and was so happy he did not die. She told me she gladly would give up her life so her little one would survive."

James went to Mary's bed and held her hand and stroked her forehead. She was burning up, but had a smile on her face.

"Isn't he beautiful?" She asked.

James agreed, although he didn't think the baby was very beautiful. Actually, he was a mess, covered in blood and afterbirth.

"I want to be buried here on this land, close to our tree," Mary instructed James. "Please don't fret for me any longer. I'm going to see my Lord soon and I know he loves me—he let my baby live! Please, fetch the boys so I can say goodbye. I know I don't have much time. And James, I love you more than life itself, always remember that. You take care of our children and make sure they grow up to be strong, honest men. Now go."

The other children, Patrick and Sean Christian (or "S.C."), ran in and hugged their mother, as she cried and slowly slipped into a deep coma. Her breathing became labored and then became very quiet as she passed away surrounded by her family.

James, laden with grief, found a suitable plot for his wife's remains in a far corner of their 15 acres of leased land, close to the only tree on their land. It was a sad day for the entire Mountain clan. All of James and Mary's relatives attended the small outdoor service. Catholics at the time were forbidden to attend a church or confer with a priest or minister because of the harsh penal laws that existed in all of Ireland. That left James and his brother-in-law Patrick to officiate at the funeral. Mary was only 24 years old at the time of her death. She and James had only been 16 years old when they were married, which was common at that time in rural Ireland.

It was a rainy, cold day in January with a strong westerly wind that blew at 20 miles per hour, making the temperature feel like it was below freezing. The ground was near frozen and the men of the

Mountain clan had to dig somewhat of a shallower grave than normal, because of the hardness of the dirt. The digging was difficult on that cold and rainy day, but the men were used to hard labor and the very poor conditions. It would have been better to have Mary buried in a cemetery in the town of Killeagh, however the weather conditions were not conducive for the four and half mile trek into the town, and there was not a Catholic Church, nor a Catholic priest, to officiate at the burial. The only cemetery was designated for Protestants. Catholics and Presbyterians were not welcome to bury their dead there.

Patrick would be the first to speak. He was very emotional about Mary's sudden and unexpected death, since she was not only his sister but also his twin. Patrick, who could not read or write, recited what he had prepared from memory.

"What a fine, young, beautiful woman my sister was. She was a wonderful mother and a faithful wife. She was courageous, and was fearless in the face of her death. She faced her untimely death as a woman of the Catholic faith, knowing that God would take care of her and knowing she was going to a better place."

James was next to speak, but had not prepared himself as Patrick had done. James could feel the tears building up and he choked up several times before he could speak.

"Ireland is a horrible place to live and a horrible place to raise a family," he stammered. "Mary's death is a fine example of the squalor that we live in. If Mary would only have had some professional medical care during her ordeal, she might be alive today. My children have lost the most important thing in their short lives, the love of a mother. My beautiful wife is gone and the only thing I have left is this godforsaken land that offers so little for my family. Please, dear Lord, take my Mary into your kingdom and watch over my three sons as they will need your guidance and direction. Amen."

Since the Barony of Imokilly lacked any significant stand of trees, lumber for coffins was at a very high premium. Mary's coffin was made out of old timber that was donated to the family by some of the neighbors and friends. It was constructed by the hands of Mary's brother Patrick, who six months previously was forced to bury their parents without coffins because of the lack of timber. Their parents had apparently died of some type of pneumonia or black lung disease, but no one would ever know the exact cause of their deaths since there was no attending physician. Their deaths were a very sad event for members of their community, but their daughter Mary's sudden death stoked the reality that a person's life in Ireland was undoubtedly very short.

James, along with his brothers William and Michael and his brother-in-law Patrick attended to lowering the casket into the gravesite. After everyone in attendance had said their goodbyes and their short prayers, the four of them filled in the grave.

After the burial, members of the family and neighbors sloshed through the cold and wet mud to congregate at the Mountains' sod and mud hut. The hut consisted of two small bedrooms in the back part of the hut and a living room/dining room with a little kitchen attached. The roof was a thatched one that kept out the rain but not the cold. There was a small brick oven that heated the entire home poorly and was also used for cooking the family meals. There were no windows, just a wooden front door that was provided to the young couple by James's father Edmund. There was a small corral that housed the few animals the family could afford, and behind the corral, away from the water supply and hut, was the privy or outhouse.

Home-brewed cider was served to the adults, but nothing else. Food was not served to anyone because there was barely enough food left in the house to feed the young Mountain family. The cider was enough to warm the adults' bodies and bring a glow to their personalities.

The men and women talked about Mary's beauty and striking figure. Her hair was long and curly and was the color the darkest black earth. She had dark brown eyes and her nose and cheeks were covered with light brown freckles. She was thin, but not frail, and was the envy of all the women in the area because of her natural beauty. The women commented about her commitment to her family, as well as the community. She was always available to help out her neighbors in their time of need and was always more than willing to attend social gatherings at the different homes for the (albeit unauthorized) prayer services.

The little Mountain children did not understand all the commotion that was taking place in their little hut. The boys did not understand why their mother was not with them. They rarely had any company except grandparents and never had they seen any of their extended family or neighbors imbibing in alcohol. Although alcohol was a demon for many of the Irish people, in this area of Ireland, where there was little money for food and poverty was rampant, alcohol was normally an afterthought.

As darkness fell around five o'clock in the afternoon, the last of the neighbors left as well as the remainder of the close relatives. James's mother Margaret, his father Edmund and his unmarried sister Elizabeth (Libby) Mountain remained behind. The conversation quickly changed to the well-being of the children. Libby told James that she would be willing and able to help out with the children on a daily basis. She would continue to live with her mother and father across the road, but would come to his hut every day to look after the children and work on their education. In addition, Libby said her friend Teresa, who had lost her baby to consumption a few days before, would be asked if she would volunteer to be a wet nurse for baby William. All agreed that the children would be well taken care of.

James, however, still being in shock over the death of his wife, said something very disturbing to his mother, father and sister.

"Please take that damn baby with you and raise him. I don't want him around. All he will ever be to me is a reminder of his mother's death and that he was the cause of it."

James's mother was stunned to hear such a proclamation from her son.

"We will not and cannot take care of an infant!" Margaret said angrily. "He is your responsibility and you will honor your wife's memory and love and take care of that baby."

Edmund also spoke. "I realize the sorrow you must feel, but that little boy in there had nothing to do with Mary's passing. It was God's will and please respect that. Do what I trained you to do all your life, be a man and take care of all your responsibilities, including little William here. Do I make myself clear?"

James reluctantly agreed with his mother and father, but for the life of him, he could not see how he could ever love that child.

Margaret and Edmund lived just across the dirt road from James. In addition, his brother William and his wife Sarah also lived with his parents and helped farm the 30 acres of leased land with his father. James's Brother Michael and his wife Ellen also farmed 15 acres of leased land just adjacent to the parents.

The Mountain clan leased all of their land from the same individual, a wealthy English Lord by the name of Charles Webb. Lord Webb possessed large tracts of land throughout County Cork, particularly in the surrounding area of Killeagh Township. The Mountain clan leased their land for one life, or 21 years, or for whichever would last the longest. The cost of the yearly lease was two pounds per acre, and most of leases in the area were for 15 acres, at a cost of thirty pounds per year.

The land that was leased was originally raw land that had to be cleared of rocks and tree stumps by hand, with very primitive tools. The farm came with no livestock, no seed, no grain, no house, nor any enclosures for livestock. All the Mountain clan got for their 30 pounds per year was a raw track of underdeveloped land, whereby they might be able to make a meager living.

The farmer in England, however, was provided with stock and implements and entered a farm already in a high state of order, requiring no preparatory expenditures. He was also provided a house, with enclosures for his livestock and a furnished shop including tools and anything else that he might need for the betterment of the property. In other words, an Englishman leasing land in England has all the tools necessary to achieve his goals, pay for the lease, and provide a comfortable lifestyle for him and his family.

Lord Charles Webb (the leaseholder) was a 30-year-old tyrant of a man. The entire community feared him because of his ruthlessness. Webb inherited his land from his family, and his family received the land in a settlement with Englishman General Oliver Cromwell in approximately 1650. The land that Cromwell gave to the Webb family was for services rendered during the Irish Civil War and had previously been owned by the Mountain family and several other local families for nearly two hundred years.

Cromwell was a fundamentalist Protestant and an extremely cruel man. After coming from Dublin in 1649 with 12,000 heavily armed men, he killed over 3000 Irishmen along the way to the South. He marched on Wexford town and massacred several hundred people there, and the surrounding towns of Cork, Banden, Kinsdale and Youghal. When he left Ireland in 1650 he had dealt a severe blow to the uprising of the Irish.

The problem of concern to Cromwell after the Civil War was that most of the soldiers in the army still needed to be paid for their time served, but the English Parliament had no money to give them. Cromwell decided to pay them in land. He forcibly moved thousands of Irish from their homes in Munster and Leinster and resettled them in counties Clare, Galway, Mayo and Roscommon. In 1652 the newly cleared land in Münster and Leinster was given to Protestants in what was called the "Cromwellian Settlement." There was now no part of Ireland where Catholics owned more than half of the land. He claimed to be acting on God's behalf and expelled about 1000 Catholic priests from Ireland. From 1653 to 1658 General Oliver Cromwell ruled Ireland. In 1660, Cromwell died and the people of Ireland rejoiced.

Lord Webb insisted on a partial one quarter of a percent payment at mid-year (June 30th) and full payment by the year's end (December 31st) every year, regardless of the outcome of crop production. If one of his tenants did not have the proper payments on either date, they would be immediately evicted from the property. The Mountain family lived in fear of not having a sufficient potato crop at midyear, and a complete crop of wheat, corn and potatoes by years-end to pay the 30 pounds in rent that was due. The families had toiled for many unproductive years on their properties and the fear of losing it because of one poor crop was a constant reminder how fragile their situation truly was.

After hearing of Mary Mountain's passing, Lord Webb, accompanied by several hired hands, rode their horses directly to the Mountain farm and informed James that nothing had changed and he was still required to pay 7 1/2 pounds due on June 30th. If he did not, he and his children would be forced to leave the homestead.

"There will be no exceptions or excuses to our contract and if it is not fulfilled to the letter, I will exercise my authority and evict all of you shanty Irish. I have several Protestant families lined up that would gladly take up this tract of land and pay me in a timely manner," threatened Lord Webb.

After having relayed his message to James, Lord Webb crossed the road to pay a visit to Edmund.

"I will tell you the same thing that I just told your son James. If you or any of your family members choose not to pay 25% of your lease on June 30th you all will be evicted from my land. There will be no exceptions and no excuses," said Webb. "Do you understand?"

Edmund said that he understood, and there would be no problems paying the first half-year's lease. Webb left with the smile on his face.

"I've explained the conditions of the lease to you and if you and your families don't comply, you know what the consequences will be. My overseer Dante Wright will be here on June 30th to collect all the monies that are owed, so be prepared," warned Webb.

When James and Mary married in 1811, Mary's family provided James with a small dowry, which was common for the time. Although her family was far from rich, they had prepared for her marriage many years before and took great pride in having enough of a dowry to help sustain the couple for their first few years. Like many poor Irish farmers, hoarding of gold and silver was common. The Irish traded in English currency and English coins for necessities, such as rent and fuel, but hoarded things with more of an intrinsic value.

The entire Mountain clan hid gold and silver coins on their homesteads, as did all the successful farmers in the area. These people were not wealthy, but frugal and they saved their precious coins for the days in the future where their hoard may well save their farms, or their lives. Mary's dowry provided the couple with a bit of security during lean years on the farm.

After Mary's death, James and the rest of the family mourned the loss for years. James was a red-haired, handsome young man, who turned the heads of all the single ladies as he passed by. But James had no inclination to re-marry, although there were several single women that were eager to take on his ready-made family. He would remain single for the rest of his life and tend to his young family by himself. James was a distraught and depressed man who spent most of his time alone working in his fields. He paid little attention to William and showered most of his attention on sons Patrick and S.C.

The days turned to months and the months into years as little William grew steadily to become a inquisitive young boy. His aunt Libby was there every day to take care of the boys and to instruct them on their reading and writing skills. Catholics were forbidden to attend school, therefore home schooling was a necessity to educate Catholic children.

Late one afternoon, James went to visit his father and mother across the road. He told his father he had enough silver left from Mary's dowry to take care of any of his financial issues that might arise. He thought that the wheat and corn crops were not great, but would suffice, and thought the potato crop was sufficient to pay off that bastard Webb without having to use any of his hoards. Edmund showed James the gold and silver coins he had concealed in the walls of their hut. The coins were to be used for family emergencies and nothing else. Since James was the oldest son, Edmund had willed all they had to him, but expected him to also take care of his sister and brothers, if need be.

On June 30th at 12 o'clock, Dante Wright appeared at the front door of the Mountain sod hut and was asking for the 7 1/2 pounds that was due Lord Webb. Wright was an ugly, fat man with a pocked face and a very surly disposition. He had worked for Lord Webb for the past five years and enjoyed the confrontations that he usually had with tenants. He liked nothing more than to be able to evict people from their properties and to get into physical confrontations with them in the process. He always traveled with four companions that were heavily armed, and that garnered great delight in being able to use the weapons they carried. Wright was mightily surprised when James immediately handed him the 7 1/2 pounds paper money for the rent that was due. Wright informed James that Lord Webb had told him that the likelihood of payment would be remote, and to prepare his men for an eviction.

James replied, "You go back and kindly tell Lord Webb, that the Mountain clan have always paid their debts on time and will continue to do so."

James detested Dante Wright and his men more than he detested Lord Webb. He knew that Webb would try everything in his power to evict the Mountain clan from their properties. But James was fearful of Dante Wright. He had heard rumors about some of the atrocities that Wright and his men had performed on other Irish men and women that were being evicted from their properties. Not only had they maimed and killed men during his tenure as a henchman for Lord Webb, he had also taken great delight in killing the women after raping and torturing them. James knew that Wright and his men could not be reasoned with and any confrontation with them would more than likely end in death.

Wright and his men rode their horses to Edmund's farm across the road. Edmund promptly opened the door as they approached. In his hands he had the required lease payment. He hid his contempt for all of them and put a smile on his face as he thanked them for stopping by. Wright told Edmund the same story that he had told James. That Lord Webb was sure the Mountain clan would be unable to make their half-year payment. But since they did, they could remain on the property. Wright and his men continued down the road to Edmund's other son Michael Mountain's farm, where he was met with the same warm reception and the amount of the lease was promptly paid. Thankfully, this would be the last time the Mountain families would hear from Dante Wright and his thugs, or from Lord Webb, for the rest of the year.

CHAPTER 2

William Mountain

THE MOUNTAIN BOYS CONTINUED TO GROW big and strong. They were very helpful around the little farm as they hauled water, dug potatoes, weeded the fields and tended to the livestock. The livestock consisted of two horses, one named Ned and the other named Ed. They also had two sheep and a cow. The horses were needed to help plow the fields and for their excrement, as it was used as fertilizer which was in great demand in that area. The sheep and cow also provided much needed fertilizer for the farm. Most farms lacked ample fertilizer for the crops, and used sandstone, seaweed and ocean sand as a replacement for manure. Crop rotation was not common in this area, for most of the farmers were not educated in that line of agriculture. The ones that did understand crop rotation, such as the Mountain clan, survived and were able to scratch out a meager living on their farms. The rest failed miserably in a few short years and were evicted from their farms.

William's younger cousin Mark lived across the road, and the two were inseparable, spending every moment they could together. William also enjoyed Mark's family and got along very well with his parents, William and Sarah. He was invited for dinner whenever he paid a visit to their home and also was invited to stay overnight, whenever it got too late for him to trudge home. William realized long ago that his father was not fond of him, and he did everything in his power to avoid confrontations with him, unless it could just not be avoided. Whenever his father wanted something that seemed unreasonable to him, he wouldn't do it, knowing full well a beating would be coming. He never cried or showed any emotion during his routine beatings, but he bore the scars mentally, where no one could see them. His brothers could not for the life of them understand his defiance and worked hard to please their father. James was not a poor father, he just had no patience with William and the thought of his Mary dying because of this child was more than he could bear. He wanted to love him as he did his other sons, but he couldn't get Mary's death out of his mind.

One morning, ten-year old William took his father's flintlock rifle out of its hiding place under his father's bed. He had watched his father load the gun many times, and being a bright young boy, he knew exactly how to load it himself. After loading the gun, he went outside to shoot a rabbit that was standing by the small corral that housed the family horses. The thought of rabbit for dinner was more than he could resist and since he had seen his father kill rabbits occasionally in the yard, he thought his father would be proud of his ingenuity. William took aim while his brothers watched in amazement as their little ten-year-old brother pulled the trigger.

The recoil set him directly on his ass, and the shot hit one of the horses a ricocheting blow in the hindquarters from off the fence post. The horse went berserk and the boys scrambled for cover. James heard the shot and came running from a remote part of the homestead. It took him several minutes to arrive at the sod home. He found the horse still bucking around, but was calming down a bit. He knew right away that the boys had been up to no good. He went into the corral and assessed the damage to his horse. Since it was a ricocheting blow, the damage was at a minimum. The horse named Ned was stunned, but not harmed a great deal.

James immediately confronted the boys. It took no prodding to get William to own up to what he had done. James knew his son's personality well, as he possessed a major stubborn and defiant side. He would never lie and always told the truth regardless of the consequences. The consequences in this case would be more severe than usual, since this almost cost the family a valuable tool in maintaining their farm. James told William he would get the strap, which was an unusual punishment, even for William. The strap was a leather belt that was used to sharpen blades, such as a straight edge blade used in shaving.

William didn't flinch when his father said he'd have S.C. go into the house and fetch the strap. The strap was housed in the empty washbowl beside his father's bed. He stood straight up and stared into his father's eyes.

"I'm sorry for what I did, Pa, and I won't do it again."

S.C. reluctantly handed the strap to his father. "Please Pa, leave him be, he meant no harm. He is just hungry like the rest of us, and the thought of not having that rabbit for dinner was more than he could bear."

James ignored his son.

"This little son-of-bitch has to learn a lesson from this, and I cannot and will not tolerate this type of behavior from my children."

William got three lashes that day from James and the strap. It hurt his pride more than it hurt his ass. He would not cry and he would not shout out, no matter how much it hurt. His brothers couldn't believe his strength and determination. They were in awe of their little brother. James was not. James had mixed emotions regarding William. He was proud of the way William handled his punishment, but hated his defiance and his confident demeanor.

It was too bad that he missed that damn rabbit; it would have been a pleasant surprise to have a rabbit to go along with their evening meal of potatoes.

CHAPTER 3

The Hunter

FOR WILLIAM'S FOURTEENTH BIRTHDAY, HIS GRANDFATHER Edmund gave him a ten-inch long knife and a sheath to carry it in. Edmund explained, "All men must carry a knife as a tool while working on a farm." But William had better plans for his new weapon. He was determined to use the knife as a tool for hunting, as well as for protection - just in case he needed protection. He began throwing the knife relentlessly at posts in the yard, at the only tree on the property, and the walls of the outhouse, as well as at every wild animal that was careless enough to walk across his path. Working on his accuracy led him to forget to do his chores, which led to more beatings from his father, and his father threatened to take the knife away. William didn't mind the beatings, but losing that knife would be more than he could handle. He knew his father was serious and he would be happy to see him suffer a bit, so his chores came first and foremost. He continued to hone his skills with the knife and he began to amaze his brothers and his cousin Mark with his throwing accuracy.

William began to carry the knife in its sheath strapped to his back and a bit lower than the nape of his neck. It was attached with rawhide he found on a fence post down the road toward Killeagh. The rawhide was long enough to use as a strap to go around his armpits and under his shirt to hold the sheath in place. He could just reach behind his head and grasp the knife handle and pull it out in less than a second. He then began to practice grasping the knife and throwing it in one motion. He became so efficient with that knife that all the boys tried to imitate him, but to no avail.

After two years of practice throwing the knife with either hand, the sixteen-year-old William was able kill his first rabbit. The throw hit the rabbit in the neck and it died instantly. William was so happy with meat for dinner. Although James was happy to have rabbit for dinner, he could not bring himself to praise the boy. He just sat down, said nothing, and ate the rabbit. William could hit any animal within 10 to 20 yards of him. Birds such as grouse, quail, and pheasants were no challenge to him. He just needed to get close enough to throw the knife. Squirrels were also fair game, but he enjoyed the taste of rabbit a bit more. Squirrels he gave to his grandparents and aunts and uncles.

When William reached the age of twenty, he began regularly to supply some of the relatives with fresh wild game. His chores around the farm became less and less important, as the extended Mountain family began to depend on him to provide them with an occasional rabbit or squirrel dinner. His father was happy that he was gone most days with his hunting, as it provided less time for James to be irritated with him.

William took his younger cousin Mark along on many of his daily hunts. They would roam far away from the homesteads in search of wild game. The many years of aggressive hunting by William had depleted the supply of rabbits, squirrels, and birds around his homestead. Most often they would reach the foothills or the mountains where the Killeagh farmland ended. They knew better than to kill game on any of the farmers land. But the unattended land by the foothills was always full of game. Lord Webb owned the land and they had to be careful not to be seen by him, or Dante Wright. If seen poaching game the consequences could be death. William did not fear Webb, or Wright for that matter, but Mark was petrified of being caught by them. William just assumed they would not be seen and if they were he knew how to protect himself.

William was also becoming a more skillful hunter. He learned how to patiently wait for game without moving a muscle for hours. He learned where certain game congregated and how close he needed to be from it to make a good, swift kill. He learned to disguise his scent by smearing mud on his body and to be aware of the direction of the wind that could potentially carry his scent ahead to warn his prey. He learned to gut and skin his kills immediately, so they would not spoil. Having them skinned and gutted also meant they would be lighter to carry. This was important, since the demand on him to provide meat for the family was increasing.

He enjoyed the solitude of the foothills and the mountain range. He enjoyed having Mark with him from time to time, but he found he was more productive without him. However, Mark was useful, he was strong, and could carry several heavy bags of cleaned game and never complain.

When William reached the age of twenty-two, he began to stay away from the homestead for a night, or two nights in a row, if the hunting was good. This enabled him more time to find the elusive game. He had secured another knife from his uncle Michael that he attached to his right forearm, with the handle facing down towards his palm. He worked for months learning how to drop the knife out of its sheath and into his hand and throw it in one motion. He could now throw either knife with pinpoint accuracy. His grandfather Edmund also gave William another knife as a gift, to be used as a spare. He also gave him a good sharpening stone. He had refused to use his father's leather strap for sharpening, as he despised it for all the pain it caused him. He had been using rough rocks as a sharpening tool, but often times it would dull the blade. Now the blades were razor sharp. He carried a small blanket for sleeping and leather bags for the game he would bring home. Since it was always cold and rainy, he also carried a tanned leather hide he'd use to keep himself dry while camping, also given to him by his grandfather. When going for more than a day trip he was always alone, for the family thought he could probably handle any problems that might arise, but the rest of the boys could not.

William was now going further than ever before to find new areas to hunt. He was in peak physical condition, and had a chiseled body to go along with great stamina. He could walk or run all day without getting tired or winded. He could carry large quantities fresh game in his backpacks and not slow down a bit. He found less and less game within five miles of the farm and he knew it was the result of his over hunting this territory. He knew he would definitely have to go further away to fill his backpacks.

CHAPTER 4

The Flynn Girls

IN LATE MAY, WILLIAM LEFT FOR a hunt expecting to wind up a long way from home. He had walked many hours in the cold and rain and had no idea where he might end up. He was not sure exactly where he was, but he was pretty sure he was not on Lord Webb land any longer. He was surprised by the different game he encountered. He saw a deer for the first time in his life and swore he would take one down, if he could only get close enough. He wished he had his father's flintlock, but that was out of the question. His father would never let him use that gun again after almost killing old Ned.

William settled in above a small lough (lake) by a heavy wooded area. He could see large waterfowl swimming in the lough below. He had never seen a wild goose before, but its immense size made his mouth water. There were also ducks swimming on the lough, and he remembered his grandfather said that they were good to eat. The ducks were in the middle of the lough, but the geese were close to shore. William had never learned to swim and the thought of having to swim after a downed bird made him shudder. He questioned himself; how deep was the water, and if he misses the geese would he be able to retrieve his knife? What would he do?

A half hour passed when he heard two female voices in the distance talking and laughing very loudly. They were having a great time, but they surely would disrupt the wild life. The geese flew away, ending any chances he might have one for dinner. They came to the lough with long poles in their hands, and they took off their shoes and stockings and began to wade out from the shore. Their dresses became soaked to the knees. The water was cold and they screamed in delight as they inched further out. They baited the hooks with worms they kept in small cloth bags in their pockets. The fish were biting and the girls couldn't bring them in fast enough.

The two types of fish the girls were catching in this lough were the dace, a small silver fish with yellow eyes, and the perch, olive-green in color with vertical stripes on their flanks. Both fish weighed an average of about a half-pound. The girls used a fairly long thin branch of a tree as a stringer to hold the fish, so they didn't have to leave the water after each catch.

William walked down to the lough where the girls had entered the water. The one that he had his eye on was the one the other girl called Anne, and she was a beauty. She was about twenty years old, had long coal black hair, freckles galore, deep brown eyes, a dark smooth complexion and a figure that was definitely that of a full-grown woman. Her sister was younger by two years and was a nice appearing girl. She did not have her sister's stunning good looks, but was very attractive. William was smitten immediately. He yelled, "Hello" and asked what they were doing. He knew of some loughs close to his farm, but the Irish Catholics were forbidden to enter them by penalty of death. He had never seen anyone catch a fish before, but he did know what they were and that they were edible.

Anne turned to see the handsome, young, freckled-faced William standing near the water. She was surprised to see him and was immediately intimated by him. She screamed that their father was close at hand and he always carried his saber with him. William tried to calm them.

"I mean you no harm, please do not be afraid of me. But, by the way, what are you doing in the water and what are you catching on those poles?"

"Where are you from? You are not from around here, you speak a bit different than us and who does not know what a fish is? You are one strange boy," Anne responded.

William said that he knew what a fish was and had seen them in the village of Youghal, by the ocean. He said he hadn't thought that they might exist elsewhere. He also said he was surprised at their small size. Anne and her sister Margaret's fright of him subsided a bit, after hearing him innocently speaking about his lack of knowledge on fishing. Although they were unaccustomed to socializing with young men, they were getting comfortable with this naive acting young man.

Anne told him to come closer and look at the fish they had caught. They were clearly not as large as the fish he had seen in Youghal, but they looked like they were big enough to eat. Anne said she and her sister planned to eat some of the fish before heading home and he could help them clean, cook and eat them, if he liked. William agreed, as he was always hungry and also very anxious to spend as much time with Anne as humanly possible. Anne asked him if he knew how to build a fire. William responded that he could indeed do that. After he got a fire started they would both show him how clean and fillet the fish.

After William gathered small, dried twigs and branches from the forest, he then started the fire by using a flint that he carried with him, and struck it repeatedly against a rock to create a spark that ignited the twigs. In most cases, starting a fire was a major undertaking for most Irishmen, but for William it was easy. The days he spent away from home, hunting and camping out, made his being able to start a fire in a short time a survival necessity. The girls watched in amazement at his fire starting skills.

After the fire was burning the girls showed William the two ways they knew to clean the fish. The first was to scratch the scales off with a knife, chop off the head and scoop out the innards, and wash off the blood and guts in the lake. The second, which appeared to be the easiest to William, was to fillet the fish. Using one of his thinnest knives, Anne held onto the fish head with one hand and made a cut just below the gills and then straight down to the tail. She folded the skin back without detaching it from the tail and then cut just the meat off the skin, leaving just a nice piece of fish meat. She turned the fish over and did the same process on the other side. William was amazed at her skills with the knife and was anxious for his turn. It took him several tries, and he finally succeeded in doing a fairly good job, according to Anne.

As William and Margaret filleted the fish, Anne placed the fillets on a small thin skillet and placed it on the fire. The girls always carried the skillet along with them on their fishing trips in order to cook their lunch. After all the fish were cleaned and cooked and placed on a tin plate, the three of them sat down around the fire and devoured them. William had grown up living on mostly potatoes, some bread, a little corn and rarely a piece of squirrel or rabbit meat. Although in the last few years he and his family members had tasted more wild game than ever before, their diet was very limited.

William thoroughly enjoyed the fish, as well as the female companionship. He introduced himself as William, but said his family members called him Bill. Anne and Margaret then introduced themselves as well, but concluded that they did not like his nickname, so they would refer to him as just William.

The girls explained how to use the fishing pole and to how to hook the worms. After lunch William tried his luck fishing and began to be quite good (or lucky) in a short period of time. He really enjoyed the new sport and asked the girls how he could transport some fish home to his family. The girls said he should fillet the fish immediately after finishing fishing and wrap them in the large wet cotton towel they were prepared to give him. He should leave for home as soon as possible after packing the fish in his leather bag. The girls explained that the cool weather and the wet towel would help keep the fish fresh until he got home. He told the girls he thought it would take him somewhere between eight and ten hours to get home, so he'd leave tomorrow morning after fishing.

The sisters said they had to leave now for their trek home. They had to be home by five o'clock as expected, or their father would worry about them. Anne told William they would try and come back next weekend and she hoped that maybe he would be able to meet them again. William smiled and thought to himself, if they only knew, nothing could keep me away. William and the girls said their goodbyes and they told him how much they enjoyed their day with him and hoped to see him soon.

The night was cool by the lough, so William moved closer to the wooded area to get shielded by the wind and to build a small fire for some warmth. He had difficulty falling to sleep, as he tossed and turned most of the night, not being able to get Anne off his mind. He woke early and ate a piece of leftover fish and a slice of raw potato. He had some tea with him, but he felt he did not have ample time to restart the fire and complete all of the tasks that lay before him.

William went to the lough as soon as he finished his little breakfast. The girls had left a pole and worms for him and he was to leave it by a tree near the lough for use next week, when he was done. He waded into the cold water, baited the hook with a worm and began to fish. The fish were slow to bite, and William thought that maybe it was to early or to cold for the fish to be hungry. He spent the better part of an hour in the cold water and all he had to show for his freezing feet were three dace and one perch. He left the water to warm up and while sitting on a large rock, rubbing his feet; he heard a familiar voice call his name. He looked up and it was Anne approaching carrying a fishing pole.

"I thought you might need some help catching the fish and properly packing them for your trip," Anne exclaimed in a shy voice.

William had butterflies in his stomach since she left yesterday, just thinking he may never see her again. He couldn't hide his happiness and Anne could not either.

But Anne was all business at first. She ordered him back into the lough and she began to take off her shoes and stockings. William tried to convince her that the water was too cold, but she just laughed at him. She waded in and began to fish alongside of him. She must bring me good luck, William thought, as they began to catch fish every time they threw their bait into the water. The stringers were full and they both decided they had enough fish and enough of cold feet.

After drying off their feet, they put on their stockings and shoes and went right to work on filleting the fish. Anne was not afraid to get her hands dirty and worked right alongside of William. After the filleting job was completed, Anne told William to get the leather bags ready and she would wash and place the fish in the damp towel she had given him the day before. He did what he was told and stayed out of her way as she washed and packed the fish.

After her tasks were completed and William was packed, she encouraged him to leave on his long walk home. William was not concerned about getting home and didn't care when he got there, he just wanted a few more minutes with Anne. She was insistent that he leave now, since she was worried about him traveling throughout the night. She was also concerned about meeting up with a sheriff, or the possibility of running into one of the landholders or their henchmen. William surprised her by saying he could handle any problems that might arise with his fists and his knives. He reassured her he'd be careful and would not take any chances.

Anne walked him to the forest and said goodbye.

"William, wait," Anne called as he began to walk away. "Come back. I want to tell you something."

William set his pack down and strolled back to where she was standing.

"I want to whisper something in your ear," she said.

William turned his head so his left ear was facing Anne, and she put her hands gently on his face and gave him a slow, loving kiss on his left cheek. William blushed, his face turning a bright red, as he stammered and stuttered.

"Th-thank you, that was the nicest thing that has ever happened to me," he said.

Anne confessed that he was the first boy she ever kissed and she hoped he would not think her too aggressive. He smiled a nervous smile, and said he would see her next week, for sure. He told her he would also see if his younger cousin Mark could come along and meet Margaret. The couple parted ways, both as happy, with big smiles on their faces.

William's trip home took longer than he thought it would. Carrying a hundred or more fish fillets did slow him down somewhat, but the thought of Anne's sweet kiss made the lonely trip more than bearable. He could hardly wait until next week. But he was concerned; what if she didn't show up? How would he find her? Where did she live, what was her last name? She had neglected to tell him anything personal about herself or where she lived. He was worried, but the kiss was given, he thought, to make sure he would show up next week. I will not worry any longer, he thought; she'll be there.

William entered the family hut at about midnight. His father woke and quietly asked him where he had been. He told his father the truth, which he always did, but neglected to say anything about Anne. He told him of the fishing experience, just stating some folks from Fermoy showed him how it was done. He told his father in his pack he had over a hundred fillets for the family to enjoy, but they would need to eat them tomorrow. His father questioned the edibility of freshwater fish and said he didn't know that people ate fish from loughs. James was also concerned that Lord Webb, if he found out they had fish, would accuse them wrongly of entering his loughs and they could all could face a severe penalty. William assured his father the fish would all be eaten tomorrow after their Sunday morning religious service at grandfather Edmund's home. He said he would show the women how he was instructed to cook the fish and they would all be pleasantly surprised with the taste.

At Edmund's home the family congregated for their homemade Sunday service. The service included only the Mountain clan, with Edmund officiating. No outsiders were included for fear of repercussions from the English. Catholic services and prayers were not permitted under the Irish penal laws, but Catholics, in defiance of the laws, continued to hold their services in private.

Afterward, William showed the all the family the fish he brought home with him. He explained that if they enjoyed the fish, there would be more in the future. He showed the women how to fry them in grease and how long they should be cooked. The ladies, seeing the results of the fried fish, decided to roll the fish in a small amount of flour and then fry them. The consensus was that this was better and if they had flour that would be the preferred way to cook the fish, and they all concluded this was a very tasty meal. James was happy his son had provided the fish for the family, but he could not tell him so. The rest of the family freely told him how proud they were of him. They all encouraged William to go again, but not to take any chances getting caught. If someone were to approach him while carrying the fish, he was to leave them and run. He agreed to everything they said, but he knew in his heart he would never run from the English in his lifetime.

CHAPTER 5

Mark Meets the Flynn Girls

WILLIAM TOLD MARK OF HIS ENCOUNTER with Anne and Margaret. He explained that the two girls showed him the finer points of fishing, as well as engaging in some wonderful conversation. He did not tell him about the kiss, nor did he tell his two brothers. He asked Mark to ask his father William if he could go on a three-day trip with him the following weekend. William knew that the family thought it might be dangerous, but they also knew William could take care of himself and Mark. Having two boys making the trip would ensure more fish for the family, as well as the possibility of a few rabbits or squirrels.

The family agreed that Mark could go along with William, but they should not be gone longer than two nights. William argued that they needed at least three nights to make sure they could catch enough fish and maybe kill a few rabbits. His request fell on deaf ears; they could be gone no longer than two nights. If they were not home then, the other boys would be sent to find them. William knew that was a bluff; the family had no idea where they were going.

On Friday morning, June 4, 1841, the Mountain cousins set off for the Fermoy region of southern Ireland. Mark slowed William down a bit, but he was glad to have his cousin along for company. The walk, half-run, took much longer than William had remembered, or expected. They trotted for more than twelve hours, through some dense forest and some thick wetlands. William forgot the exact route he had taken the week before and that was the main cause for their delay. They reached the lough around ten o'clock that night. They bed down in the same spot William had the week before and decided not to start a fire since they would just eat some raw potatoes and would save their tea for tomorrow morning. They curled up in their blankets and fell fast asleep. They were exhausted from their walk and not cold, but very anxious for the next day.

They woke early as the sun was coming up. William had Mark gather some small kindling wood and a few branches for a fire. It was much colder this morning than last night and they both welcomed the warm fire. As the boys reminisced about their travels the day before, William heard someone in a soft voice call his name. The girls saw the fire and ran to warm themselves, even though it was a ways from the lough. Both girls had big smiles on their faces as William introduced Mark. Mark was not unlike William in his experience with girls: he had none. He was nervous, and as his father would say, 'nervous as a whore in church.'

Margaret tried to start a conversation with Mark, but he could only mumble and couldn't make eye contact. William, on the other hand, was beaming with confidence. He looked right into Anne's eyes and asked her all kinds of questions he failed to ask the week before. Where do you live? What is your last name? Do you live on a farm, or in the town of Fermoy? Do your father and mother know you're here? Do you have any other brothers or sisters? The questions came so fast and furiously, that poor Anne tried to open her mouth to speak, but before she could, he would blurt out another question. Finally Anne told him in a firm tone to be quiet and slow down, and she would answer all his questions.

"We live on a small farm near the town of Fermoy, with my father and brother. My mother, God bless her soul, passed away ten years ago and we don't know why. She just got sick and died. Our last name is Flynn and my father and brother are both named Patrick. My father and brother do not know we are meeting you two, and they would not approve. We told them we were just going fishing. I hope that answers your questions. Now I have a few of my own," said Anne.

Anne was eager to get some answers about the life of this strange but interesting boy.

"What area do you both come from? Do you live on a farm or in a town? Do your mother and father know that you're here and if they do, what are you here for? You couldn't be here to fish, because you told me you live a long ways away. Do you have other family members, and what is your last name? Those questions will be just the start, because I have lots more," she said.

William had calmed down and was ready to answer all her questions. Mark still had not said a word; he let William and Anne do all the talking.

"We come from near the township of Killeagh, about eight miles east of the coastal town of Youghal. Both Mark and I live on farms, me with my pa and my two brothers, Patrick and S.C. Our last name is Mountain. My ma died when I was born, in childbirth. Mark lives with his ma and pa. My whole family and Mark's know we're here for the fishing. I am the hunter in my family and I have taken on the chore of trying to provide wild game for us all to eat. I only told Mark here about you and Margaret. No one else in our families knows about you two. Does that help answer your questions?" asked William.

"This is a lot to digest, but that should hold me for a while," said Anne.

There was one thing, however, could not wait for later.

"You said you are the hunter for your family and you provide wild game. Just how do you do that? You have no flintlock, and you do not appear to have any snares. How do you hunt with no weapons, and aren't you a bit young for that kind of job?" questioned Anne.

William reached behind his head and drew out the long bladed knife; he then dropped the knife that was concealed in his sleeve into his hand.

"I hunt with these. I hunt mostly small game such as squirrels and rabbits. I can kill birds on the ground, but they are most difficult to hit in the air. I was going to try and hit one of those large birds I saw in the water last week, but since I cannot swim, I didn't know how I would retrieve the bird, or my knife. I am young, but I have been doing this since I was fourteen years old. I taught myself. That's the truth, Mark here will vouch for me," said William.

Anne's eyes turned slowly to Mark. He lowered his head sheepishly.

"William can hit just about anything he wants with those knives. Let him show you," said Mark.

"That isn't necessary," replied Anne, although she didn't believe either of them. The thought of a person throwing a knife at a bird in flight and hitting it was absurd.

"Let's get to work and get some fish," Anne said. She was clearly in charge. She told her sister and Mark that their job would be to fillet the fish. She and William would catch the fish. When their feet got cold they would switch places. They all agreed with the plan and Margaret said she would teach Mark how to clean and fillet the fish. Margaret told Mark that he'd better get over his shyness right now, for she was not going to spend the day with someone that could not look or speak to her.

"Trust me, I won't hurt you," said Margaret.

Mark tried to speak but words failed to come out. He turned red at her comments and just stood there looking down at his feet. Margaret grabbed his hand and led him down close to the lake. She told him to take off his shoes and wade out to where the others were fishing and bring her the fish after they were caught. Mark immediately felt more at ease and did what he was told.

Anne and William were catching mostly perch, which was unusual, because the week before the dace fish made up the majority of the catch. The type of fish did not matter to the kids; it was important just to catch as many as they could.

The stringers were continuing to fill and Mark waded out more often to retrieve the fish. Margaret couldn't keep up with the supply of fish that Mark was bringing in.

"Get your skinny ass over here and help me fillet these fish!" She told him, in no uncertain words.

A stunned Mark watched her fillet a few fish and said he'd try. He butchered several fish before finally getting the hang of it. He worked alongside Margaret and began to laugh out loud thinking about her comments.

"Skinny ass, the way you talk, girl!" exclaimed Mark.

"Haven't you ever heard a girl swear before?" Margaret asked.

"I've never even spoke to a girl before in my whole life, so no, I never heard one swear," Mark answered.

"How about your mum, or other relatives?" Margaret asked.

"Oh no, never, not my family, they are too sweet and nice to swear," laughed Mark.

He was laughing uncontrollably when she smacked him in the arm.

"You dumb ass," said Margaret.

Then the two of them began to laugh harder, and their laughter became contagious, and both William and Anne began laughing uncontrollably too. The four of them ended on the shore laughing even harder. The tension they all felt earlier disappeared and they began talking and teasing one another. Mark was the easiest target, but he didn't care, he was having the time of his life. He realized he was getting over his shyness and was more comfortable talking to Margaret, and looking straight into her cute freckled-faced was a sheer pleasure he had not experienced before.

The fishing and filleting went on for several hours. He had filleted sixty-five perch by the time they had finished for the day. The boys divided up the fish between the girls and themselves. They cooked about ten for lunch and the four ate until they were stuffed. The talk and teasing was robust and all four joined in the banter. The girls frequently used a little profanity, and after a while the boys grew accustomed to it.

After lunch Anne became a bit serious, and asked both boys what they intended to do with their lives. Mark said he would just work alongside his father and brother on their farm. William was not so sure what he would do. He said he didn't particularly like farming and couldn't see himself working alongside his father.

"I guess I never gave it much thought," William said.

He asked Anne what she intended to do with her life.

"We will not live here in Ireland," Anne answered for both of them. "We are planning to go to the Americay with our father. We have family in a place called Whisk-con-sin in the Americay. They say the land is lush and free for the taking. No Englishmen to tell you what you can do, or not do. You are free there."

Mark and William had never heard of such a place.

"How does a person get there, can he walk?" asked Mark.

"No," the girls echoed at the same time. "You must take a ship and the voyage can take a month or longer!" Anne exclaimed.

A whole month was a very long time. "What do you do when you get there?" asked Mark.

"First, you cannot take a ship directly to Whisk-con-sin, you must land in a place called New York City. Then you walk to a place where you get on another ship, and go across a big lake, a lake as big as the ocean. Then you walk, I guess," Anne said.

The Mountain boys fell silent for a short time trying to digest what Anne had just said. William was spellbound by her tale. He said that it sounded like a wonderful adventure.

Mark was less impressed. He might be a dumb-ass in Margaret's mind he thought, but this dumb-ass Irishman would not be making such a trip that far away from home.

The girls had to return home; it was beginning to get dark. The boys said they were going to fish again all day tomorrow and might leave the next morning. Margaret said they'd be back tomorrow to help if they could. Anne grabbed William by the hand and walked away from the other couple.

"Now it's your turn to kiss me," Anne said.

William didn't need to be told twice. He lowered his head, moved in close and gave her a soft kiss on the lips. Anne smiled, and reached up, put her arms around his neck and kissed him right back. Hers was not a soft kiss, but a more passionate one, which startled William for only a second, and he returned the favor. The two giggled and laughed and were a bit embarrassed, but not enough to stop kissing one another. After a few minutes Margaret called Anne's name and she grabbed William's hand and returned to where her sister had called.

Mark looked confused and bewildered. Eventually, Margaret had surprised Mark with a kiss too.

"You tight ass, you are supposed to kiss me back, not stand there like scarecrow," teased Margaret.

Mark was mad at her accusation, took a step forward and gently grabbed her hand and pulls her close to him. He lowered his head and kissed her on the lips. They both closed their eyes and the kiss lasted longer than it should have.

"Don't treat me like an idiot again, do you understand?" said Mark.

Margaret understood and took his hand.

"Yes sir," she said.

They all laughed and the girls ran off for home.

"Do you think they'll come back tomorrow?" Mark asked his cousin after the girls were out of sight.

"They would have, if you didn't scare them off, you dumb-ass," William said as he grinned and reassured Mark. "They'll be here. If not, I'm going looking for them."

CHAPTER 6

Patrick Flynn

THE BOYS ROSE EARLY AND STARTED a small fire. They heated up some fish from yesterday's meal and made a pot of tea. The teapot, tin cups, tin plate and skillet were part of William's new travel gear that were now essential. The girls showed up an hour later, by eight o'clock. They were all very happy to see one another. William asked the girls if they told their father about them.

"Hell no, do you think we're crazy? He would not understand befriending the likes of you two. We can't even talk to boys from our own town without him getting upset," Margaret replied sternly. "He says you can talk to all the boys you want, when I say you can. When we ask, when is that, his reply is always the same – when you turn thirty, not before."

They all laughed.

"If he only knew we did more than talking," Mark said.

Margaret smiled and smacked him a good one on the arm and told him he was maybe getting too brave. She reminded him her father was a very large man and was an expert with a saber.

The kids went about their work realizing that time was running short. It was cold and fishing was going to be hard on their bare feet. William and Anne took the first shift on the lough, with the others filleting and cleaning. After a few hours they had as many fish as they felt they could carry. As the girls packed the fish for the boys, William and Mark gathered small sticks and branches for the fire. William had the fire raging within a few minutes. The girls put the fish in the skillet and the fish fry began. As the kids ate they talked more about the Americay and wouldn't it be nice if they could all end up there. After finishing the meal and storing the leftovers in the boys' backpack for later, the girls said they were expected home a long time ago and they'd better get going. They promised to meet in two weeks if everything went well.

Just as they were separating for their good-bye kisses, they heard a very deep voice yelling behind them.

"What in the hell are you doing?"

It was the girl's father, Patrick, and he was raging with anger. He ran at Mark and grabbed him by the back of his neck and dragged him along to where William was standing. He reached out to grasp William by his neck, but William's strong arm and hand slapped it away. Shocked by the boys' strength and agility, he let go of Mark and took a full swing at William. William ducked out of the way and the girl's father's momentum carried him to the ground. Patrick blinked once and then realized William was on top on him, with the blade of his a knife pressed against his throat. William, not realizing this was Anne's father, warned him that the knife was sharp and he knew how to use it. Anne and Margaret were screaming at him to stop.

"He's our father!" They cried.

William carefully replaced the knife in its sheath and jumped up.

"I apologize to you, I didn't know who you were, I was only trying to protect my cousin and these girls," said William.

Patrick backed away from him and moved toward the girls.

"You two bastards stay away from my girls! You don't know who you're fooling with. I have many friends and relatives who would like nothing more than to end your worthless lives. If I find you've been around here again, you'll pay the consequences. And for you two sluts, you should be ashamed of yourselves! Your mother is turning over in her grave right this minute. I thought I raised you better than this. Get on home before I punish you here and now," said Patrick.

The girls turned and ran for home. Patrick walked backwards for about ten feet with his eyes fixed on William and Mark.

"This had better be the last that I see of you two bastards," he exclaimed.

"I think that went as well as we could have expected," Mark said to William after the girls' father had gone.

William didn't laugh and was remorseful of his attack on Patrick.

"I just should have let him grab me and try and explain to him that we were just fishing. He really surprised me and I could only think of protecting the girls. Goddamn him, he could have talked to us as adults instead of attacking. He is quite a prick," said William.

But Mark's sense of humor was working overtime.

"Is that the way you should be talking about your future father-in law, calling him a prick?" said Mark.

"You're a prick too, but at least you're a funny one," William responded.

The boys put on their backpacks and headed for home very depressed about the way things ended.

"We'll probably never see them again, but I will come back in two weeks, just in case she shows up," William said.

Mark said he would like to come along too. They agreed, in two weeks they would make a last effort to see the girls again.

The walk home was long, cold, wet and tiring. They knew they were getting closer to home when there were fewer and fewer stands of trees. William hunted for a short period of time and killed three squirrels, but the two boys did not see any rabbits. They cleaned the kill and added to their already full backpacks.

CHAPTER 7

First Kill

JUST AFTER LEAVING THE PROTECTION OF the trees, a rider approached the boys. He jumped off his horse in an intimidating manner and asked what they had in their packs. William said it was some game that they killed in the forest and some camping things. The man was fairly small in stature, very dirty and well- armed with a long sword attached to one side of his belt and a small saber attached to the other. He told them to open the packs so he could see for himself. Mark was scared to death, but William was not. He opened the packs and the man looked in.

"So you've been poaching fish from Lord Webb's loughs, you goddamn foolish Irish bastards," the man said.

"How fuckin stupid are you?" William said in a tone that set the man back at bit. "Webb's loughs are three or four miles straight south of here. How the hell could we poach fish from him when we are coming from the opposite direction?"

"You young bloody Irish have not yet learned to respect your betters, have you? I will now teach you a fuckin' lesson that you won't learn, because you will both be dead when I finish with you. I always say the best Irishman is a dead Irishman," said the man.

The man began to draw his sword out of his belt, when out of William's hand a knife rocketed into the man's chest. A surprised, confused look appeared on the man's face, as a second later another knife hit an inch above the first with so much force the man toppled over. The man was dead on impact of the second knife.

The boys stood silently for long while.

"You killed him, William, you crazy son-of-a-bitch, you killed him!" yelled Mark.

William just stared at the body for a long time, contemplating what to do next.

"Mark," he said finally. "You stay here with the backpacks and I will take this asshole's body way back into the forest and hide him the best I can. I'll take his horse along and let him go a long ways from the body. Closer to Fermoy. You wait here until I get back, do you understand?" asked William.

Mark agreed and said he'd wait, but he would hide in the forest just in case someone was with the Englishman. Mark and William walked the horse with the body slung over it to the forest and William left Mark alone.

William trudged alongside the horse and body for over an hour. When the forest was at its most dense, he slid the body off the horse and onto the ground. He dragged it into a thicket and covered it with branches and leaves. He buried the man's sword and saber in a shallow hole and covered it up. He thought the body would decompose or be eaten by wildlife within a few weeks, which was enough time for anyone looking for him to give up. He took the saddle off the horse and also buried it. He then walked miles with the horse and shooed him away, careful not to be close to the lough where the kids had fished, in fear of running into Patrick Flynn.

It took William four full hours, running as fast as he could to get to where he had left Mark. Mark was sleeping when he arrived. He woke and asked William how things went. William responded that the body should not be easily found, but his main concern was the horse. It would be found and if the finder just kept it they'd be all right, if not there would be problems for all the Irish.

"Pray they don't find that horse," William said.

Mark and William agreed to never, ever tell anyone what had transpired that night.

"I couldn't believe you could kill a man so quickly. He never saw the knife coming," Mark said to William.

"He deserved what he got. That prick would have killed us without blinking an eye, just over a few fish. I guess he was not as superior an Englishman as he thought he was. A poor, stupid Irishman killed him with only a knife. Fuck him and the horse he rode in on, I'd do it again in a heartbeat," William responded.

The boys arrived home mid-morning, exhausted from lack of sleep as well as lack of food and water. Luckily, Mark noticed the blood on William's shirt and pants and William took them off and replaced them with fresh clothing he had brought along. His problem was how to get the old washed without anyone seeing them. He didn't want to throw them away, but he did not see how he could wash the blood out. He took a chance and brought them in the hut and waited until his father and brothers were working to wash them. He knew Dante Wright would be looking for his hired hand and finding a bloody shirt and pants would be a certain give-away. The clothing cleaned up pretty well and if questioned about the stains he could always say it was from a rabbit he killed and cleaned.

Three weeks later Wright and his men came to the Mountain farm. They had plenty of questions for the Mountain family, but they were mainly concerned with their whereabouts in the last week. Wright thought his man had gone missing in the last week. James stated that they all had been home working for more than the last two weeks and they had relatives that could vouch for them, if necessary. William had on the stained pants, but Wright said nothing about them. Wright and his gang moved on to the rest of the family farms and all the neighbors. They found no traces of the hired hand, not even the horse.

Mark and William finally had a chance to talk in private about the happenings on their trip. Mark asked him if he felt any sadness or remorse about killing the hired hand.

"Why should I? That man was intent on killing both of us, and I wouldn't let that happen. We must be able to protect our families and ourselves, and you are my family. I will do it again and again, if I need too. I will never hesitate," William said.

Mark asked about going back to see if they could find the girls. He said he planned to go in a couple of days. The family had been asking the boys when they were going fishing again; they were developing a taste for fish. Mark said he wanted to come along and William agreed to take him.

CHAPTER 8

First Love

THE BOYS LEFT EARLY ON THURSDAY morning, the 1st of July. They ran most of the day, only resting once every couple of hours. The boys were not tired after all the running; they were just anxious to get to Fermoy and see if the girls were around the lough. The boys passed the place where William hid the hired hand's body. They checked the spot and could find no evidence of the body. The creatures of the night had disposed of the remains. Both boys felt relieved and relaxed a bit and kept moving forward. They reached the lough late in the day and as expected the girls were nowhere around. The boys camped in their usual place near the woods and started a small fire. For the first time that day, they ate a small potato.

The next day things began slowly as the boys took their time going close to the lough, half expecting the girls to show up. They didn't, however. The boys fished all day with the new poles they fashioned out of tree branches. The kids had brought string with them and Mark dug the worms and put them in the cotton bags. It took almost two hours to get prepared to fish. When they finally started to fish it was close to 11 am. The fishing was good, but not as good as when the girls were with them and clearly not as much fun. Both boys missed the girls very much. They realized they were in love with the sisters and thought they would never be able to tell them of their love. They worked hard catching the fish and filleting them before dark. William said Mark should start fishing tomorrow and he would try and kill a few squirrels and maybe a few rabbits to go along with the fish. He would come back around noon and help Mark fillet and clean the fish and then be on their way. Mark agreed, but didn't like the idea of being left alone by the lough. William assured him he would be all right.

William left very early to hunt and Mark slept for a while longer. After getting up an hour later, Mark ate a raw potato and went to the lough. He caught a few perch and decided to warm his feet and fillet the fish he had caught. He heard footsteps behind him and jumped to his feet expecting to see Patrick Flynn in a rage. Instead he saw both Margaret and Anne with their fishing poles in hand. Margaret ran to Mark and jumped into his arms. She kissed him several times and told him how much she had missed him. Anne stood back and waited for the exchange to stop. When it stopped she asked Mark if William had come with him. He said William had gone into the woods to hunt this morning and they would be leaving this afternoon. She said she would go and search for him in the forest and said they should continue fishing.

Anne walked for over a half hour before she heard a rustling of leaves behind her. She turned around and there stood William with two squirrels and three rabbits in his hands. Neither of them said a word, Anne just stared; she then dropped her head to her chest and began to cry. William dropped the game and rushed to her and held her in his arms. She choked back tears and tried to apologize for her father's actions. She was so ashamed and said she wanted to die after the confrontation. They sat down and talked and talked until they began to laugh. He told her that they were afraid to come back too soon. She said that the Flynn family lived on fish and a few potatoes a day. The rest of their crops went for sale to save enough gold or silver to go to the Americay. She and Margaret fished the next week without their father present, hoping the boys would return. They both had a heart to heart with their father when they got home. He apologized to both of them for calling them sluts, as well as attacking William and Mark. The girls had told him they had done nothing wrong and that the boys were perfect gentlemen, all the time. They confessed that they had both kissed the boys, but did nothing else. Their father said his emotions got the best of him when he saw the boys, and he thought they were trying to take advantage of his daughters.

Anne had told her father that she and Margaret planned to see the boys again and that they would bring them home for a proper introduction. William was a little skeptical of the idea of meeting their father on his home turf, but told Anne he would gladly meet with him. She kissed him passionately and held the kiss for a long time. William was bursting with emotions he hadn't experienced before. Not knowing what to do next, he put his hand on one of Anne's breasts. She responded by pulling away from him and he was embarrassed with her reaction.

"Please William, I'm not ready for that type of thing," Anne said. "We must slow down and take our time."

"I have no problems with that, I didn't know what to do next anyway," William said with a grin.

Anne told him that she thought she had fallen in love with him and he told her he had fallen for her too. They walked back to the lough hand in hand.

After the four of them had caught and filleted an ample amount of fish, the girls said that they had to return home. Anne announced in an authoritative way that the boys would come along and be properly introduced to their father. They would both stay for dinner and would also stay the night on the floor of their small hut. Neither of the boys wanted to get reacquainted with the girl's father, but if their romance was to continue to the next level, they had better do as they were told.

The walk to the girls' home was not far away. It was a simple mud structure with no windows and a thatched roof. The layout of the inside was not much different than William's home, with the exception of three small bedrooms instead of two. The fireplace was a bit larger and the hut felt much warmer than William's home ever felt. Patrick was warming himself by the fire when they walked in. The boys stood behind the girls and stared at the floor.

"Well, it's a pleasure to meet you two lads under better circumstances. I apologize for my actions the last time we met. I didn't know my daughters had befriended two boys and I reacted poorly. I'm just thankful I still have my head attached to my body," Patrick said in a kind voice.

He laughed and the kids chuckled along with him. He shook both of the boys' hands and asked them to stay for dinner. The girls said they had already invited them for dinner and asked their father if they could sleep on the floor that night. Patrick thought that would be a good idea, and said he did not want these young men to have to sleep outdoors. He did not, however, worry about their well being - they could certainly take care of themselves, he laughed to himself.

They dined on fish and potatoes as usual and the girls' brother, Patrick Jr., joined them too. Patrick Jr. was the oldest and he looked much older than his twenty-six years. His face had aged from all the time he spent in the sun and from all the hard labor he had done all of his life. He was a pleasant lad and the boys grew fond of him immediately. After dinner, the talk was mainly about Americay.

"It's the land of milk and honey," Patrick Sr. quoted The Bible, "and I want that type of life for us."

William was mesmerized by the conversation. He could see himself on that type of adventure. Mark, on the other hand, wanted no part of that. He was staying put.

William asked Patrick Sr. when they planned on leaving. He explained that at the end of this year or early spring they would trek to the Cove of Cork, also called Cobh, and find a ship to take them to Americay. Patrick told him there were many ships that traveled to Americay and they left every week and some monthly. Their plan was to find one that would go into the port of New York. From there they would find a boat and leave for Whisk-con-sin as soon as possible. William asked if Whisk-con-sin was a city, or a village. Patrick said he thought it was called a territory and it was a very large landmass, much larger than their surrounding areas of southern Ireland. He said that they plan to settle in a place called Washington County, named after the first president of Americay. He also said it was a township of Erin, named by Irishman a few years ago who had moved there from Ireland. William made a mental note of what Patrick had said, for without a doubt, his plan was to go to Whisk-con-sin.

After the lengthy conversation about Americay, it was time to turn in for the night. Both Patrick's had their own bedrooms and left the boys and girls alone and said goodnight. The girls said their goodnight without so much as a handshake, not wanting to press their luck with their father.

William slept, but it was a restless sleep. He kept waking thinking about Americay. What a place it must be. Freedom for everyone to do what he or she wanted to do. It was the place for him. He wouldn't tell Anne of his plan to get to Whisk-con-sin, in case he was too late and she would have found someone else.

Patrick had to admit to himself, he liked the boys. They had a good sense of humor and treated his daughters very well. They were polite and well-mannered. Although they were brought up in an all male family, they must have had some female influence at some point in their lives. He also appreciated William's hunting skills, his ability to protect himself, as well as Patrick's family. This kid had it all and he had to admire him. He now saw what Anne had seen in him. Now Mark was a completely different person. He really liked his laid-back demeanor and quick wit. He didn't see much drive in the boy, but figured he was a hard worker and could provide for his daughter, if she chose him as her mate. All in all, he was happy that they patched up their issues. The next day he invited the boys to come and stay at his home whenever they were fishing.

The kids left for the lough together to fish for the day and to say goodbye. The girls were so happy their father accepted the boys and the boys were happy they didn't get the shit knocked out of them - which was what they expected.

Anne, Margaret, and Mark fished and filleted for several hours, while William went into the forest to see if he could kill some additional game. William walked a long way from the lough to find a quiet spot to lay in wait for some game. He had killed two rabbits on the way to his new location, but nothing else. He had gutted the rabbits and left their innards where he killed them, as he did not want to carry the scent of blood with him as he continued to hunt. He found an opening and leaned against a tree. He had one knife in his right hand, which he considered his strongest throwing hand, but also had the other knife ready in the left hand as he waited quietly for more rabbits to appear.

He stood still for over an hour when three doe came into his view. His heart raced and he had to close his eyes for a moment to calm himself. The deer continued to feed; unaware that William was within ten feet of them. William marveled at their beauty and wonderful coat of fur. He had been told that any four legged animal's heart was on the left side of their body, just right of the front leg. William used his quickness and deft accuracy and threw the knife so fast it appeared to have been shot out of a cannon. The deer he hit did not jump or act startled after it had been struck, it just keeled over. The other two deer just looked at the fallen doe and were going to keep eating until William moved away from the tree he was standing by. They were finally spooked and ran away. William knew he could kill a deer if he could get close enough, and by God he had. He wanted to gut the animal immediately and get back to Mark and the girls. He worked hard and fast and was happy it was cool so the bugs wouldn't drive him crazy. He completed his work, put the deer across his broad shoulders and also grabbed the rabbits off the ground. The deer would bring welcomed meat to both families.

When William approached the lough he had a big smile on his face. Mark was the first to see him and his eyes bugged out in disbelief.

"Where in the hell did you get that?" asked Anne.

William was a bit embarrassed, but said he killed it with his knife. The four of them just stood in amazement at the magnificent animal at their feet. Never had any of them, or their family members, tasted venison.

William didn't know exactly how to cut the animal up. Anne suggested they get her father to help, as he had butchered a calf that died accidentally a few years ago and might be of some help. Margaret and Mark ran to get Patrick. When they returned, they found William had begun to butcher the animal. Patrick used one of William's sharp knives to help. They divided up the animal, William taking two-thirds and the Flynn's taking the other third. The hide went with the Mountains. Patrick cut off the head and legs, and ran into the woods to dispose of them. Killing a deer could bring about some problems for the Flynn's, but since there was no shot to be heard, Patrick felt they'd be alright.

Patrick told William he had never heard of an Irishman killing a deer with a flintlock, let alone a knife.

"You have some skills that few men will ever possess. You are truly a hunter." Patrick said.

Anne was so proud of her boyfriend; she gave him a kiss right in front of her father, who said nothing. The boys bid the Flynn family goodbye and promised they'd be back within two weeks.

CHAPTER 9

The Killing Continues

WILLIAM WAS CONCERNED WITH THE TRIP home. He was fearful of running into some more of Webb's men. His fear was not that he couldn't protect the two of them, it was that someone would find out what he had done and the repercussions it would have on the family. He instructed Mark to walk and run at least a mile ahead of him. Mark would carry the fish as well as the rabbits, and William would carry the deer meat.

"If you are stopped by anyone, just tell them you are by yourself, and you had been snaring game and fishing near the Township of Fermoy," said William. "Whatever you do, don't panic, I'll be right behind you. Do you understand?"

"Yes, I understand if I have a problem you better come running fast. Make sure you get your head out of your ass and pay attention to where I am, so there is no problem. Do you understand me?" Mark responded.

"I understand you, you stupid prick," William said, as he laughed out loud.

"I'm sorry William, but I've lost my sense of humor, I'm just so scared. I don't want anything to happen like last time," Mark said.

William reassured him he was in control and nothing major would happen. Unfortunately, as William would soon find out, he and Mark, as well as the rest of the Mountain clan, were headed for a life-changing event.

After the boys had completed their hike through the woods, they approached the marshland. William gave Mark a head start of a half hour, thinking that would leave them about a mile apart, as the game they carried would surely slow them down. Mark trudged through the wetland and was facing some flat land that was spotted with a few trees. He did not see them at first, but the two riders coming from the east saw him. The riders were coming at top speed as they approached Mark, who was attempting in vain to become invisible, as he hid behind two trees. They saw him and dismounted on the run and came up upon Mark with flint-locked pistols cocked and sabers drawn.

"We remember you. You're a member of the bloody Mountain clan. How in the hell do you dare trespass on Lord Webb's property, after all he's done for your family?" they asked.

Mark was so afraid he wet himself, and he was so tongue-tied he couldn't pronounce a single word. The two screamed at him at the top of their lungs and one slugged him across his face with a closed fist, dropping him to the ground with a gash over his eye.

"Do you know what we are authorized to do with trespassers? They get twenty lashes and if they don't die we slit their throats," the larger man asked in a loud demanding voice. "Drop the bags and let's take a look at what you find so valuable."

They opened the leather bags and found the fish fillets and the rabbit meat. "No wonder you're scared shitless, you've been poaching, as well as trespassing. We are going to enjoy teaching you and all of the other goddamn Irishmen in this county a lesson they won't forget. When we're done with you, we'll take what's left of you back to your family, and we'll burn the house to the ground, with you and the rest of them in it. This is all we needed to get all you worthless Mountains off the Webb estates."

The smaller man tied Mark's hands in front of him with a leather strap. He then took a rope and tied it in the leather strap and threw the end over a tree limb. He grabbed the loose end and tightened it as Mark's hands rose high in front of him and his toes were just barely touching the ground. He tied the rope end to the tree and ripped off Mark's shirt, while the larger fellow took a whip off his saddle. After doing a couple of practice lashes at a tree, the larger man asked his partner to also pull down Mark's pants.

"His ass looks as soft as a baby's butt, this should make him scream," the man said.

The large man uncoiled the whip and lashed out at Mark's behind. Mark screamed in horror at the excruciating pain. The man continued lashing Mark, but after the fourth lash, he stopped dead in his tracks. To the right of him, on the ground lay his partner, with a knife lodged in this throat and a gurgling sound coming from his throat, but not making any recognizable words. The man was confused at what happened to his partner. One second he was standing there laughing and enjoying the whipping and the next he laid almost dead. Then William stepped out of the shadows.

"It looks as though you stupid-ass English never learn when to leave well enough alone," William said.

The man retorted, "You will suffer greatly for what you have just done here."

He quickly pulled the pistol out of the waistband of his pants and in one motion attempted to fire at the surprised William. The pistol, however, failed to go off. The powder had gotten damp from the man's sweat that soaked through his shirt, causing the pistol to misfire, leaving him reaching for his saber. William took his time. He walked over to the now dead man and pulled his knife out of his throat. He wiped off the blade on the man's shirt and placed it back into its sheath.

"I know who you two are, and believe me, you and your families will suffer greatly if anything happens to me," said the man as he stepped forward.

William dropped the knife from his forearm sheath into his hand and threw it underhanded with blazing speed, directly into the man's stomach. The heavyset man bent at the waist and fell to the ground trying to pull the knife out.

"I purposely used your stomach as my target and not your heart, I wanted you to experience the same pain you were so happy to dish out on my cousin here and the many others of my countrymen that you tortured," William said.

William cut Mark down from the tree and placed him on the ground by their backpacks.

"If you have anything more to say to me, now is the time, you are not going to last much longer," William taunted the dying man.

The man was bleeding profusely and was dying an agonizing death. He asked William to put him out of his misery. William refused.

"Die like a man, you English coward," he said.

A few seconds later, Mark staggered to get off the ground and reached for the saber that was still in the dead man's belt and shoved the tip into the dying man's heart. The man sagged forward, and died instantly after the saber pierced his heart. William showed no emotion to Mark's deed. Mark, however, dropped to his knees and cried. The pain and the killings were more than he could take. William tried to comfort him but to no avail. He just continued crying.

"I'm just not like you. I'm just not like you," said Mark over and over again.

William had enough.

"Mark, pull yourself together right now. I'll take care of your wounds and then we need a plan to get rid of these assholes and get back home and warn our families," William said.

William ripped the shirt off the first dead man and found some standing water in the marsh. He soaked it in the water and returned to aid Mark. He patted the wounds gently with the shirt and ripped the shirt into strips to make bandages. He went through both man's saddlebags and found a shirt in the larger man's bag. Mark put the shirt on and grimaced in pain. He found the trousers that were ripped off him and put them back on. William thought they would suffice until they got home.

William told his cousin that he would find a place in the marsh where Wright and his gang would not find the dead men. William laid both men over one of the horses and tied them on with rawhide strips. He then led the horse deeper into the marsh. He was gone for over an hour when he returned soaking wet and covered with mud.

"I found a place deep in the marsh and buried the two of them in the mud and water. I don't think they will be found. Now all we need to do is get on these horses and ride close to home and then let them run," William told Mark.

Neither boy had ridden a horse before, so the going was slow. Mark was also slowed down because of the excruciating pain he was in. A few miles from home the boys let the horses go not knowing if Wright or Webb would find them and suspect the boys.

When the boys reached William's hut it was close to 10 pm and everyone was in bed. They woke James and the brothers up immediately after entering the hut. James could see that Mark was in tough shape and he sent S.C. to fetch Mark's parents and grandparents. James figured Mark was in need of medical help and they would provide it.

"I'm not going to ask you two any questions until the rest of the family gets here and after Mark is attended to. But I want you to be truthful and tell us exactly what happened," James told William.

All the family members rushed to James's hut. After the women attended to Mark's wounds with salve and fresh bandages, the questions began. James figured that William had instigated whatever had happened to the two of them.

"What happened to Mark? Was he whipped?" asked James.

William responded that indeed he had been whipped by some of Wright's men.

"How in the hell did you two get away from them without them killing you? And what did you do to make them whip him?" said James.

"Pa, I have never lied to you before and I won't now," said William. "This is all my fault and I take responsibility for it. We had met some friends a few months ago near Fermoy by a lough. They taught us to fish and that is how I was able to bring home fish every few weeks. I also hunted in the forest in the same area. Do you remember a few weeks back when Wright and his men came looking for a missing member of their gang? Well, he attacked us on our way home and I was forced to kill him. Believe me it was him or us. I laid him on his horse and walked back to hide the body deep in the forest and then I let his horse run away close to Fermoy. Thankfully someone found the horse and kept him."

"Mark and I thought all this had passed and Wright had just thought his man had left his employment," William continued. "We were wrong. I had killed this deer in the forest, and several rabbits. We also had caught and filleted all the fish in our packs. Because we had so much game and fish, I had Mark walk ahead of me in case someone questioned us. Well, two of Wright's men attacked him. They were whipping Mark when I arrived. I killed the first man I saw with my knife. I hit him in the throat, I was aiming for his chest and he moved suddenly. I intentionally threw my second knife into the last man's stomach, I didn't want him to die too soon, and I wanted him to suffer. Mark finished him off. That's what happened and now we're afraid that the horses we rode here will run home and Wright will come looking for us."

The Mountain elders said nothing for a long time. They were all trying to digest what they had just heard. Grandfather Edmund was the first to speak.

"We will need to get the boys out of here as soon as possible. In fact, we'll need to get all of our young men out of here," said Grandfather Edmund. "Wright and Webb will not stand for this, they will want revenge and some of us in this community will be punished. We must warn all our neighbors that Wright will be coming and he will be coming soon. William and Mark, I do not condone for one minute the taking any man's life. You were both brought up in the Catholic faith and you both know it's a mortal sin to take a life, any life. You will both have to face God and ask His forgiveness. I realize you were just protecting yourselves, but killing is wrong."

"Boys," said James with a heavy heart, "You have done a terrible thing and more than likely this will hurt our entire family and maybe the rest of the community. Both of you will stay here until Mark has healed and can travel, but do not go outside until then. When he can travel, William will take Mark and his brothers S.C. and Patrick and will head to the town of Cork or to the Cove of Cork to find employment and a place to stay. If and when things get better here, we will find all of you and will bring you back."

"Under no circumstances," Grandfather Edmund said, "are you to confront Wright and his men. Stay hidden,"

CHAPTER 10

Carnage In Killeagh

A WEEK AFTER THE CONFRONTATION WITH Wright's men, James heard someone screaming on the road that separated his home from his fathers. It was Emmett O'Keeffe, a young neighbor man from down the road, with tears steaming down his cheeks. He jumped off his horse and told the Mountain family the news he had overheard in Killeagh. Dante Wright and his gang found the bodies of their men in the marshland, just west of Killeagh. The horses had made their way home on their instincts. Wright correctly assumed foul play. While searching for the two men they saw carrion circling the lower marsh and discovered the bodies. O'Keeffe said they then killed his mother and father and his two sisters yesterday and they are headed this way. James tried to comfort Emmett, but he could not be comforted.

"They raped my mother and my two sisters and then they slit their throats," Emmett said. "My father was stretched out and whipped to death. They were all tied naked, high on a tree limb, as an example to what happens when the Irish break the law. I was in Killeagh for the day when this happened and I'm leaving now and I'm not coming back. There is no law to protect us now."

Edmund handed Emmett a few silver coins.

"God be with you," he said. "We will bury your family if we can."

Emmett thanked them and rode off.

In the distance they could see smoke billowing from some out buildings on the Sean O'Connor farm about two miles away. The O'Connor's were shirttail relatives of the Mountains through marriage.

51

Edmund, his sons James and Michael, along with William, Mark's father, discussed their options. There was no place for the family to run or hide and Wright would surely find them anyways. The only thing they could do was try and reason with them. Edmund said they should confront them at his homestead and for James and Michael to bring their flintlocks just in case. Edmund said the young boys would remain at James's house and should hide there and not come to their aid.

"Take all of these coins with you and the four of you hide somewhere in the hills and don't come out until this is over," Edmund spoke directly to William. "It's your job to carry on our family name and our traditions. Please do as we say. We love you all and remember us always. Pray God takes care of us and if we must die, pray it will be a swift death."

The boys went back to James's hut and prepared for the worst. William knew they had no time to run for the hills, or any place else for that matter. He had sharpened his knives and set the bags of coins in the privy. He thought they'd never look in there. Just then he had a brilliant idea; why not all of us hide in the privy? It would be disgusting, vile, and they would all probably get sick, but it was clearly large enough for all of them. William thought, we'd all be sick in the beginning, but we'd get over it. He told the boys about his plan. Although William was the youngest of the brothers they accepted him as their leader, so whatever he asked of them, they agreed to do.

The smoke continued to billow from the surrounding farms. They could hear screaming echoing coming from all the women and children. There was chaos everywhere. People were running from the men on horseback that were wielding swords. The Englishmen just slashed at everyone that ran, killing most instantly. The men and the older women that didn't run were rounded up and were whipped until dead. The younger women were raped and then their throats were slit. It was a complete and utter blood bath.

William wanted to help, knowing full well he could kill at least three of them. But instead he remembered what his grandfather had told him and he took his brothers and cousin to the privy. He told them to remember what their family is going through, so a little shit on their heads and in their ears and mouths should tolerable. Mark was the first in, followed by Patrick, then SC and lastly William. It was crowded and the smell was choking all of them, and the flies were driving them crazy. They all vomited whatever little was in their stomachs.

"Now we're done with being sick, all of you be quiet and breath lightly. Cover your bodies deep in the shit; rub it on your faces and into your hair," William instructed them. "Keep your eyes closed. If they look into the holes they will not be able to see us, do you understand? Get used to it, it will save our lives. We'll get our revenge soon enough."

The boys could hear voices coming their way. They were sure that their family members had been slaughtered and they all choked back tears and vomit. If they were found out, they be dead soon. They could hear their house being ransacked. They heard two shots fired. Their horses Ned and Ted were deemed too old and worthless, so they were shot. The cow and the two sheep were to be taken to Webb's compound. Wright's men set fire to the thatched roof and pulled down the corral. They put a rope around the privy and toppled it over. The boys were well hidden in the shit, and covered by the toppled boards from the outhouse. Wright's men had no appetite to jump into a shit pit to search for anything or anyone. No one, not even an Irishman, would be low enough in their minds to hide there. After spending twenty minutes dissembling the James Mountain farm, the thugs left.

The last of the Mountain family cleared away as much of the outhouse as they could and dragged themselves out. It was a slow process as they were close to chest high in human waste. As they expected, the farm was in ruins. They walked to the well and pulled bucket after bucket up to clean themselves. They were still gagging from the smell and their eyes burned from the amino acid in the urine. After washing quickly, the four of them ran across the road to their grandparent's home. There they saw the blood bath. James had been mortally wounded by gunfire after he shot one of the intruders with his flintlock. He was one of the lucky ones. Edmund and sons William and Michael were whipped until nearly dead, and then their throats were slit. Men on horses trampled Grandmother Margaret. The remaining women fought like hellcats, and refused to be used by Wright's men. The Englishmen were forced to kill the women with their swords and sabers. All the Mountain men stood their ground and killed or wounded five of Wright's men in the process.

The boys could not believe the carnage that the English had brought upon their family. Mark, SC and Patrick all wept uncontrollably and just stared at what had taken place. After a short while, William urged them to get over their grief and start thinking where to bury the family. The boys decided on a spot behind their grandfather's burned out home close to an evergreen tree. They wrapped the bodies in as much clothing as they could find and carried them to their final resting place. The four boys silently dug the graves and place each family member in their appointed one. Patrick said the prayers as the rest of the boys looked on. They all shared the duty of filing in the graves.

"Grandfather told us to go to the hills and hide out," Mark said. "I think that is a very good idea."

"What then?" William chimed in. "Do you think they will just leave us alone? They know they didn't kill all the Mountains and they will be on the lookout for all of us. The way I see it," he continued, "We need to meet in Cork in a few days and find a ship that will take us out of this English infested country. I don't know about all of you, but I'm going to Americay, with or without you. We'll divide up the coin equally and we all should have enough for good start."

"You prick, you've been planning to leave Ireland for Americay ever since Anne told you about it," Mark said.

The other boys wanted to know who was Anne and what is this Americay he was taking about. William told the boys about their adventures and all that the girls had told them. William told them they really had no choice but to leave Ireland, and they reluctantly all agreed.

CHAPTER 11

William's Revenge

WILLIAM ASKED THE THREE OTHER BOYS to leave immediately for the town of Cork. He told them to stay together for protection and off any main roads. They were not to talk to anyone unless they had to. He said he would meet them in four days' time near the harbor or by the ticket agent's office at the Cove of Cork, where he thought the ships would depart. He told them to buy four tickets on any ship that would take them to Americay.

"Pick the one that is first to leave next week," he said. "If I'm not here, leave without me."

"Just what the hell are you going to do? Are you going to the Webb estate and try to kill all the assassins that killed the family?" Mark asked.

"Not all of them, but I plan to kill enough of them so that the Mountain name will be remembered in this part of Ireland," said William.

Mark wanted to go with him, but William said he could move more swiftly without him and he didn't want to worry about anyone but himself. The boys said their goodbyes and told William to be careful. They parted ways very nervous about their future, if indeed they had one.

Lord Charles Webb's family constructed a stately manor just north of the Township of Killeagh on the River Dissour in approximately 1760. The estate was not graced with a castle, but with a very large stone house set back on the property, with many other buildings to house armed guards, servants and a barn for livestock. The buildings were surrounded by a massive five-foot thick wall that enclosed the entire compound. The wall was eight feet high and had loopholes for light and the use of flint-locked rifles in the event of an attack. Several buildings were used as a continuation of the wall. Those building were primarily for armed guards and servants. The buildings also had loopholes for light and rifles. The estate was approximately six miles north of Killeagh and about eight miles from the Mountain homesteads.

William did not know where the Webb estate was, but he had heard it was somewhere on the River Dissour. He would find the river and follow it north to the Webb estate. He didn't know exactly what he was going to do when he got there, but was sure he'd take out his rage on some of Wright's men.

William walked to the outskirts of Killeagh in less than two hours. Along the way, all he saw were burned out farms and dead folks laying naked in the yards. He assumed that Wright and his boys surprised all these poor folk and killed them on the spot. He could see that the women got the worst of it and he promised himself he would get retribution for all they had done. He was saddened by what he had done that led to the massacre of all these poor people. If it weren't for his grandfather's insistence that they hide, he and the other boys would be dead too. It was clear to him that Webb and Wright had planned to rid the community of the Irish farmers for a long time. The killing of two of Wright's hired hands would relieve Webb of any criticism from English gentry for retaliating against a few Irish farmers. Webb had bragged to William's father that he had many Protestant families more than happy to take over productive farms. As William walked forward his anger raged. He didn't care if he lived or died, but if he were to die, he would take many with him.

It was late in the day when he came upon the Webb estate. There was a wonderful stand of trees on both sides of the river. The banks of the river were much higher than the river itself and the water was running at a slow speed and was not deep.

William waded out to the middle of the river and submerged himself and took off all his clothes. He needed to fully bathe himself and wash his clothes to get rid of the odor of the outhouse. He chose a hiding place behind some shrubs and several small trees to dry his clothes, as well as himself. In hunting for game (or in this case, men), he knew he must get rid of any odors that might tip off his prey to his presence.

He estimated he was about four hundred yards from Webb's compound. He could see the top of buildings and its fortified walls, but could see nothing inside. There was a great deal of activity going on outside the walls, with servants trying to deal with the unruly, frightened livestock that had just been acquired from the dead Irish families. The gates were wide open as the servants were trying to assess which animals should go into the barns or which ones would be left in the outside corrals.

Darkness fell and all activity slowed, but the gates remained open. William figured that Wright left the gates open on purpose; he must have believed that there was no threat of an attack. The Englishman thought all their enemies now lay dead or near dead. In Dante Wright's wildest imagination, he would have never, ever thought, a single strong-willed Irishman could be transformed into an assassin and turn Lord Webb's compound into a burning, bloody killing field.

William waited until it was completely dark and very late before moving toward the compound. Clouds covered the reflection from the stars and moon, making it almost impossible to see. William approached the wall from left of the gates. After reaching the wall, he crept along until he reached the open gates. He was amazed to find that there were no guards stationed by the gates. Darkness concealed him, although it was not necessary. There was no one around. Wright's men must have been exhausted from the carnage they performed on their Irish tenants. William checked his weapons. The knife behind his neck was in place, as well as the one in his sleeve. The third was in his waistband above his buttock.

William entered the gates with the knife from his waistband in his hand. He saw one sentry standing near the first building on the left. He walked softly toward the man, but he was either sleeping standing up or was in a daydream-like trance. William walked right up to him, put his hand over his mouth and shoved the knife deep into his chest. His eyes opened and closed in an instant as he dropped to the ground. William stepped over the sentry and proceeded into the first building. He was uncertain how many men Webb employed, but knew there were many. His goal was to eventually get to both Wright and Webb, but he intended to kill at least one of them.

He entered the first building and let his eyes adjust to the darkened room. He heard men snoring and tossing and turning in their sleep. They must have been overtired from all the work they performed today. William knew if he were to maximize the death toll on the English, he had to remain very quiet and kill silently. He reached his second victim, covered his mouth and slit his throat. He waited until the man bled to death before moving on. He went down the line and killed a total of five men silently, all by slitting their throats.

Outside again, he saw another sentry about twenty feet away. The sentry saw him and it was the last thing he saw in this life. William's first knife entered the left side of the man's chest just below his nipple, the second one made a direct hit to the man's heart. William wiped off his knives on the man's shirt and proceeded to the larger buildings. He bypassed another barracks, but figured he would look for higher-ranking Englishmen instead of just rapists and killers.

The third building down is where he thought Wright and some of his second-in-command might be residing. He entered the main floor but found no one there. He could hear snoring upstairs and decided he would take a chance. The wooden steps creaked as he went up. At the top of the stairs he saw three rooms. He looked in the one to his left and saw two men sleeping in separate beds. The beds were very close together and he feared he would wake both of them while attempting the first kill. He decided to pass on the first room and moved to the second one. It was the same as the first, two men sleeping in too close of quarters. He could always go back if need be. The third room had door which was closed. William quietly opened the door. It squeaked, a fairly loud squeak.

"Who's there?" said a female voice.

William entered the room, closed the door and pressed one finger to his lips indicating she say no more. She sat there naked and motionless on the bed, just starring at William with his knives in his hands. He whispered to her to get out of the bed and hide in the far corner.

"Is that Wright or Webb in the bed?" asked William.   " M r . Wright, Lord Webb is in the last building," she whispered. "They both force us to sleep with them. When they are done with us, they give us to their men. I hope the bastard burns in hell."

"He will," responded William.

William tiptoed to the naked Wright's bed, climbed on top of him and placed his hand over his mouth as he woke up startled. He began to struggle and it was then William realized how soft this tub of shit really was. He was over fifty years old, five-foot-four and weighed about 220 pounds. He was nothing but flab. William enjoyed seeing the panic set into Wright eyes. William showed Wright the knife and he quit his struggling for a moment. Then he placed the blade of his knife just above the man's Adam's-apple and slowly shoved the knife forward. Wright wiggled his body and tried to remove William's hand from his mouth with both his hands, but he could not match William's strength. Still holding his hand hard over Wright's mouth, William pulled the knife out of his throat. He slid off the man and lunged the knife into his testicles, slicing at them until they were lying on the bed. Wright bled profusely and William just watched the horrid look on his face, as he let him bleed to death. It was not as satisfying as William thought it would be.

William was bloody from head to toe and looked fierce. The young woman just sat in the corner as William passed. He nodded at her, told her to get dressed, stay quiet and follow him. She did as he asked. They both tiptoed down the hall to the staircase. She went first and he followed, very quietly. When they got to the main floor they both emptied the oil of several of the non-lit lamps throughout the main room and on the wooden staircase all the way to the top. William placed a lit wick of an oil lamp on the floor where they had spilled the oil. The wick was used to ignite the oil after they exited the house and it spread quickly throughout the lower level and up the stairs. There were no windows on the second floor, thus the only exit was the flaming staircase. The four Englishmen upstairs died in as much pain as they had inflicted on the poor sharecroppers. William instructed the young girl to go find the other female hostages in the camp and stay hidden in the barn. He would find them.

CHAPTER 12

Molly McCarthy

WILLIAM RAN TOWARD THE WEBB HOUSE and as he reached the steps the door swung open and a single guard walked out. He died in his tracks. William was within ten feet of him and had no problem making a direct hit to the heart. Behind him he heard much commotion coming from the burning house. He just left as the hired killers had risen from their deep sleep and were panicking trying to find a way out. William pulled his knife out of the guard and had to quickly reassess what he wanted to do and where he would go next. The house fire lit up the compound and there were people running everywhere in panic. William was still hell bent on killing Webb.

He ran into the Webb mansion and was surprised not to be greeted by more armed guards. On the table in the dining room, the booty they had accumulated earlier in the day from the Irish farmers was on display. Flintlock rifles, pistols, silver cups and plates, and bags of coins all lined the table. He heard a voice behind him and turned to throw one of his weapons in the direction. He was able to stop midway through his throw. Before him stood a young woman about his age wearing rags and looking terrified. William motioned to her to whisper quietly and asked if Webb was upstairs.

"No, he left for Dublin late this afternoon after the men returned with us girls and the livestock," she said.

"Who are you?" William asked.

"I'm Irish. My folks had the first farm right outside Killeagh. My name is Molly McCarthy and Wright and his men killed my family

61

today. I'm supposed to stay in this house until Mr. Webb returns. He told me that I am now his property," she explained.

She was the most beautiful young woman William had ever seen. It was obvious that Webb decided that she would be one of his young mistresses.

William asked, "Is there anyone else in the house?"

She said, "There was a guard here a while ago, but he's not here any longer."

William cracked a smile. "We shall not worry about him any longer, but we do have work to do. We're going to burn this place down," he said.

William told her to get all the oil lamps and extra oil out of the storage cabinets and dump them on the floors, the staircase and upstairs. They worked quickly and soon had a major fire in the works. Before leaving, William looked over the dining room table for anything valuable he could carry. He handed a few bags of gold and silver coins to Molly to carry. He then grabbed several more bags as they headed for the side door near the staircase that opened into a small garden.

Once outside the burning house they ran toward the barn where the other women prisoners were waiting. Molly led the way. Inside the barn, she located the other three girls. They were frightened and bloodied and were crying hysterically. William recognized the girl he freed from Wright's bed, but none of the others.

"My name is William Mountain, and I'm also from Killeagh, where all the slaughter took place. I'm sorry for your losses and we have all suffered dearly from these men, but it stops now. Do as Molly says and you'll get out of here. Of course, if anyone wants to stay, they may."

None wanted to stay.

Molly told them to follow William and her toward the gates, but instructed them to stay well behind. The four of them followed William, but at a good distance, fearing for the worst. William ran close to the wall on his left with knives in both hands. There was much confusion in the compound closest to Webb's blazing inferno. William and the girls left the estate without being noticed.

As they walked past the corral they saw two workhorses tied to a post. William untied the horses from the post and led them toward the river. After they all crossed the river, William stepped back in and washed the blood off his face and hands as the girls watched.

They walked in silence until reaching the stand of trees on the far side of the river. William held out the coin bags to the young women and told them the coins were for them to use for a fresh start somewhere else.

"I also have bags of coins, why don't we all split them up equally, including you William," said Molly.

William was surprised at Molly's gesture.

"I don't need the coins. You all need them more than me. Use them as you wish. Take the horses and get as far away from here as you can. Go to a big city, either Dublin or go north to Belfast, but use back roads and don't let anyone know about what happened here tonight. Take the horses, they will speed up your trip. Disappear in a big city and begin a new life. Make sure you feed the horses and water them on a regular basis. If you do they will get you to where you want to be. Good luck and be careful," instructed William.

Three of the young girls were already on the horses when Molly informed them she would not be going with them. William scolded her and told her she could not stay here and she could not return home, it was too dangerous.

"I know exactly what you are saying, that is why I'm going with you," Molly said.

"What? You think I have time to take you with me? You will only slow me down, and if we get caught, you will die a horrible death because of my actions. I can't allow that to happen," demanded William.

"I have no life here, or in Dublin, or in Belfast. I will be always be viewed in the eyes of the English as just a whore. I know what I look like and I know men want me, but I want what my mother had—a husband, a home and a family. I'm not a whore and I will not go to a big city and become one. I'd rather die right here and now. So, I am going with you and if we get caught we'll both die horrible deaths," insisted Molly.

William had met Irish women before with such strong personalities, namely Anne and Margaret Flynn. He admired women with strong convictions and he admired Molly.

"You will be taking a grave chance going with me and I will tell you up front, I am going to Americay with my cousin and my two brothers. They are waiting for me at the Cove of Cork," said William.

"So be it, I'll go to Americay with you and your family, but I will not stay here. I promise I'll not be a burden to you," said Molly.

The three girls agreed that Belfast was better than Dublin. There might be a chance of someone recognizing them in Dublin, but Belfast was far enough north that there would be little chance of that happening. The girls thanked William for releasing them from their bondage and for the coins. Molly hugged all the girls and hoped that they would all find happiness. They rode away excited about their future, but so sad about their past.

Although they were very tired, William told Molly they must get as far away that night as they could from Webb's estate. The English would be looking for William or someone else for the killing of hired hands and the burning of the estate. William was sure that no one alive saw his face except the girls. He hoped that they wouldn't get caught, and if they did, he hoped they would not give out his name. Getting to Cove now was an urgent undertaking.

Besides being beautiful, Molly was physically fit and could keep up with any pace William set. Molly had dark auburn hair and a snowy white complexion. She lacked the Irish freckles, but had stunning beautiful green eyes. William could see why Webb and his men all desired her, but he did not. He liked her; he thought she was funny and clearly beautiful, but he did not feel romantically inclined toward her in any way. Anne Flynn was the only woman he thought of in any romantic way. She was the only woman he would ever desire.

William and Molly walked most of the night. They stayed as far away from the Township of Killeagh as possible. The walk took more than seven hours since both were exhausted and they had to stop and rest often. Molly never complained, and William found her to be good company. They talked about their families' deaths and about their dismal futures. They both laughed at each other and quickly became good friends. They stopped for a rest by a small pond in the field of one of their dead neighbors.

"Do you have any remorse for killing so many men?" Molly asked William.

The young woman whom he rescued from Wright had told her about the killings. William sat silent for a very long time. Tears welled up in his eyes and he dropped to his knees and began to cry. It was a hard cry, and he began shaking uncontrollably. The pent-up anger turned into tears as it was released from his body. He could not stop. Molly moved over and held him in her arms. She had no idea just how many men he had killed, but it must have been many. William was sobbing harder than ever.

"Molly, I'm so ashamed of what I have done. I should have tried some other way, but I suppose I did not really want to find another way. Killing them was the easy way for me. I didn't think twice. Oh my God, please forgive me. My poor family might all be alive today if I hadn't killed," he sobbed.

William continued to cry until he cried himself to sleep. He went into a deep sleep and slept for hours. Molly fell sound asleep too. When he woke he felt relieved.

"That was the first time in my life I've cried. Nothing's ever made me feel that way before," he told Molly.

"Everyone needs to cry sometimes. We've both lost our folks and we don't know what the future will bring. It's enough to make me cry right now, but instead I think laughing might be more suitable," Molly said.

They both smiled at one another and began their trek towards Cork.

The aroma of smoke still filled the air, and as they passed the outskirts of the farm community of Killeagh they could also smell the pungent odor of bodies decaying. The carrion birds that filled the air made both of them sick to their stomachs.

CHAPTER 13

Cove of Cork

THEY TRUDGED ON, HOPING TO REACH the Cove of Cork by nightfall. They walked in silence for a long while, trying to make sense of all that happened yesterday. William was very happy that Molly had insisted on going with him. She was no trouble, and she was a great companion - and very easy to look at. Molly also liked William, but was certain he would not be a suitable match for her. He was kind, sensitive, protective, and was easy to look at too. She knew he would never disrespect her or make advances in a sexual way, like most men did. William never worried her in that respect, but the killings and his ability to kill was too much for her.

They reached Cove by early evening. The town of Cove was situated on the south side of the Great Island in Cork Harbor. The climate in Cove was warm by Irish standards. The mild climate resulted from being open to the sea on the south and encompassed on every other side by high hills, providing shelter from cold winds. William and Molly found a suitable spot to sleep just below the top of one of the hills out of the wind and cold. They slept soundly and very close together hoping their body heat would keep them warm. They woke at dawn, and were famished. Molly had some small potatoes left in her bag that they shared. William said he would go into Cove alone and search for his brothers. Molly insisted that she go along. She was not going to be left behind.

The two walked down the very steep hill toward the town. There were many stores in the town and it was the first time in their lives that

Molly and William had seen so much activity. They found a store that sold passage for ships headed to Americay. They did not see William's brothers or his cousin. Inside the store where passage was booked, they asked the agent when a ship would leave and the cost. The agent explained all the details and said when they were ready to leave they should come back and purchase their passage. The couple then walked to the harbor and watched the sailboats move in and out. They met an old man while watching the ships and he told them the harbor was too shallow for ships to be moored there. They were all moored out in the ocean a bit farther and passengers had to be shuttled out to them, at an extra cost, of course.

William knew they were here a day early. He thought the boys were probably hiding out somewhere. He and Molly ate in a small pub down by the water. They were served a piece of boiled fish, a boiled potato and a pint of beer. Molly paid for the lunch with silver coin. Both were feeling a bit tipsy and ordered another beer. It was the first time in William's life he had tasted alcohol, and he liked it. Molly, on the other hand, had tried it before but was not fond of it, but this time the glow it gave her was remarkable. They both loosened up and began to laugh like fools. They had never felt so good. The two of them stumbled back to their hiding place on the hill and fell fast asleep.

The next morning they awoke very early with unexpected hangovers. Molly had a severe headache.

"I remember my pa telling me that such things happen if you drink too much. Did I drink too much?" she asked.

William just laughed and said, "I don't yet know when I've had too much. That was the first time I've ever had beer. Maybe we did have too much."

They just laughed as they held their heads.

William said, "I need something to drink, right now, but no beer."

Molly giggled and said she was thirsty too and would like something other than beer. The thought of beer made her nauseous.

They had hidden most of her coins under a rock close by, so they retrieved them and began their walk to Cove. They hoped they would find William's relatives soon and decide what ship to book for their passage to Americay.

The couple went to the same pub where they ate the day before. They ordered a pitcher of water, some apples, and porridge with dark raisins. The food was excellent and filling. Their hangovers began to dissipate a bit with the food and water and they both felt excitement instead of the hangover fatigue.

They found a suitable place near the harbor where they could watch the ships, as well as the booking offices. They also stayed close enough to see their favorite pub; dinner was definitely going be there again today. They thought a few more beers might just take their minds off their problems.

The couple lay down in a grassy area and slept for part of the day. They were not bothered by anyone. When they woke it was late afternoon and there was no sign of William's relatives. He was now getting worried.

"If they don't show up by tomorrow noon, we will go ahead and book passage on the first ship out," said William.

This was not exactly what Molly wanted to hear. She thought if there were five of them, no one would bother them. She knew William could take care of himself, but she was not so sure about herself. She prayed for them to show.

The two of them left their comfortable spot on the grass and headed for the pub. They sat down and ordered a beer, vegetables soaked in brine, smoked fish and potatoes.

Molly said, "What a feast we have ordered. I have never in my life had smoked fish. Is it good?"

William, acting as if he were a mature man of the world, replied, "Yes indeed, it will be a wonderful meal. My cousin Mark and I spent many days fishing in a lough near Fermoy. My family never smoked the fish. We were fearful of attracting the English landholders with the smell of the fish being smoked. As you know, entering a lough to fish was a punishable offense." William said with a smile, "We avoided everything that was a punishable offense."

Molly's blinked her eyes and said, "William, you're full of horse shit, and I mean it."

That brought about more laughter from both of them, as the beer was taking its effect.

They finished their meal, and Molly paid for it again in silver coin. William thanked her and the two of them walked hand in hand to their grassy spot overlooking the harbor. The beer had not only warmed them up, it had also loosened them up quite a bit. Molly asked William if he ever had a girlfriend.

"Yes, her name is Anne Flynn," replied William.

"You still have a girlfriend now?" she asked.

"Yes, I do and I love her very much. I hope when I see her again she will still feel that way about me," he said. "How about you, did you or do you have a boyfriend?"

"No, I've never had a boyfriend, or been in love, for that matter. Some boys showed interest in me, for sure, but I was not attracted to them in any way. I always felt men were undressing me with their eyes. It gives me a creepy feeling. I do not think of you in that way. Don't be offended, but I think of you as a big brother, a very protective big brother," she said.

William laughed and said, "I never had a sister, but if I did, I would want her to be just like you. I do understand your feelings about some men, but not all men are like that. You saw the worst when you were a prisoner of Webb. That's the past. We are now in the future and you will never have to put up with that shit again." Molly smiled and reached over and patted William's hand and thanked him.

The alcohol was wearing off a bit and the two of them got extremely tired. Molly fell fast asleep, but William kept a diligent eye on the booking agent offices. He sat for several hours after dark before seeing his three relatives walk up the dirt road to the now-closed offices. He tapped Molly on the shoulder and told her to wake up. She was a bit groggy and slightly hung over, but had a big smile on her face as the boys approached. William greeted the three of them with a big hug and a smile. He introduced Molly to them and they all politely shook her hand.

The first thing out of Mark's mouth was, "Did you kill the bastards?"

William said that conversation was for later. He told them he and Molly had a resting place up on the hill and they would go there to plan their strategy.

William told the boys that he and Molly found a ship called the Schuylkill that would leave tomorrow afternoon with room for all of them. He said the cost of the passage was three British pounds, and it would be an additional two pounds for food per person which would include the cost of the shuttle. William thought they should pay in silver for both the passage and food. He and Molly both thought they should bring as much additional food and beverages as they could carry, in case supplies ran short. That would likely cost an additional three to four pounds.

"Forgive me, Molly, but who in the hell are you and how and why do you fit into our plans?" said Mark.

Molly was embarrassed by the question and was about to speak when William chimed in. "Molly is my friend, and you all will treat her with the respect due her. Molly helped me and others escape from Webb's compound and has been my companion for several days. She lost her family as we did and now she is part of our family."

The boys did not ask any more questions of Molly.

William asked the boys if they knew exactly how much gold and silver they had in their bags. The boys were still suspicious of their new traveling companion and were reluctant to open up in front of her about their financial situation.

"All of you, listen to me, once and for all. Molly is now part of this family and will be treated as such. She will pool her funds with ours, just as families do and everyone will know exactly what we have as a family. Please don't embarrass her again. You'll all get to know her and trust her and treat her as you would a sister," said William.

Molly was embarrassed, but understood the boys' trepidation. She would have to win their trust.

The five travelers reached the passage agent's office at eight o'clock the next morning. They were all very excited and extremely nervous.

They paid the fare and were told the shuttle would leave the dock promptly at one o'clock that afternoon.

This gave the group time to shop for food and beverages as well as some new clothes. William told Molly that she should find a new dress for the trip. She was dressed in rags and William feared that after the long trip, she would have no cloth left to cover her. Molly was surprised at his generous offer, but realized he was just acting like a concerned brother.

She took all of them with her shopping. Patrick was the first to follow, S.C. second and it was obvious that they both liked her a lot. William and Mark followed at a distance behind. Mark was bound and determined to find out what happened at Webb's compound and how William became acquainted with Molly. William said he would tell him the story when they were aboard the ship, not before. He said he was still concerned Webb may send agents out looking for them.

Molly found a very inexpensive dress in a women's dress shop. She bought a light brown cotton dress that had already been made. There was also a white dress that was not yet completed. After Molly said she would take the brown one, William insisted on her taking both of them. She blushed and said it was too much money. He assured her she would need at least two dresses for the trip and travel when they got to Americay.

"Just how much coin does she have?" asked Mark.

William replied, "More than you, cousin." That shut him up.

The elderly women that owned the dress shop, a Mrs. Farrell, told Molly that she would have the second dress done within an hour. Mrs. Farrell told the boys the general store was just down the road and she would entertain Molly until they got back. She also said that they could bathe in the back of the store and wash out their clothing.

After the boys left, Mrs. Farrell said to Molly, "I have to say, your friends smell worse than an outhouse."

Molly laughingly agreed and said, "I thought it was just me, but they do smell poorly, and you are right, they have an outhouse smell."

They both laughed, and Mrs. Farrell said, "Molly girl, you don't smell very good either, take off your clothes and wash yourself in the large basin in the backroom."

Molly went through the drapes and found the basin and a small apartment Mrs. Farrell called home. Mrs. Farrell followed her with a linen chemise that was to be used as an undergarment and a tightly laced bodice to go over the chemise. After Molly had washed her hair and her body, Mrs. Farrell gave her a towel to dry herself with and the undergarments to put on. Molly put on the chemise and bodice and brushed her hair.

"I knew there was a beauty under all that dirt and rags. I have a few other things for you, child, things I'll never be able to use, but you might find them useful," Mrs. Farrell said.

"You have done enough for me. I'm someone you hardly know and yet you shower me with kindness," said Molly.

"Molly, I have some things that were left with me long ago and that person never came back for them." Mrs. Farrell continued, "There are brogues shoes and woolen stockings here that should fit you, as well as a beautiful heavy wool shawl for your trip."

Molly had never worn shoes in her life and wondered if she could get used to them. Mrs. Farrell assured her she would and they would keep her feet warm on the ship and after they arrived in Americay. Mrs. Farrell washed Molly's old clothes and put them on her clothesline to dry.

She told Molly, "You never know when you might need some of these rags for personal use, if you know what I mean?"

Molly did, and although she was accustomed to having a regular cycle, she hadn't for quite a while because of stress and hard work. She felt the rags may come in handy on the ship and thanked Mrs. Farrell again for her kindness.

Mrs. Farrell went back to work to finish the dress on time. Molly helped as much as she could, but was anxious for the boys to return. She had put on her new dress and she looked lovely.

The boys went in the general store to buy new clothing too. They all bought tight knee britches with knitted wool stockings. They purchased linen shirts of different types and bought topcoats for the cold weather. They purchased heavy shoes but kept their old ones to wear in bad weather. This was the first time in their lives that they had store bought clothes. Their shoes were always bought in a store, but most of the time the boys went barefoot to save wear and tear on them. Their grandmother and aunt had made all their clothing. The storekeeper suggested the boys bathe before putting on their new clothes. He led them to the bath area and said he would have someone wash their old clothes for them.

The boys dressed in the new clothing after finishing their baths. They looked well scrubbed and all their scraggly beards were gone too. The outhouse stench that had offended everyone was gone, and they walked back confidently to Mrs. Farrell's shop. When the boys entered the shop the first thing they saw was the beautiful Molly. She looked stunning in her new dress and combed hair. She could possibly be the most beautiful woman any of them had ever seen.

Both Mrs. Farrell and Molly complimented the boys on their new looks. They both noted that a certain smell was no longer emanating from them.

William thought Molly looked lovely, but her stunning beauty worried him. People would remember her. They would likely forget the boys the minute the ship left port, but not Molly.

He pulled Molly aside and said to her, "Molly my dear, please don't take this the wrong way, but I'd like you to wear your shawl so it covers your head and your face."

She was hurt and insulted by what William had said.

"I'm sorry you don't like the way I look and I'm sorry if it offends you."

"Molly, you are just too lovely and people will remember you, especially Webb and his men," William tried to explain. "I don't know how far reaching Webb's influence is, it might be as far away as Americay. They may try and have someone track us down there. I'm just trying to protect you and the rest of the family."

Molly smiled, kissed William on the cheek, and said, "Thank you for always thinking of my welfare. You are a dear."

All of the Mountain boys saw the kiss and their imaginations ran wild, thinking maybe William and Molly were more than just friends.

Mark thought, "No wonder William would not discuss what happened at the Webb compound, or after they left!"

They collected all the new and used clothing and headed back to the general store to buy provisions for their long adventure. At the store they discussed what they would need. They agreed that food that wouldn't spoil was most needed. Molly spearheaded the purchase of the necessities, which included salt pork, beef jerky, smoked fish, hazelnuts, plain seeds of knot-grass and goose-foot, vegetables preserved in brine, and honey mead. The boys bought leather bags to carry the food and three two-gallon goatskin containers to hold the mead. All in all, they figured they would have enough food to supplement what they'd receive on the ship and sustain them for the entire trip. The group went to the dock area to count the coins they had left. Patrick and Molly counted the combined coins and reported to the others that they had a total of two hundred and twenty-two American dollars in silver coin left after the purchases. Patrick said he guessed, according to his calculations, with land offered for sale at approximately $2.50 an acre in Americay, the Mountains would have enough to buy approximately five hundred acres. That seemed to the boys about the same size all of the surrounding area of Killeagh. They'd be rich! They would have more land than Charles Webb.

CHAPTER 14

The Voyage to America

THE TRAVELERS WAITED ANXIOUSLY BY THE loading dock in the harbor of Cove on July 20, 1841, as the shuttle boat came across the harbor to pick them up. They were loaded down with supplies and were concerned that the ships' captain might not allow them to take everything aboard.

The group boarded the shuttle with seven other travelers and headed for the sailing ship named the Schuylkill. The excursion to the *Schuylkill* took under an hour, which was a faster pace than normal, as the calm water in the harbor made easy work for the oarsman.

Upon reaching the *Schuylkill*, the travelers climbed aboard on rope ladders while their belongings were hoisted up in baskets. The Captain, Gregory Steele, greeted them and said nothing about the amount of cargo they brought along.

In his welcoming speech, the captain said, "The trip to America will take somewhere between five to six weeks of sailing time, so be prepared for a long, cramped voyage. Including all of you, there are a total of seventy-five passengers aboard, which is the smallest number we've had in two years. The *Schuylkill* was built as a cargo ship and still is, but it has been modified slightly to carry passengers too. The quarters below are cramped, but not as much as it would have been with a one hundred and eighty passengers, as we normally have. I hope you can enjoy the trip; we will try and do everything in our power to make it comfortable for you. If you have any questions or are in need of something, please see Second-Mate Michael Gorman."

The family went below with Mike Gorman to find where they would be living.

William asked Mr. Gorman, "Please don't think I'm being disrespectful, but just what are the duties of a Second-Mate?"

Gorman said, "Please call me Mike, and I am third in charge of this vessel. The Captain is first in charge, always, and First-Mate Gleason is second in charge. Gleason is responsible to the captain for the crew and passengers' welfare and safety. He is also responsible for the ship's cargo. I help him in all aspects of his job, but I am ultimately the ships navigator. We'll all do as the Captain says. He is completely in charge. If you have questions of him regarding this voyage, please ask them through First Mate Gleason or me and we will ask him privately to respond. That's all I have to say about the chain of command and it is written in stone."

The Schuylkill was a small three-masted sailing vessel that was primarily used as a cargo ship. Most ships at the time were cargo ships or war ships. They were designed to fight wars or transport goods from one place or another, not passengers.

The quarters below were cramped and headroom was so low a person had to bend in a stooped position and creep to their assigned cot or hammock. Gorman assigned the five members of the Mountain family three cots and two hammocks close together, so they could rotate among themselves for comfort. Patrick suggested that Molly be given a hammock, since it did provide a little more privacy than the cots that were crammed together.

"Please don't treat me different than any of you. I will take my turn in the cots and I promise I will not complain," she said.

William knew she would not complain and she would adjust to any situation. He knew she was happy to be with them and was very excited to be going to Americay.

Food was to be eaten in their tiny living quarters; there was no dining area. The only exercise available was on the ships' deck and that was limited. The passengers were told in no uncertain terms to stay out of the way of the crew. Women were not allowed to have any contact, verbal or physical with the crew, it was strictly forbidden. The crew was made up of hardened men that would take any contact from a woman as an invitation for sexual advancement. Most of this six week trip would be spent below on their cots or hammock, sleeping, talking and reminiscing about their past.

On the first day out to sea a storm was brewing and the waves rose to about ten foot swells. Mark was the first to experience seasickness. He threw up in one of the many buckets that were provided by Mike Gorman to all the passengers below. Gorman knew that there would be very few that would not come down with seasickness, and he was correct: fifty-five were sick on the first day out of port and that number increased daily. Molly and William were the only members of the Mountain family that were not sick. Molly tended to the three sick men; she ordered William when to dump the buckets and when to bring fresh water. All the passengers, men, women and children shared the living quarters. With seasickness running rampant, the smell of the vomit filled the air and made it impossible for those that were sick to feel better. Patrick was the most affected in the family by the motion of the ship. He lay on a cot for four days, eating nothing and only drinking a spoonful of water and throwing it up. Molly never left his side. The boys were getting nervous about Patrick's condition. They knew full well of the dangers of being dehydrated. It could lead to death.

Molly told Patrick that it was time for him to get up and go topside. She thought the fresh air would help and he needed to get some food in his stomach. Mark and S.C. helped Patrick to the steps and with their help he made it to the fresh air. Molly was right behind them. They placed him on the port side of the ship, with the wind blowing directly in his face. Molly had brought a small cup of mead with her and put it to his lips.

"Patrick, my dear, this was made with honey, it has sweet taste and will give you the nourishment you need. You will drink the entire cup."

Molly held the cup to Patrick's lips until he took a small sip. He gagged immediately and Molly told him he must keep it down. He was able to do so. She continued holding the cup to his lips until it was all gone. She told him he was to stay aboveboard until dark, when she would return to help the boys get him back to his cot. Molly knew she

77

must not stay aboveboard too long, she could sense all of the crew's eyes on her. She went below to help the women attend to their sick children.

As the sun was going down and the temperature dropped, Patrick was ready to go below. He was chilled and shaking so hard he could barely get to his feet. Molly and the boys dragged him to his cot and covered him with some blankets. He shivered uncontrollably until Molly crawled onto the cot with him and covered him with her body.

He looked up at her and smiled and said, "Molly, you can do this anytime you want, even if I'm not seasick."

Molly had a serious, deadpan look on her face, and responded, "Patrick if you don't get better, I will have to live the rest of my life without you and I couldn't bear that. So get well my dear, please."

Needless to say, that's all it took for Patrick to start eating and drinking again. The boys couldn't figure out what Molly had said to him as she lay beside him, but whatever it was, he got better.

Molly and Patrick were spending most of their time together, which pleased William. He thought Patrick would be a good match for Molly. Patrick was smart, good looking, a sandy haired young man with deep blue eyes. He had a laid back disposition and was always easy to get along with. He tried to protect William from their father when he was a young boy and often times William was spared a beating because of it. Patrick remembered his mother distinctly and frequently told William and S.C. what she was like and his memories of her. They enjoyed the time when he would reminisce with them about her.

They were three weeks into their voyage when many of the children became ill. Some of the food had turned moldy and some of the cachets of water had soured, leaving it undrinkable. Several children died without warning from high fevers and unsustainable coughs. The bodies were just thrown overboard, since there was no way to preserve a body for burial later. Several men and women also passed away from what the captain thought appeared to be typhoid. Eighteen passengers perished on the trip. The passengers moved the cots and the hammocks of the dead out of their quarters. There was fear that the cots and hammocks carried the disease of the dead. They were thrown overboard with the dead bodies.

The Mountains were happy that they brought enough food and mead with them. The supply of mead was getting low, but it appeared the food supplies would last until arriving in Americay. The family decided that they would share some of their food with families with small children, or with undernourished adults. The recipients of the food were all very grateful, especially the families with small children. It helped ease the constant crying of the children, which the adults were not getting used to.

Molly wanted Patrick to take her up top for some fresh air. Patrick was somewhat reluctant because of the crew. He had heard stories from some of the other passengers about aggressive crew-members, harassing and yelling obscenities and asking females if they would perform sexual acts with them. Patrick dreaded going on deck, but Molly was insistent on him doing so. She was still worried about his ease of getting seasick and wanted him, as well as her, to get some fresh air.

Molly led the way up the steps and Patrick followed slightly behind. He always enjoyed watching Molly go up the steps ahead of him. She was all woman, and he enjoyed the view. Once up top, they moved to the starboard bow to get a better view and to have an ocean breeze and sea mist in their faces. Molly looked radiant in her new white dress. The breeze and mist made her dress cling to her body in a very seductive way. Patrick however, was a not the only one admiring Molly's striking features.

Two of the crew-members, Toothless Jack, and his partner Jonas White were watching her too. Toothless Jack looked around to see if the captain or mates were watching them. He decided they were alone and approached Molly from the side.

"My dear, don't you look nice today in your nice white dress. We can almost see your nice titties through your dress. I think we'll need to undress you a bit to get a better view of that nice little body of yours," he said.

Molly stepped back to where Patrick was standing and grabbed his hand.

She said to him, "Let's go down below, right now."

Patrick told the two of them to leave them alone or he would go to the captain. Toothless Jack pulled a small saber out of his waistband and waved it in the air toward Patrick.

He said, "You won't be telling anyone what we are about to do to your little bitch because we are going to slit your throat and throw you overboard to the sharks. And you, you little bitch, will cooperate with us or you'll have the same fate as this bloody boyfriend of yours. Jonas, you take care of this poor excuse for a man, while I break this little lassie in."

Jonas was making a move toward Patrick with a saber in hand, when they all heard William say, "I'll give you both two options. First, you can die where you stand, or second, you can drop your weapons and we'll go find the captain. I hope you both pick the first option."

Molly said to William, "I hate these two more than you do, but don't forget your promise. Please don't kill them William, let the captain punish them."

Molly stepped behind William and Patrick followed her.

Toothless Jack studied William for a moment and said, "How the hell are you gonna kill anyone without a bloody weapon? Hey Jonas, maybe he's going to try and beat us to death with his big cock?"

William smiled and asked, "Is that your answer? You both want to die?"

The two looked confused, as William dropped the knife from the sheath attached to his forearm into his hand and threw it just above Jack's head and into a beam. The blade cut his scalp and blood flowed down his face.

William said, "That was your warning, next one will be a direct hit to your goddamn heart, if you have a heart."

They still didn't know where the knife came from, but they realized this was one Irishman not to fool with. They both dropped their sabers and William told them to lie face down on the deck, as he confiscated their weapons. Molly ran to find the Captain and found him by the ship's wheel, with Second Mate Gorman. Gorman took the ship's wheel and Captain Steele followed Molly.

The crew-members were adamant that they had done no wrong. They said it was a clear case of them being attacked by a madman.

Toothless Jack said, "Look at what he did to my head. He and his friend attacked us after the women flirted with us and we rejected her. We know the rules aboard this ship, Captain, no patronizing with passengers and we followed the bloody rules."

Captain Steele ordered them to the brig until the episode could be sorted out.

William was worried that someone could place him and Molly at the Webb compound in the future if this story got out. A young Irishman carrying knives and the skills to use them could bring Webb's agents to Americay to find him. He told Molly and Patrick of his concerns and that it would be best to tell the captain, that the men harassed them, but no damage was done. William felt the two men would stand in fear of him and would leave the family alone.

"We have maybe two weeks left at best on this ship, let's leave well enough alone," William said.

They all agreed, but promised they would only go topside if William was present. After William recanted his story to Captain Steele, Steele released the two men from the brig, but made them work only in the cargo area. When on shore they would need to find other employment. The family congregated in their small space below deck to have dinner and talk about the day's events.

Mark was most inquisitive and said, "Are you and Molly ready to tell us what happened at the Webb estate? Is this a carryover from that? Do we have to continue to fear Webb in the future?"

William spoke, "All of you should know that I killed several men at the compound, with the most notable being Dante Wright. Molly, if you'd like, you can leave us here for a time while I tell them my story."

Molly said she'd stay. She had never asked William for details, but was interested.

William began, "When I reached the compound I killed one sentry immediately, then I went into the first building and slit the throats of five men while they slept. They slept far enough apart, but I can't believe to this day that none woke up to face me. I went into the third building, which was Wright's. There was no one on the first floor, so I quietly went up the stairs. There were three bedrooms and Wright's sleeping men occupied the first two. I believed their beds were too close together to kill them without waking everyone. I found Wright naked in the third bedroom with a young girl that he had forced to have sex with him. He was a monster to all the Irish he killed, so I slit his throat and cut off his private parts and let him bleed to death while I muffled his screams. The young girl and I doused the main floor in lamp oil and set it ablaze. I sent her to the barn and I went into Webb's house. I killed one guard there and found Molly. She was going to be used for sex by Webb. He was not there, but I set that place on fire too with Molly's help. We took some of the gold and silver Webb stole from the families he slaughtered and divided it among the girls. There were four including Molly and we sent three of them off to Belfast to start a new life. That's the whole story. Molly, do you have anything to add?"

Molly began, "I knew William had killed several by the blood all over his shirt, trousers and his hands and face. He was covered with it. I was very afraid of him, but he was so calm, I just did as he said. I am not, that I know of, responsible for killing anyone, but I helped start the fire. I don't regret it, but I pray no one perished in the fire."

Patrick was the first to speak. "Is that why you pleaded with William not to kill the crew members?"

"Yes, William promised he would not kill again. I was sure he would kill that bloke, Toothless Jack, but he didn't, and I am proud of his restraint," Molly said.

William said, "Molly dear, don't be too proud of me. I did try to kill him, but I missed. I think my aim is off a bit, not having practiced in many weeks. I aimed for his eye and just grazed his head. I was lucky the knife hit the beam or I might have lost it. No one will ever hurt my family again and if they do they will pay a severe price."

Most of the family felt uneasy about William's last comments. Molly later told Patrick and S.C. she was worried that William was beginning to enjoy the killing and the sense of power that came with it. None of them responded to what she said, but they were beginning to feel the same way. They felt safe with William being their guardian, but they were also afraid he might go too far and get them all in trouble.

CHAPTER 15

Perils in America

THE NEXT TWO WEEKS WERE UNEVENTFUL as all the passengers aboard were anxiously awaiting their arrival in America. When the ship was within a day of New York harbor, First Mate Gleason and Second Mate Gorman had an informal meeting below with all the passengers. Gleason and Gorman had recited their rehearsed script on many voyages before this one to many Irish emigrants. They liked this group and were very concerned that these poor Irish farmers were not worldly enough for New York City. They were sure they would be targets for thieves, con men and cutthroats. The forthcoming lecture was to prepare them for what might lie ahead for these poor, unprepared, farm folk.

"After you exit the ship with all your belongings, please hold on tight to them. Also, keep your money, if you have any, in a safe place and not in your pockets," Mike Gorman told them. "There are people who can pick your pockets without you knowing it's happening. Go past Five Points as fast as you can. Don't stop and talk to anyone. You have no friends in New York. Get to the tenement housing just past Five Points and find a place for the night, week, or whatever. The regular rate for one room is $1.00 per week for as many family members you have. Food in the summer and fall at the markets is cheap, but buy only what you can eat that day; otherwise it will spoil. Jobs are plentiful, but you men will work 12-hours a day, seven days a week for seventy-five cents a day, if you're lucky. If you're not lucky, it will be fifty cents a day. So, your room will cost $4.00 per month, food will run you about $2.00 to $2.50 a week, or $8.00 to $10.00 per month. You will need wood in the winter months for heat and cooking that will likely cost $1.50 per month. Your fixed costs should be around $16 to $18 per month, leaving roughly $4.00 to $6.00 for you to save. Hide your money carefully and never give it to anyone to hold for you. The women should stay in the room as much as possible and should never go to the markets unescorted. Don't talk to strangers and get a weapon as soon as possible - a pistol, knife or saber; anything to protect yourself. New York is a dangerous place to live. Get out to the countryside as soon as you can. Find the Erie Canal and take a ship on one of the Great Lakes to a rural community like you just left, but don't stay in New York."

The men asked Mike what types of jobs were available to them.

Gleason responded, "I'll answer that. Take anything that is offered, but your competition for work will be with the Negroes and they will work cheap. The common white folk in New York will not take the jobs that will be offered to any of you. Go to the shipyards, steel mills, warehouses or with the construction gangs that are building canals and railways. The Irish are always wanted to lay track. It's a backbreaking job, but it pays well, upwards of ninety cents to a dollar a day, but it is dangerous. They say for every tie laid, one Irishman will die laying it. Most of the construction gangs like Irish workers. They don't bitch and they work harder than anyone else."

First Mate Gleason asked if there were any questions. Most hands in the room were raised. There were questions about food and safety.

"Why would I have to remain in the room all day? What would happen if I go out?" a woman asked.

Mike answered, "We're not saying you can't go out. But going out unescorted, even in daylight could be a risk. There are ruthless men living in the surrounding area of Five Points and they make a living by taking innocent women and making whores out of them or selling them as slaves. A women can be kidnapped in broad daylight and their families never see them again. Unfortunately, those are the risks that lie ahead for all of you. And all of you - make sure you know where your children are at all times."

A quiet hush fell over the room as the brutishness of their new country became a reality.

"I'm so sorry to frighten you, but you all need to know the facts of life in this country. Just be extremely careful," Mike said.

After the meeting, William spoke to his family privately.

"The two things I learned from Mike and Gleason was that we will need more weapons and Molly will need to be protected at all times. I suggest we work in the railroad business, which seems to be the most lucrative job for us. You three will rotate and take every third day off to be with Molly. I intend to work every day until we can leave New York. The way I figure, and Patrick will correct me if I'm wrong, with three of us working seven days a week, we'll earn on the low-end $80 per month. And if I figure our expenses high at $25 a month, we'll net approximately $55 a month. In one year we would have close to $700 additional dollars for our land and travel expense," said William.

The group recommended that William, even if he didn't want too much time off, take at least three days a month off.

"We'll see how tired I get, but I want to get to Whisk-con-sin as soon as I can," said William.

Molly was inquisitive about William's hurry to get to Whisk-con-sin.

She point blank asked him, "What is the reason you need to get to Whisk-con-sin in such a hurry?"

William was a bit embarrassed, but he told Molly, Patrick and S.C. his reason.

"It's a woman, Anne Flynn. As I told you she is the most beautiful woman I have ever seen. Mark knows her and she has a sister, Margaret. I got the idea of Americay from them. They are leaving this year or next and will go to Whisk-con-sin. I hope someday to see her there."

Mark interjected, "I'm in love with Margaret and plan to wed her if she'll have me."

Molly laughed and said to William, "No wonder you never seemed interested in any of the girls we've seen. You've been in love all this time?"

"I have, and I'm not ashamed to tell you. Anne is so special and I have to get to Whisk-con-sin before she might find someone else to marry," William said.

"If she loves you, she'll wait," Molly said.

CHAPTER 16

Five Points New York

THE *SCHUYLKILL* DOCKED IN NEW YORK Harbor on September 3, 1841 and the gangplank was lowered for the passengers to disembark. The families lined up with all their belongings and nervously walked down the plank to solid ground. It had been over six weeks at sea and many passengers were so used to the rolling of the ship that they fell upon reaching the dock. Although most were hesitant and worried about life in their new country, they found humor in their inability to stand without falling over.

This happens every time we reach port," said Mike Gorman. "It always amazes me that after so long at sea, the Irish can still smile and laugh at themselves in the face of so much uncertainty."

The Mountain family was no exception. They were all staggering as though they were drunk and laughing along with the other passengers.

After a short while the passengers found their footings and began their trek to find suitable lodging, all the while keeping in mind the lecture that Gorman and Gleason gave them on the perils of New York. The group walked as fast as their legs would carry them, past the barkers on the pier that were trying to sell them clothing, food, liquor and women.

The Mountain clan, with no children to slow them down, was ahead of the others by several blocks when they reached the area called Five Points. As they walked into Paradise Square Park, where the five streets of Mulberry, Orange, Gross, Anthony and Little Water all intersected, they were greeted by the roughest bunch of humans they had ever seen.

They walked briskly along trying not to make eye contact with anyone that might accost them.

Molly walked with Patrick, a bit behind Mark, S.C., and William. As they reached the far side of Paradise Park, a large ugly man with a dirty salt and pepper beard and a pistol in his belt came up behind Molly and ran his hand up under her dress and grabbed her buttock. She screamed and turned to slap the man when he drew his pistol from his belt. Molly pulled away and he released his hand from under the dress. All the traffic in the Square stopped immediately and stared, wondering what would happen next. This was a common event in Five Points.

The man said, "My name is Desmond Delaney, and this is my square. What's your name, lass?"

Molly said, "Please go away. I have nothing you want."

He replied, "Oh yes you do. You will come along with me, I have a very high paying job in a store for you and all you have to do is lay on your back. You're a beauty and you'll be in big demand here in Five Points. Now I won't say it again, what is your name?"

Patrick stepped forward in front of Molly and said, "This is my woman that you are disrespecting. She is not and will not be your whore."

Desmond cocked the pistol and took aim at Patrick and said, "You poor country boy, you're in the big city now and you'll all do as I say. Do I make myself clear?"

William looked around and saw that there were two others that were grinning ear to ear. He assumed they were with Delaney. He knew he'd have to stop all three if they were to move on safely. William stepped from behind the group and faced Delaney.

Delaney laughed when he saw William and said, "Now what the fuckin' hell do you want? Do all of you country boys want to die today? Even if you do, the girl will still go with me."

William didn't say a word. He just stared at his enemy with a look of contempt on his face. William judged that Delaney was not going to back down from a few Irish farm boys, so he dropped the knife from his forearm into his hand and threw it with all his might—directly into Delaney's right shoulder. Delaney fired his pistol and the ball struck

William in the left hip. William winced in pain but stood his ground. Then he wheeled around, reached for the knife behind his head and launched it into the chest of the second man. As he was hit, the man fired his weapon at William and hit him in the right side around the waist area. William staggered and dropped to one knee. Lucky for William both balls went through the fatty tissue and exited without hitting anything vital. The third man fled into the crowd. Desmond Delaney lay on the ground in excruciating pain with his pistol laying five feet from him.

William pointed to the second man and told S.C. to get his pistol, gunpowder, and the balls. S.C. also found a very large knife with a twelve-inch blade that had to be five inches wide.

"Here's something that will test your skills. Have you ever seen a knife this large?" S.C. asked.

William limped to Delaney and kicked his pistol toward Patrick.

"Patrick pick up the gun and come over here and take his powder, and balls", said William. "We might need these weapons in the future."

William stood over Delaney, leaned down and yanked his knife out of his shoulder. He screamed and swore at William. As the screaming and profanity continued, William pressed his foot squarely on the injured man's wound with all his weight and pressed the point of his knife on Desmond's throat.

"Desmond Delaney, you fucked with the wrong person today," William warned. He leaned down and whispered softly, "I've killed many men in my life and you and your friend were lucky today. I chose not to kill you because I want a fresh start here in Americay, but if you push me again, I will kill all of you. You may get a shot off, like today, but by the time you try and reload, I'll send three knives in your direction, and as you can see I am very accurate. Now you'll do exactly as I say. Stay away from my family or I will kill you and I'll make you suffer. You might get me, but I'll take you with me. Stay away from the girl. If I ever see you or your men even look at her, you will die. Now, do I make myself clear?"

Delaney was shaking in pain as William released his foot from the injured man's shoulder and said, "We'll leave you alone for now, but I wouldn't stay in Five Points very long if I were you."

William limped over to the other injured man and pulled his blade out of his chest. He stepped on the wound with all his weight and the man screamed. He told him the same thing he told Delaney

"I will, I will, so help me God, I will!" the man yelled in panic.

The crowd began to disperse and they kept a good distance away from the Mountain family. In the distance they heard cop whistles. The cops would wait until the shooting stopped before going into Five Points. Four men came to the aid of Delaney and the other fellow and dragged them away from the park. As William limped away he told his family to keep walking and get as far way from this park as they could. Molly was fearful that William would bleed to death from his wounds. She made him stop so she could look at them. William dropped his trousers so Molly could examine the wound on his left hip. The ball tore a chunk of meat off his hip and it was bleeding profusely. She took some of her old clothing rags from her bag and put them on the wound. She then looked at the wound on his right side. She was much more concerned with that one. It was bleeding more than the one on his hip. She applied as much pressure as William could stand and then wrapped the rags tightly around his waist, hoping they would stay in place until she could dress the wounds properly.

The five of them had to move along very slowly with S.C. and Mark holding up William.

William demanded, "Leave me and go on and find a place to stay. I cannot go further."

"I'm sick of you telling me and Patrick what to do," S.C. said. "For God-sakes you're our younger brother and not the fuckin' boss. We will not leave you, or anyone else, and stop telling us what to do. You're acting like a goddamn martyr, which you're not, so stop that bullshit now! We will carry you, but we shall not leave you."

S.C. and Mark continued to carry William about a mile past Five Points, where there were many tenement houses with rooms for rent.

Patrick said, "Let Molly make the decision where we'll stay, it's more important to her than us."

The family looked at a few close by, but they were all the same—one room, one window, no beds, no water, dirty with a common outhouse in the back yard. Molly chose a room on the third floor, since there was only one other room on that floor. Molly also saw a young woman in the other room and liked the way she smiled at her. The man who rented them the space wanted one month's rent in advance. Patrick said they'd pay one week in advance and that would be $1.00, take it or leave it. He took it.

S.C. and Mark had stayed a short distance from the new room so the landlord would not see William's condition. It was difficult getting William up three flights of stairs, but they understood Molly's reasoning. The room would be safe from intruders. It had only one other tenant on the floor and they could keep track of anyone coming up the creaky staircase. They all felt safe, at least for the time being.

Mark went downstairs to the street to where he had seen a man selling bales of straw. Mark bought two bales and went back upstairs. He brought them in and Molly and Patrick helped him make beds for everyone. William asked for the space in the corner where he would have a good view of the door and the landing area. Molly looked at William's wounds and redressed them. They continued to bleed but the bleeding had slowed a bit. William closed his eyes and fell asleep.

After getting settled in their new room, the neighbor from next door rapped on the open door. She was a slender young lady with a beautiful face and an infectious smile. She sheepishly introduced herself as Emilia Campbell from County Tyrone in Northern Ireland. Molly liked her immediately and asked why she was in New York. Emilia said she came here a year ago with her grandparents. Her mother and father sent her along with her father's parents to find a better life in America. Thus far, that hadn't happened. Her grandfather was working as a laborer on the docks, unloading cargo from ships. Her grandmother and she stayed in their room most days and seldom went out. Emilia said she was an artist and a writer and was bored out of her mind. She amused herself drawing pictures of New York and its inhabitants. Occasionally, someone would pay her to draw pictures of their children. It kept her busy and did provide a little income for her family. S.C. liked her smile, as well as everything else about her.

Emilia felt comfortable with the Mountain family and brought her grandmother, Mrs. Kathleen Campbell, over to introduce her. She was an elderly, thin woman who was quick to smile. Emilia and Molly liked each other right off and Emilia said she could stay with her and her grandmother during the day while the boys were working. Molly was slightly embarrassed to say she would have company for a while since William was injured. Emilia and her grandmother were concerned and asked what was wrong with William. Molly explained the incident to them, not going into great detail, but told them as much as she thought they could handle. Kathleen said shootings were a common occurrence in this part of New York City and most residents had a gun or a knife pointed at them one time or another.

As the Mountain family was getting to know the Campbells, someone was walking up the creaky stairway in a hurried manner. William rose off the straw bed and told the women to get back away from the door. William lifted the pistol off the floor and aimed it toward the door.

A happy voice said, "Where are my girls?"

It was Emilia's grandfather Bradan, home from work.

William fell back into his bed and said, "Sorry, I thought it was someone that meant us harm."

Kathleen asked if she could look at William's wounds. He allowed her to look, but knew Molly had done all that could be done.

"This boy needs a doctor, he's bleeding to death," Kathleen said.

William protested, saying, "No doctors and no one from the outside. That's final."

"We need to cauterize the wounds. It will be painful, but it's the only way to stop the bleeding," said Bradan. "Do you have a steel knife?""

"Do I have a knife?" said S.C. "Yes I do."

He brought out the bowie knife that he had picked up off the man in the park. Bradan told Kathleen to stoke up a fire in their small stove. When the coals were red hot, he slid the knife into them and waited for the steel to turn red. He told Molly to undress the wounds and for the boys to hold William down.

"That will not be necessary," William said. "Just get this over with."

Bradan held the knife over the wound on the right side first. He had to cauterize both the entry and exit wound. William stared straight ahead and never blinked his eyes. The bleeding stopped immediately. Bradan turned him over and did the same to his hip injury. William never made a sound, he just passed out. The girls covered all the wounds with an ointment and applied rag bandages.

The family thanked the Campbells for their help and for not asking questions. S.C. told Bradan they were going to go look for work in the morning. Bradan suggested that they come with him to the docks. He said he thought he could have them all working on a temporary basis. He said they wouldn't be seen in the Five Points area. He had learned his lesson taking Emilia there. He always walked on the outskirts going to and coming from work. They all agreed to meet at five o'clock and head to the dock.

Molly said she should keep one of the pistols for their safety at home and the boys should carry the other for their protection. Emilia suggested that since they lived just across the hall on the top floor, with no other rooms, they could just leave the two doors open and move back and forth as they pleased. That way someone would always be on the lookout for invaders. When the girls went to the privy, Molly carried the pistol. Molly liked the living conditions and felt safer than she had in quite a while.

S.C., Mark and Patrick met Bradan at the scheduled time and left for the docks. Molly had packed the boys and Bradan leftover jerky and a few apples. They were pleased and said their goodbyes. William remained unconscious for several more hours. When he awoke he was thirsty and asked Molly if they had any water in the room. Emilia told them not to use the water from the pump in front of the tenement houses because it was contaminated. They were to use the well in the back yard; it was away from the outhouse and as pure as any water around here. Molly took the gun and the two of empty cachets the mead was stored in and went to get water. She saw a few men while at the pump and they seemed harmless. She filled the two cachets, went out to the front of the building, and looked around. Nothing out of the normal, she thought, and went back in. William devoured the water and he couldn't get enough. He was still running a fever and the wounds were leaking pus. Mrs. Campbell offered William some tea that had an ingredient in it to lower a fever. He drank it and fell fast asleep.

Bradan Campbell and the boys returned at six o'clock that night and were all very happy. They each received $1.00 for their work that day and were given several apples, a gunnysack of oatmeal, raisins and some dried jerky. The food was taken or stolen from the ships' cargo by the dockworkers and was divided among them. Bradan said this was a common event and that was the reason he continued to work there. The pay was excellent and the food offset a big part of their expenses. Otherwise he would love to get out of this dangerous area. The boys agreed they would return the next day and would remain until William could travel. When they looked at William, they realized that he would not be traveling for a long time.

One week later, William was still alive, but very weak. The fever had subsided a bit, but would return without any warning. Molly fed him jerky, but he had a hard time keeping that down. The fruit was refreshing, but he couldn't eat much as it bothered his stomach. The oatmeal was his savior; he could always keep that down. The boys continued bringing home food almost every day and they were earning between seventy-five cents to a dollar per day. They were happy and had not been bothered by anyone. Molly and Emilia went to the market two times a week in the early morning. They figured the men that could, or would cause problems, were likely sleeping off a drunken stupor and were too hung-over to go out in the early morning.

Emilia and Molly became fast friends. S.C. and Emilia also became close and were more than friends. They really liked each other. Emilia asked Molly if she thought the boys would take her along to Whisk-con-sin. She said that her grandparents encouraged her to ask. They loved their granddaughter, but wanted her to find a better life than what was here in New York. They also liked the Mountain boys and felt she would be safe with them. They told her that they had enough coin to pay her way. Molly told her she would ask and was sure S.C. would be all for it.

A few days later after the boys had left for work, Molly told William that she and Emilia were going to the market for some smoked fish. She was always worried about leaving William alone; things were too good and too quiet. She had not been carrying the pistol any longer and neither had the boys. William knew that things were not over with the Five Points gang. He kept both guns loaded at all times.

Molly and Emilia went to the market and had a wonderful time. They bought the smoked fish and some fresh bread that would be a treat for all. Molly noticed two men watching them from a half block away. They weren't gawking like most men, but were pretending that they had no interest in the girls. Molly thought that one of the men looked like the man that ran away after their encounter with Desmond Delaney. Molly took Emilia's hand as she was asking some questions of a woman selling the bread.

"Emilia, we are leaving now," Said Molly.

Emilia immediately understood, and walked away with Molly.

"Act as if there is nothing wrong," Molly told her. "Walk slowly and look at all the goods for sale, but head for home. We must warn William and your grandmother."

The girls went the long way home trying to lose the two men that followed them. They finally went to their tenement house and ran upstairs. They rushed to William and told him about the men that followed them. Molly was certain that one was the man that fled after the shootings in the Park. William told Emilia to go to their place and sit in the far corner with her grandmother.

"Give me both of the pistols and the big knife," William told Molly. "I have my other knives."

William struggled to stand up in his corner with both loaded guns in his hands and his knives well hidden. Molly sat across the room, hopefully out of gunfire range.

William was the first to hear the footsteps on the stairs. Whoever it was, was taking his time, but the creaky staircase gave him or them away. William saw a shadow cross in front of the door with a man following it. When he turned the corner, William shot the man in the face at close range. He screamed and fell to the floor holding what was left of his face. William looked up from the injured man and saw Emilia pointing at someone about to enter his room. He sat down and waited for the man to expose himself. He turned into the room and blindly shot in William's direction, but missed by four feet as William remained seated.

William fired the second pistol and hit the man in his stomach. He crawled up the walls to his feet and threw his knife into the man's throat, killing him. William could hear more noise on the steps and waited for an attack. He thought he heard someone starting to quietly, slowly go back down the steps. William limped to the door and with knife in hand, swung to the hallway and threw his knife. The knife lodged in the third man's leg as William drew another knife out of his waistband, but didn't throw it. William slowly came down the stairs. The man was crying and screaming in pain. William pulled his knife out of the man's leg.

"Hand me your pistol," William demanded. "You are all just a bunch of cowards, aren't you?"

Still crying, the man said, "I'm only the tracker, not a killer."

"Did Desmond Delaney send you?" asked William.

"Yes, Desmond sent us. We all got a $10 gold piece for the job, but we had to bring the girl back. He really wanted the girl. He had offered a reward to the man that found her and I found the beautiful girl in the market," the man said.

His comments upset William even more and he said, "Now get the hell out of here and tell Delaney I'm now coming after him. But before you go I'll have that $10 gold piece, since you did not complete the job."

The man handed over the gold piece and limped down the stairway and into the street where a crowd had gathered after the gunfire stopped.

Surprisingly, no police, no landlord, or concerned friends of the deceased showed up and had the nerve to walk up the steps.

William and the girls dragged the first body into their room. As William went to fetch the second man's body, he asked Molly to search the dead man's pockets for a gold piece and bring him the sack that contained his balls.

Molly stopped in her tracks and screamed, "Are you delirious, I wouldn't touch this dead man's balls!"

William laughed out loud and said, "Molly my dear, let me rephrase myself. Please bring the sack that contains the lead balls for the pistol."

In this time of great stress, his comments broke the tension and the girls all giggled.

"While you're at it please get the powder as was well," said William.

William dragged in the other man with Kathleen's help.

Molly said laughingly, "I suppose I should get to work on this bloke too. I'm sure he has no need for his balls or gold coins."

William now had four flintlock pistols, balls and powder; enough to wage a war. He also had a new knife that S.C. called a bowie knife for some reason. After they emptied their room of food and all valuables, William asked the women to close the door. He said they would stay in the Campbells' room until the men arrived home from the docks. Molly wanted to go and fetch the boys so they could get as far away from this area as possible before dark.

William said to her, "Molly, I love your spirit, but if you think I'd let you go that far with the likes of Desmond Delaney looking for you, you are daft," William said. "That is just what he wants; we'll just have wait until they get home."

Nothing was said for a very long time, when Kathleen broke the silence and said, "William, you would be doing Bradan and me a big favor by taking Emilia with your family to your Whisk-con-sin. We have nothing but fear for her here. We watched how all you boys care for each other and we know she would be treated well. She cannot stay here after what happened, they know her face."

"I'm not leaving here anytime soon, I have some debts to repay," William said. "I'll ask Patrick, Molly, S.C. and Mark if they would accept her and I'm sure they will."

"I've already told Emilia she will come with us, as well as the other Campbells, but you're not staying here under any circumstances. They will kill you," Molly told William.

"I thank you for offering to take us with you, but we are staying too. Bradan has the best job he could get anywhere and we'll just move closer to the docks," said Kathleen. "They like him there and we get enough food and income to take care of us. We are happy, our only concern has been for Emilia and now that has been resolved. We cannot thank you all enough."

William waited for a long time before answering Molly. He said, "I cannot allow a man to get away with treating people the way Delaney does. Women are all whores for his personal pleasure or for his mate's pleasure. He makes all men do his bidding. He's a coward."

Molly smiled and said, "William, your intentions are good, but you cannot change the way things are here in Five Points. Maybe we can change things for the better in Whisk-con-sin."

The family returned home around six o'clock, anxious to tell everyone about their day. Things had gone well and they brought home several bags of vegetables and fruits. Molly told them the entire incident that had occurred in their room and that was why the door was closed. She suggested they all look in.

"What the hell happened here, were you attacked?" S.C. exclaimed.

William said, "Yes, we were attacked by those dead in our room, Delaney sent them to kill me and bring Molly back to him. I let one man get away and told him I would come for Delaney."

"But he's not going after anyone, he's coming with us to Whisk-con-sin," Molly said.

"Let's get out of here tonight, before the authorities come and find these bodies," S.C. said.

Patrick suggested that they pack up immediately and head to an area near central Manhattan, where he had heard they could camp out. Molly explained that Emilia would be going with them and the Campbells would remain in the Five Points area. Emilia and her grandparents cried and said their goodbyes. Kathleen handed Emilia some silver coins that they had saved since arriving in New York. Kathleen and Bradan told her to use it for her expenses to Whisk-con-sin, and for a new start in her life. They hugged and kissed and the Campbells went in the other direction toward the docks.

The group headed north toward central Manhattan, where they would determine where to go next. William was in poor physical shape. He was coughing, limping and holding his sides as he tried to keep up.

"Please go on without me, I'll find you up the river soon, but I need to rest," William said.

S.C. replied, "We will not leave you or anyone else, get that idea out of your mind. We're all in this together."

Mark and S.C. both grabbed one of William's arms and dragged him along. His breathing became labored and he was definitely losing all his strength.

"We need to get him to a place where he can lay down and Molly can re-dress his wounds," S.C. said.

"Let's get as far away as possible before we stop," said Patrick. "I know he needs rest, but we don't know who is looking for us. A place called Seneca Village is our destination tonight, let's not stop until we get there."

CHAPTER 17

The Pratt Family

THE FAMILY REACHED THE OUTSKIRTS OF central Manhattan around ten o'clock. It was dark, but the full moon and stars helped them along. They saw what they thought was a campfire and approached it with caution. Mark and Emilia entered the area slowly.

"Hello, can we join you folks?" asked Emilia.

A voice said, "Please do."

Mark went in first followed by Emilia, with the rest of the party remaining in the dark. There were two adults and two children surrounding the fire for warmth. The family was of Negro descent and appeared to be happy for company. The man introduced himself as Eldon Pratt and his wife as Marcie. Mark asked them if the rest of their family could join them.

"Of course they may," Eldon said.

The rest of the family came into the light and the Pratt family were shocked at the sight of William.

Marcie said, "Please lay him here by the fire. What is wrong with him?"

Molly told the Pratt's that William had been shot twice and was slow in recovering.

"Please don't be alarmed by what you see here," said Molly. "We mean you no harm. We need a place to rest and we have food we can share with you. We'll be happy to pay you for your hospitality."

"Please sit down and rest yourselves, I can see you are weary and cold," said Eldon. "We don't have much, but you can share what we have."

None of the family had ever seen a Negro before, let alone an entire family. They had heard that Negroes were all slaves, but this family didn't appear to be slaves. They were clean, well groomed and very articulate. In fact, they were far more articulate than any of the white New Yorkers they had come in contact with.

Molly opened one of the leather backpacks that contained some fruit and offered it to the Pratt children. They were very polite and looked at their parents for approval before taking the fruit. Eldon smiled and nodded his approval. The kids ate melons and apples with abandon and giggled with enjoyment. Molly offered some to the parents.

"We'd rather not," Eldon said.

"Why not, it's very good fruit?" said Patrick.

"We are free folk and we don't take handouts from people that likely need food more than we do," said Eldon. "I mean no disrespect to any of you, but we realize times are hard."

"Thank you for being so polite, but we have more than we can eat and will be a pleasure to share it with you fine people," said Patrick. "Besides the fruit, we have many vegetables and plenty of jerky for everyone. Please join us."

"Thank you, I will," said Marcie. "Forgive Eldon, he just doesn't trust many whites."

Eldon responded, "Marcie and the children and I are all free blacks. We were given our freedom from a generous man and his wife, Mr. and Mrs. Edgar Lipton. They bought Marcie and me in New Orleans when we were young. We were house slaves; we did all the domestic chores including the cooking for the Lipton's. The Lipton's allowed us to marry and educated us and our children. When Mr. Lipton died a few weeks ago, Mrs. Lipton said it was his desire to free my family and me. Mrs. Lipton did as he requested and freed us; we have the papers."

"What are your plans in the future?" S.C. asked Eldon. "Can we help you in any way?"

"You are very kind and I will join Marcie in sharing your food. I sincerely appreciate this," said Eldon. "After we eat, I will share our plans with you."

The Pratt children, 12-year-old Eddie and 10-year-old Sue, had their fill and went to Emilia and Molly, entertaining them with several folk songs.

While the children were busy, Eldon said, "You asked what we intend to do? I'll share our future with you. Mr. Lipton, besides freeing us, left us some of his fortune. We inherited a nice sum of money. We bought 10 lots of land for $500 dollars in Seneca Village just north of where we are now. We will transfer our money for the property tomorrow. It is the only place in New York where a black man can own land. In the State of New York slavery ended in 1827 and that gave us Negroes more opportunities to own land if we had the money. There will be several more free blacks buying property in the area soon and there are many already there. I plan to build a home and a small farm on my 10 lots and with the money left over we will have some security."

"Eldon, we came from a society that treated us the same way that Negroes are treated here in Americay," S.C. said. "Only we could not own property and we had to obey the English in everything they said. We came here for freedom, but have had nothing but problems since we got here. Just look at my brother, William. He was just trying to protect our sister Molly when he was shot. Americay is becoming a worse place to live than Ireland."

Eldon asked S.C., "What are your plans?"

"Our plan is to get to the Hudson River and find a boat or a ship of some kind to take us north to a town called Albany," said S.C. "It's supposed to be a long trip to Albany, more than 150 miles. From there we take another boat on something called the Erie Canal to a place called Buffalo, and then to Lake Erie or to another area called the Great Lakes. We're not exactly sure of all the lakes or towns, but we will eventually find a place called Whisk-con-sin. One problem, we should have begun this journey long ago, not in September. By the time we get to the Great Lakes it may be frozen and we'll have to wait until spring to continue. I have no idea where we'll stay until spring."

"If you left in late February or early March, would that make the trip easier?" asked Eldon.

"Leaving in late February would be ideal, but we can't stay close to Five Points," explained S.C. "There are people looking for us."

"Let's get some sleep tonight and talk about this problem tomorrow," said Eldon. "I think I have a solution that may be beneficial to us all."

The next morning, after a breakfast of porridge and fruit and while everyone was still seated, Eldon began his proposal.

"You folks are in need of a place to stay for the winter months and a place that will provide you safety and comfort. I need help building my house and beginning my gardens," said Eldon. "I'll need to clear some fields and build some stonewalls; I could use your help. All of you could stay with us here in Seneca Village, where you will be safe from whoever shot William. People from Five Points know enough to stay away from Seneca Village."

The Mountain clan looked at one another with relief on their faces.

Patrick spoke, "Eldon, that is a generous offer and we will accept, providing all of us are in agreement."

"I don't want my being here with your family to bring you any harm," said William. "I don't see that it would be an option for me. I think I'll have to leave, but the rest of the family should take your offer. They are all used to hard work and with all helping, your house, stonewalls and gardens should be completed before the snow falls. Me, I'll leave tomorrow."

"Bullshit to you, William! Eldon said we'd be safe and I believe him, he is a man of his word," said S.C.

"I don't doubt Eldon being a man of his word, but how in the hell is he going to stop Desmond Delaney from finding me within a ten mile radius of Five Points?" William argued.

"William, I don't think you understand the black community here in New York," said Eldon. "We stick together. If we befriend a family of white folks, or black folks for that matter, all the community will accept that family. Also, your Desmond Delaney will never come within five miles of Seneca Village. He knows better. I guarantee you will be safe.

However, none of you can go near Five Points again, and for sure not seek revenge."

Later that morning the Mountain clan and the Pratt family walked straight north until they reached the area called Seneca Village. They went to see Mr. John Whitney, who was selling off parcels of his farm to black families. Mr. Whitney asked Eldon if he had the $500 in silver to complete their deal. Eldon handed Whitney the coins. Whitney asked Eldon and Marcie to sign the deed and he would file it at city hall. They were now property owners in the first community of black property owners on Manhattan Island.

After taking ownership, Eldon walked the property with the entire group. He and Marcie pointed out just where the house would be built and where the gardens and walls would be placed. Eldon said he had negotiated to have lumber delivered by wagon within the next two days. It was coming from Albany where there were several lumber merchants and sawmills. He had a vision in his mind of what he wanted in his new house. Two stories, with two bedrooms upstairs for the children, a bedroom on the main floor for Mr. and Mrs. Pratt, a kitchen, living room and a porch attached to the front of the house. He had helped the Liptons build several wooden structures in the past and was familiar with the process. The Mountain boys told him they knew how to build mud huts, but not a wooden structure.

"You boys just follow my lead and we'll get it built," said Eldon. "First, we need to dig the cellar and build a stone foundation, the cellar floor will be dirt, and we'll have to level and flatten it. The cellar will be approximately six feet deep and will be used for the storage of food and a place to hide in case of severe weather. We'll start today by digging the hole for the cellar. The ladies and children will begin to clear the area for the garden. We'll use the stones cleared from the garden and elsewhere on the property for the foundation. Nothing will go to waste."

Eldon had purchased shovels, picks, and a wheelbarrow from the local blacksmith. The general store carried manufactured tools such as hammers, levels, ladders, saws and nails by the pound. The store also gave the Pratt's a credit account, a very unusual thing for a black family to receive. The account was to be paid in full at the end of 30 days in order to maintain it. This would be no problem for the Pratt's as they had sufficient funds.

The digging began immediately after Eldon outlined where the cellar would be. S.C., Patrick, Mark and Eldon did the hard labor, as William sat below an apple tree and just watched or slept. He was unable to move, he was so weak and sore. Molly kept an eye on him frequently and brought him water and food even though he never asked for anything. She was worried, but Marcie told her his wounds were healing. The bleeding had stopped and it would just take time.

Eldon and the boys built a temporary lean-to for shelter out of the timber that was delivered the second day. As the house was built, they would tear apart the lean-two and use the lumber for the house.

Digging the cellar took three days. The group enjoyed the work; it had been a long time since they had done this type of labor. The girls and children gathered up all the larger rocks and put them in the wheelbarrow for the men to haul to the site. Eldon began to build the foundation by placing the rocks and boulders in the appropriate places. He had built cellars before and knew the correct placement of the rocks was very important. S.C. and Mark did the heavy lifting.

After the work on the cellar was completed and the cellar floor was leveled, the support beams for the house were installed. The main level floor was built and attached to the support beams. The lean-to was taken down and the cellar was now enclosed and used as the living quarters. S.C., Mark and Patrick were assigned to dig the privy and their past experience in an outhouse reminded them to dig it deep and wide, to accommodate as many as four if they needed a place to hide. The memory of that part of their last days in Ireland brought a smile to all their faces, including William's.

The boys finished the hole for the outhouse and Eldon, with the boys' help, built a fine house on top of the hole. They all stood and admired it for a while and were grateful to have some privacy for a change, especially the ladies. Eldon even placed a small hook inside the door for a lock, to ensure their privacy. Things were looking up, but the weather was changing.

Eldon bought a stove from the general store and brought it home. He was afraid to bring it down to the cellar for fear of not being able to get it up to the main floor again. It was heavy and would also lack a stovepipe in the cellar. It was decided that the stove would remain above ground and construction would start immediately on the main floor.

Eldon and the Mountain boys framed in the main floor of the house and then went to work on the upstairs. It took over a month to frame the entire house. Eldon's friend Maurice Stokes helped with the construction. He had built many homes in the area and was glad to help. Stokes was also a black man and thoroughly enjoyed the constant banter between the young Irishmen. He referred to them all as Micks, since he couldn't remember their names and they all looked alike.

"How in the hell did you ugly Micks latch onto such lovely women?" Maurice teased. "Are they blind, or were you four the only Micks left in all of Ireland?"

"The girls are not blind, at least I don't think they are, but they know that all Irishman are well endowed and we Mountains are all Irish, if you get my point?" S.C. rebutted with a smile.

Emilia came along after that comment and cuffed S.C. across the top of his head. "You're not impressing me at all," she said, "If you get my point?"

They all laughed, even William, who appeared to be feeling better.

As the work on the house, garden and wall progressed, the weather was getting much cooler as the end of December was quickly approaching. Eldon was in a hurry to get the house capped and the stove in place in the kitchen. They had also built in a small fireplace in the living room, using Maurice's expertise and rocks from the property. The house was taking shape and was getting more comfortable every day. Most of the group had moved up to the main floor, but Mark and William remained in the cellar. They felt the new couples, Molly and Patrick and S.C. and Emilia, needed more privacy to get better acquainted. They seemed to be in love and both Mark and William would want that privacy if Margaret and Anne were there.

The house was now a solid structure, however the interior was not complete. Eldon felt they could work on the interior during the winter, but they would have a warm and comfortable home where they could all live, as promised. The Pratts and the Mountains were satisfied with their new home and were looking forward to relaxing a bit during the winter months.

William was almost fully recovered from his injuries and was spending more time outdoors practicing throwing his knives. At first, he realized he was not accurate and had no strength left to make the throws. He worked several hours a day to regain his strength and his throwing accuracy, but found it to be a longer process than he expected. The injury to his side made throwing very difficult because of the pain it caused him while turning his hip. The pain was so debilitating it forced him to stop most days after just a few minutes. William was stubborn and never had an injury slow him down before. His body was telling him to go slow, but his mind wanted him to go fast. His body was winning the war. At the end of December, he only had about half of his strength back and it worried him. Molly told him to slow down and enjoy life.

"That's easy for you to say," said William. "You have what you want: Patrick and a future. I do not. The only thing I was ever good at was hunting and killing Englishmen. I have no love, as you do and I doubt if I'll ever have one. I'm seriously considering going after Desmond Delaney. If I could throw these goddamn knives better, I'd have been gone long ago."

"William, you must not even think about him," Molly said. "We are all safe here, thanks to the Pratts. You cannot bring Delaney's wrath on these people."

"There will be no wrath, for he will be long dead when I'm through with him," William told her. "I also expect to get rid of many more of his cohorts."

A tearful Molly said, "Your brothers will not allow this. William, you are just lonely and depressed. Things will improve once we start on our trip to Whisk-con-sin, you'll see. Please William, for me, please don't do this, please! You mean so much to me; I couldn't bear to lose you. You are like my big brother, and my only family; what would I have ever done without you? I love you so much and if you were to die, a part of me would die too."

William just stared into that beautiful sad face. He said, "It's nice to know that someone still loves me. Molly, I love you too, as a little sister. I would have never dreamed the day we met, that you would become such a large part of my life. I respect you more than anyone I've ever met and I promise, if it will make you happy, I will not seek revenge."

How William lied that day.

William got melancholy and said, "Molly, my ma died the day I was born and my grandmother told me while Ma was dying she said, 'Isn't he a beautiful baby? I love him so much and I am so happy he will live.' I never knew her, but I'll always remember those words she said. My father didn't love me, and that was hard for me. When I met Anne, I experienced real love for the only time, the kind I know you feel for Patrick. It breaks my heart now knowing I will likely never see her again. I want to feel that love again, Molly, just once more in my life."

"We will get to Whisk-con-sin and find her," Molly said. "Her family were the ones that told you about Americay, they will get here and you will see her again."

Molly hugged William again and he needed her comfort. William knew deep inside that if it were not for Anne, Molly was the only other woman for him. He also knew she was Patrick's and he would never do anything to separate them from one another.

The Mountains told the Pratt family that they were going to begin preparations for their journey to the Erie Canal and then on to Whisk-con-sin. Eldon said he had a friend at his church named Franklin James that had experience traveling on the canal and other waterways in New York. He said Franklin would be happy to explain things to the family. The Mountains gladly accepted the offer.

Franklin was a very large black man, at least six-foot four-inches and weighed about three hundred pounds. He was a very jovial man with deep devotion to God. He assisted the minister at the newly formed Seneca church and also owned a home in Seneca Village. Franklin had met some of the Mountain family before on his visits to see Eldon and was happy to be of assistance.

"The easy part is finding a boat to take you all to Albany," Franklin said. "The cost is modest, around fifty to seventy-cents per person and the trip will take less than two weeks. If you can get on one of the boats that are powered by steam the trip would cost about $2.50 per person, but you'd get to Albany in approximately two and half days. The steamships are more comfortable for passengers than the regular barges or flatboats."

The family agreed that if they could find a steamship that would take them, that's the way they would travel. Franklin explained that when they got to Albany, they would need to book passage on a flat bottom boat, that would carry them up the Erie Canal to the Great Lakes. This trip would be more expensive, about $3.00 or so per person.

"I have no idea how long it will take, but I assume it will be a long, slow trip," Franklin said.

CHAPTER 18

Leaving Seneca Village

"On another topic, a few days ago a white man came into the general store in Seneca Village," Franklin said. "He was bold and unafraid and announced to everyone there that he and some very important men in Five Points are looking for a beautiful woman traveling with four Irishmen. He said one of the men was badly injured with gunshot wounds. He posted a $1,000 reward for their capture, with no questions asked. Now, I know they are looking for Molly and you four Mountain boys. I'm also glad to report that not one person in that store said they knew any of you. Our community here will protect the Mountains in Seneca Village. However, we must ask you to leave for your next destination as soon as possible. In addition, I'd like you to rest comfortably knowing that no one in the community will ever tell your destination."

"Thank you Franklin," Molly said, "for telling us about the reward and more importantly, thank all the community for their friendship and kindness. We will leave immediately, just as soon as we can get some supplies, pack and say our goodbyes."

"We do not want to bring any trouble into your community," S.C. said. "We will never forget you people. Eldon and Marcie, you will never know how much we appreciate all you two have done for us. You have made our lives bearable in a country that was almost unbearable, thank you so much."

Emilia and S.C. were chosen to go to the general store for supplies. The family needed food, additional clothing and warm blankets. The boys still had their overcoats, but the girls had only their shawls. Emilia said she would see what the store had and report back to Molly. The family was worried about Molly or William going out in public with the reward offered by the Five Points gang fresh in their minds. Little did they know that the gang did not see the difference between Molly and Emilia, both were beautiful. Emilia looked around the store while S.C. purchased food; pickled vegetables, jerky, cider and fresh fruit. S.C. was in the middle of purchasing the blankets when a man approached Emilia and asked her what part of Ireland she was from.

"I'm from Northern Ireland, I came here with my grandparents," Emilia responded.

The man said, "I believe there are some people from my neighborhood looking for you and your friends. I'd like you to take a stroll with me."

S.C. heard the conversation and said, "She'll not be going anywhere with you." S.C. lied when he said, "This is my wife, stand clear of her or you will have to deal with me."

The man pulled a pistol out of his waistband and said, "I'd be real careful if I were you with whom you threaten. The girl comes with me, as well as you. There is a healthy reward for you two and I plan on collecting it today."

Walter Jones, the storekeeper, came up behind the man, placed a flintlock pistol to his temple and said, "No one will be leaving with you today or any day. I'll take your pistol and you can go, but if you come back into Seneca Village you will meet your maker. This is our community now and we will not tolerate anyone from the outside telling us what we can, or cannot do. These folks are our friends and you and no one else will force them to leave here. Now get the fuck out of here and don't come back. If you come back, there will be a war you can't win. We are free men here in Seneca Village and no white man will give us orders any longer, now leave."

The man handed his pistol to Walter and said, "I won't be coming back, but I assure you someone else will. I was only interested in the reward. People in Five Points know the Irish are here and I'm sure the reward will now be offered, dead or alive."

After the man left, Walter said the Mountains must leave soon. The last thing the folks in Seneca Village wanted was a war in their streets. S.C. gathered up the supplies and Emilia bought two woolen coats for her and Molly, hoping Molly would approve. They thanked Walter for being so protective of them and said they hoped to be underway by late in the afternoon.

S.C. and Emilia reached the Pratt home in less than fifteen minutes and were visibly shaken. Emilia explained what happened, how she was mistaken for Molly and how the man was going to take her and S.C. to Five Points for the reward. She told them how Walter saved their lives and asked them to leave immediately.

"Although we would love to have you stay with us forever, that is not possible any longer," said Eldon. "The safety of the entire village is at stake and we must ask you to leave. Please forgive us."

The family said their goodbyes, everyone hugged and tears were shed. At first no one realized that William was not present.

"William was here when you two arrived, but he has just disappeared," said Molly.

"His clothes are still here as well as his overcoat, but his knives are gone," Patrick said. "I suspect he is going after the Five Point gang."

"He will have to catch up with us, for we need to leave now," S.C. said. "He knows where we're headed and where the steamboat will leave for Albany. Eldon, if he returns here, which I don't expect, tell him we will wait for two days by the dock on the Hudson River and if he doesn't show up we will have to leave without him."

CHAPTER 19

Sarah and Maggie O'Grady & The End of Desmond Delaney

WILLIAM HEARD THE STORY THAT EMILIA had shared with the group about being accosted at the store. While they were all engrossed in her story, William slid out the door without being noticed. He knew they would be continually hunted for the reward. They may be hunted as far away as Whisk-con-sin. He could not take that chance. He knew where the family was going and knew they needed to leave for the docks now. He would find them—that would be the easy part. He also knew if he told them where he was going, they would try and stop him or would want to come along and help. William had been planning this move since Franklin told them about the reward. He would find Desmond Delaney and collect the reward himself and do away with Delaney in the process.

William's accuracy had improved to almost 100% and his confidence was back. Also in his favor was that he didn't care if he died. He had little to live for and was jealous of his brothers who had found happiness with Molly and Emilia. He looked back on his life. He had no mother, a father who hated him and the only love he ever experienced was from a woman he'd likely never see again. He just didn't care whether he would live or die any longer.

He had to find out where Delaney spent his time, most likely some pub in Five Points. As darkness approached, he made his way to the Paradise Park area of Five Points. Surrounding the park on every corner was a pub. William counted fifteen pubs in just the five streets that intersected the park. William slowly entered a few pubs from a rear or side door, trying to locate Delaney or some of his men. He had no luck in the first pubs he entered. Most of the patrons were older Irishman and a few black men that all looked down on their luck. William just looked around the pubs, but did not order any alcohol. He wanted to remain completely sober so he would have an edge on the likely intoxicated Delaney.

William found an all night bar across the street called the "Cellar Dwellers" and entered through the only door, the front door. This was the kind of place he was looking for. No old men, but a younger rough crowd looking for trouble. William was immediately approached by a woman that looked about five years older than him, wearing a worn out dirty dress, a face full of makeup to cover a swollen cheek, and a mouth with a tooth missing on her left side. She was obviously a whore looking for her next customer. William smiled at the woman and asked if he could buy her a drink.

She said in a rough tone, "You bet your sweet ass you can, if you don't, I'm not allowed to even talk to you."

William went to the bar and ordered a shot of brandy for the woman and a short beer for himself. After sitting down beside her in a quiet corner, he asked her name.

"My name is Sarah O'Grady from Ireland. I charge ten cents for a lay, payment in advance and two cents for the use of the room."

"Sarah, I'm not here looking for a lay, but I will gladly pay you double your charge for some information," William said.

"What type of information?" she asked. "Anytime someone asks for information around here there are risks, and I don't intend to take any risks again today. Just look at my face."

William tried to change to tone of the conversation and said, "Where are you from in Ireland? Your dialect sounds like you are from the south."

"I'm from a small town called Fermoy in County Cork," she replied. "I came to this hellhole about five years ago with my husband and daughter."

William asked her what happened to her family.

"My husband was killed right here in Five Points by a member of the Delaney Gang," said Sarah. "They took my daughter, and I haven't seen her since."

"Wait here, I'll get us more drinks," William told her.

Sarah smiled and said, "Good idea, you can loosen me up a bit. I talk more when I'm a little toasted."

William returned with the drinks and continued with their conversation. He asked her if she knew the Flynn family from Fermoy.

"Oh yes," replied Sarah. "I remember a Patrick Flynn, his wife died suddenly and he had three kids. The boy was a bit younger than me, but I remember him. They were a nice family, they lived a short way from my ma and pa's farm."

"Anne Flynn is my girlfriend and I hope to marry her as soon as she gets to Americay," William said.

William changed the subject of the conversation and said, "What I need from you is information about the different gangs here in Five Points. I need their names, their leaders' names, and where their members hang out. I need this information immediately."

Sarah didn't quite understand why he needed the information and said, "Are you expecting to join a gang or what?"

"No, I will not be joining a gang, but I'm here to destroy Desmond Delaney."

Sarah smiled and responded, "I'll gladly help you with information, but I want to be paid $5.00 in silver coins in advance. But first you need to pay me for a lay and we'll need to finish this conversation in the room. The bartender has been watching us and I'm afraid I'll get a beating soon, if I don't get to work."

William paid the ten cents for the lay and two cents for the room. Sarah said they'd have between fifteen minutes to a half hours time. If he wanted more time it would cost an additional ten cents but the room would be free. He gave her the additional ten cents in advance; he knew he'd need more time. She promptly gave the money to the bartender and they walked hand in hand to the room. The room had a small bed with a dirty sheet covering the straw mattress. There was an oil lamp in the corner on a small table and that was all the furnishing.

Sarah said, "If you'd like I can douse the light, that way you don't have to look at me."

"Leave the lamp on," William said. "But I do not intend to lay with you. Please don't be offended. I'm here on business and my business is Desmond Delaney. What I'm about to propose to you may frighten you, but will give you an opportunity to change your life. Here's the $5.00 coin for your information."

Sarah took it, thanked him and said, "I'll listen."

"I need to know where I can find Delaney," William explained. "Where does he live? Does he always have armed guards with him? Please tell me as much about him as you can."

"He has not been around much in the last few months. He had a mishap in the Park a few months ago and his arm was injured. It became infected and he lost the use of the arm and well as the hand. It's just dead. He has been in a drunken, surly mood ever since." Sarah continued, "I haven't had anything to do with him since he took me in after my husband was killed. I had no place to go, so Delaney told me to stay at his place. It was a mistake. After he used me for a few days, he handed me over to the bartender, his brother, Oscar. Oscar abused me for more than a month and then he put me to work as a whore in this bar. They took my daughter, where I don't know, no one would ever tell me. I don't want to think of the terrible things that they are likely doing to her. Delaney lives across the street in the wooden building on the second floor. His brother Oscar lives on the first floor. We are open all night so Oscar will leave here about 4:00 am. Delaney may have a woman with him, but everyone in Five Points is still afraid of him, so he's an untouchable and needs no guards."

William asked Sarah if she wanted to get out of Five Points.

Sarah replied, "How in the hell am I going to do that and where would I go? If I left they would find me and kill me on the spot. I can never leave this place."

William said, "I can help you get your freedom, but first I need your help. If you help me, I will help you."

Sarah was interested, but skeptical and said, "Just exactly what would I have to do?"

"Just deliver a few notes to the leaders of Delaney's rival gangs," said William.

Sarah quizzed William, "What the hell are the notes going to say and how do I know you'll help me get out of here?"

Sensing Sarah's doubts William said, "The notes will offer a reward for Delaney's death as well as his brother's death and most of his men. If my plan succeeds, you will have some money and your freedom. I promise on my dead mother's grave."

Sarah said she would be willing to help, but if things got out of hand she would turn on him.

William laughed and said, "At least you're honest."

"I'll meet you back here around 1:00 am," said Sarah. "You'll have to pay Oscar again to get me away from the pub."

William agreed to be back at 1:00 am. He left by the front door and was not accosted by any drunks. As long as he paid for the time with Sarah, it appeared he did not raise any suspicion from Oscar, the bartender. Once outside William checked to make sure his knives were in their proper places. The knife behind his head was secured as well as the one up his sleeve. He had attached another knife to his lower right leg and the bowie knife was in its sheath, tucked behind him into his waistband. He was armed and dangerous and prepared to kill.

William walked to the wooden structure and saw that the only lamp that was lit came from the top floor. William's plan was to kill Delaney and try to find any coins or other valuables worth taking. He would approach the other gangs and offer a reward to kill off Delaney's crew, with Delaney's own money. He figured there would be at least the $1,000 reward money for the Mountain family nearby.

After entering the house by the front door, William walked softly up the wooden staircase to the top floor. William wondered why he never felt stress or fear when he was facing death. He guessed it was because he just didn't care.

Once on the landing on the second floor, he opened the door and found Desmond drunk as a skunk lying passed out across a bed. Sitting on a small chair with her arm folded was a young girl about twelve years old.

William didn't even bother whispering, he said, "Who are you? Is this man your father?"

The young girl said, "My name is Maggie and he is not my father! My Pa died when we got here and I'm all alone. I think my Ma died too, that's why I'm here. He's supposed to take care of me until I get a little older."

"Has this man abused you in any way?" William asked.

"He hits me all the time if I'm slow to do what he wants. It's been worse since he lost the use of his arm, now I have to help dress him too. He is so mean," said Maggie.

"I'd like you to trust me, if you will. Mr. Delaney will not live much longer, so he will not bother you anymore," William said. "Please tell me if you know where any coins or valuables are hidden in here?"

"I know where all the money is hidden, I have to put it in the hiding place for him each night," said Maggie. "All his men come by in the early morning to make their daily deposit to him. Mr. Oscar collects the money and brings it to me to hide. Mr. Delaney is normally passed out, but sometimes he watches me. He told me if I stole anything he'd kill me, but first he'd hurt me real bad. Are you planning on stealing his money? If you do they'll kill you, for sure."

"Yes little Maggie, I plan on stealing everything Delaney has including his life," William said. "But now I think I may let someone else do the killing. Where are the coins hidden?"

Maggie showed him where two large floorboards could be pried up. Beneath the boards was more gold and silver than William could ever imagine existed anywhere. There was a flintlock pistol on top of the hoard that he quickly put into his waistband. He reached in and grabbed bags of the gold coins. He realized immediately that the gold was plentiful and more valuable, so he would not bother with something of lesser value. He knew he would be limited in his ability to carry the gold, but he would make several trips to get as much as he could. Desmond was snoring loudly and William was sure he was out cold for the night.

William loaded up as much gold as he could carry out the door when Maggie asked if she could help. He said he'd be delighted to have her help. He asked if there was a back door to the house and if she knew a good place to hide the loot. There was a back door and she said they could hide the gold about three blocks away under some rocks in an empty field. She confessed she had stolen from Delaney before and hid the coins there. William laughed out loud not worrying about waking Delaney. They took as much as they both could carry and went out the back door. They reached the deserted hiding place and William was pleased with the location. They made several trips back and forth and began to take the silver too. When the floorboards were empty, they put the boards back in place.

William had a brilliant idea and asked Maggie if she could get him some paper and quill. Both paper and quill were close by and were used to keep track of the daily take from the bars and whores. William wrote a note, it read:

My Dear Desmond,

If or when, you read this note, you will realize that I have stolen all your coins. I want you to also know, that I have offered all your enemies a reward for your dead body of $5,000 in coins— your coins. I also offered $3,000 in coins for your brother's dead body and another $2,000 for anyone else that supports you. So you see, I didn't have to kill you myself. I'll have someone else do it. Also, just in case you're interested, I'm the asshole that took your arm from you, and I'm also the asshole that will take young Maggie way from you. My name is William Mountain, I'm from the Village of Killeagh in County Cork Ireland, and I am only a farmer, just in case you want to know who killed you. Rest in hell, you bastard.

William pinned the note on Delaney's chest. Before leaving, William wrote three additional notes, which read:

I am offering a reward of $5,000 in silver coin to the person or persons that kill Desmond Delaney tonight. In addition, I will give a reward of $3,000 in silver coins to the person or persons that kill his brother Oscar tonight. And an additional $2,000 in silver coins for taking out his gang members. You will now control more of Five Points with the Delaney gang out of business. Delaney is at home sleeping off a drunk on the second floor and is unguarded. Brother Oscar will be home at 4:00 am with the days take. This will be easy pickings for you boys, so hurry and don't make any mistakes.

He also gave them directions to a location where they would surprisingly find another note, but not the silver. The next note, which was quite a distance from the silver, explained the hiding place. William did this ploy to insure ample time for them to all get away.

"Maggie I need to leave you here close to the gold," William said. "Will you be safe here?"

"This is the loneliest place in Five Points," said Maggie. "Notice there are no pubs. I'll be safe here."

"I'll only be gone for a short time, I'm bringing back someone to help you," said William.

William headed back to the pub and found Sarah. He asked her to give Oscar fifty cents and tell him that her customer was so happy with her performance earlier he wanted her for the rest of the night.

Sarah gave Oscar the money and he looked surprised.

"Is that dumb fuck blind? He can have you all of tomorrow too for that much money," said Oscar. "Now get to work you stupid worthless bitch, you'll finally pay for your keep."

When they reached the room, William asked her if there was a different room they could use, one with a window.

"Since it's real slow tonight, we can use the back room for a short time, but it's for the more attractive whores and the room rents for five cents a time," said Sarah.

William handed her the nickel and told her to go and pay Oscar.

The new room had a small window, a bed, a lamp and a table. William asked Sarah if she had anything she wanted to take with her because they were leaving tonight through the window.

Sarah was concerned. She said, "I don't know you at all. What the hell are you going to do with me if I leave with you?"

"You're right, you don't know me," said William. "But whatever I have in mind is better than this life. You will not be harmed if we can get away, but I cannot promise you anything. You'll have to trust me. I need you to deliver some notes I penned to three of the gang bosses."

Sarah agreed to go, but her life now was tolerable, except for the beatings. She liked the drinks and had become addicted to them. She also liked the men, at least most of them. They made her feel wanted. Maybe, she thought, this young fellow might become interested in me, too? It was worth a chance.

Sarah climbed out of the window first. William told her to follow him as they took the four block walk to the empty field. Sarah could see the figure of a shorter person in the moonlight as they approached the field. Her eyes widened as she realized it was her daughter. Sarah ran to her child and cried violently. Maggie showed little emotion or reaction to her mother's presence or embrace. Sarah continued to wail away, squeezing Maggie relentlessly.

William let Sarah embrace Maggie for a short time longer and finally said, "I'm sorry, but we have limited time to execute my plan. I realize you two will have a great deal to talk about, but please, can you do it later? Sarah, will you go with me now to the pubs and give the bosses my notes?"

Sobbing, Sarah said, "I will."

William told the girls that they would need to count out the $10,000 in silver coins for the reward and place it under a few rocks in the open field. When the counting was completed and the reward hidden, the three of them took the remaining gold stash and hid it well beyond the current location. Sarah was completely shaken from the reunion, but knew she had to compose herself to complete the next stage of William's plan.

William gave Maggie some instructions on what he wanted her to do. When her task was completed, she was to return to the field where the gold was hidden and stay out of sight. Sarah led William to the pubs where the other three gang leaders would likely be. Sarah went in each one and spoke to a gang member that she was familiar with. She handed each man the folded notes and said they must take the note to their boss immediately. As William waited patiently outside each pub, he was not accosted in any way, which he thought was unusual. What William didn't realize was that most of the gang members remembered him from the confrontation with Delaney a few months back. They wanted no part of the fabled "Knife Man," a nickname he acquired unbeknownst to him. They all acted as if he were invisible.

The gang bosses received each note. Errol Duffner, the boss of the Canal Street Gang, was the last recipient of a note and read it with delight.

He did not share its contents with his troops, but said, "You boys get on over to Delaney's house around midnight, he's sound asleep and alone. Be the first one to kill Delaney and you get a $100 in silver coin as a reward. The Paradise Squirrels gang and the River Rat gang will all be looking to kill Delaney, as well as his brother Oscar. I'll give $50 in silver to the person who kills Oscar first. $25 in silver will be paid for every other member of the Delaney gang that we kill first. Get to work and report back to me as soon as the job is completed. I want three men to come with me to the fountain in the Park and bring some shovels and pistols."

William had instructed Maggie to run back to Delaney's house before the notes were delivered and wake him. He told her to shake him hard until he was awake and run away after he regained consciousness. Maggie shook Delaney until he woke up, and she said several times, "Read the note! Read the note!" As she ran down the back stairs.

Delaney tore the note away from his chest and read it. He laughed out loud in his drunken stupor and said to no one, "Fuck that bloody Irishman. I'll have him killed in the morning."

Desmond Delaney died that night, along with his brother Oscar, both from shots to the head. Fifteen Delaney gang members were also killed in the bloodiest battle ever in Five Points. Twenty more Delaney gang members joined forces with the remaining three gangs. After following William's decoy note, the gang bosses all raced and got to the silver at precisely the same time. They decided there had been enough bloodshed that night and they would split the coins equally. As far as taking over the Delaney pubs, whorehouses, tenement houses and other property, as expected, there would be a fight.

William and the O'Grady girls began to walk northeast to the Hudson River. They had their hands loaded down with bags of gold coins. There were enough silver coins to pay the gangs the $10,000 reward. The rest, all in gold coins, was over $15,000.

William told Sarah that she and Maggie would get $5,000 of the gold, $2,500 a piece for their help and for all they had endured. William felt sorry about the girls' condition. They were a mess. Neither had bathed in a long while and their clothes were nothing more than rags. They both had been beaten badly, but at least Maggie had not been sexually abused. William said that they could join his family if they wanted to, but his family was leaving to go to Whisk-con-sin as soon as possible. Sarah said after what happened in Five Points, they would be killed or worse if they remained there. They said they would have no choice but accompany William and his family.

Sarah pulled William out of earshot of Maggie and asked, "Will my past be a problem with the ladies in your family?"

"Neither our women, nor our men, will judge you by your past," William assured her. "If you ever feel comfortable telling my family members what happened to you go ahead, but they will not hear it from me. We all have done things we are not proud of and I am one of the worst. You two will fit in nicely and you both will be accepted."

CHAPTER 20

Travel on the Hudson River

WILLIAM AND THE GIRLS REACHED THE docks on the Hudson at midday and were very tired from carrying their heavy load. William saw his brother Patrick first, holding hands with Molly. Molly was the first to see him and screamed with delight and ran to him and gave him a big hug. She was still mad at him, but she kept her anger in check for another time. Patrick, S.C., Mark and Emilia ran to him and asked what happened to him and who were the girls?

"These are my new friends, Sarah and her daughter Maggie O'Grady. They helped me take care of some business in Five Points," said William. "As you probably assumed, I went to take care of the Delaney issue that arose. You'll all be happy to know that I did not personally kill Delaney, his brother, or any members of his gang. But with the O'Grady girls' help, we engineered it. They will not bother us again. As for the bags we carry, it's Delaney's gold and it will help us all to settle in Whisk-con-sin. Sarah and Maggie will get a share of the spoils."

Molly and Emilia immediately embraced the girls and thanked them for helping William. They said that they didn't have proper clothing for them, but they would all go back to the Village store and get appropriate attire for the trip. Molly said that they could also clean up at the Pratt's' home. Sarah thought things were looking up for them.

Mark and S.C. stayed near the docks with the gold and their baggage as the rest of the group went back to the Pratts'. The Pratts greeted them with open arms, but were afraid that something bad had happened. William explained that all was well and they need not worry about Delaney any longer. Molly asked if the girls could wash up before going to the store for clothing.

"Of course they may," Marcie said.

The O'Grady ladies cleaned up nicely and Maggie's beauty rose out of the dirt and grime she had carried. Sarah was still bruised and battered, but looked better.

The entire group walked to the general store and purchased clothing, shoes, and shawls for the girls. It was the first time in several years that they had clean, store-bought clothes to wear. William paid for the clothing and bought Maggie some hard candy. She had never tasted anything that good in her life. Things were indeed looking up.

After again saying their goodbyes, the group headed for the docks on the Hudson River. They met up with Mark and S.C. and asked if they had found a boat to take them up the river. They had found transportation up the river, but the steamboat wouldn't leave for two days.

"We have food and water and a bit of mead, so we have enough to sustain us," said Emilia. "It will give us a chance to get acquainted and find out what happened in Five Points, if William is willing to share with us."

The steerage cost was $3.00 or a total of $24.00. Molly and Patrick had become the money managers and they kept detailed accounting of all spending. They offered to go over their expenses and funds with the group, but no one was interested. Everyone agreed that Molly and Patrick would handle the money and expenses. No need to issue a report, unless they spent all of it.

The group found a comfortable spot on the banks of the Hudson River to camp. There was a large oak tree for shade and a stand of trees nearby in case of high wind or rain. They were relieved to have Five Points behind them, especially Sarah and Maggie. Maggie had missed much of her childhood in the last few years and it appeared she was going to make up for lost time. She smiled and laughed and was a prankster. She would hide items from the family and would laugh a silly laugh when they realized she was the culprit. She chased and teased S.C., Mark and Patrick all the time. She was in awe of Molly and Emilia because of their beauty and their loving demeanor. Maggie would spend as much time with the girls as possible and looked upon them as big sisters. She was, however, very standoffish to Sarah.

Maggie could not understand why her mother left her to the likes of Delaney and his brother. She tried to forget what they did to her, but she was unable to. She had nightmares every night and would wake in a cold sweat. She did not scream out when the nightmares occurred, she had learned by Delaney's hard hand that was not acceptable behavior in his house. The beatings remained forefront in her mind, but the sexual connotations about what would happen when she got older, frightened her more than everything else. Delaney bragged to Oscar and his men, in front of Maggie, that he would be her first and that day was soon approaching. Maggie promised herself she would kill him with his own flintlock pistol while he was in one of his drunken stupors before he could touch her. She had stolen money for her getaway, but had no idea where she was going. Delaney had told her he had killed her mother and father and if she didn't do what he said she would join them. Maggie however, knew her mother was alive, she had seen her many times coming and leaving the pub.

As the group was preparing to begin their journey, Sarah asked Maggie if she was excited about the upcoming trip.

"I would be, if you weren't going," Maggie responded.

Sarah and the Mountain family were all shocked by her response. She knew something was bothering Maggie, but thought it was because of Delaney, not her. She thought Maggie was happy because she was still alive after been presumed dead.

"What have I done to make you say such a thing?" asked Sarah.

Maggie said in a stone-cold voice, "You left me, you didn't try to find me and I was good as dead. Don't tell me you couldn't do something to help me. You could have, I hate you as much as I hated Delaney. You are dead to me."

Maggie walked away. William followed her down to the river. Maggie just stared right ahead with no expression on her face.

"Maggie my dear, you are being very hard on your mother," said William. "She was in the same predicament as you were. She didn't know where you were and she was also forced to do things she didn't want to do.

Maggie said tearfully, "I knew she was alive. I saw her many times coming and going into that dreadful pub with a man on her arm. She was always staggering like a drunken fool. William, I was only across the street! If I took the time to find her, she could have certainly found me. I hate her and God as my witness, she will never be my mother again and as far as I'm concerned she is dead to me."

William put his arm around her and tried to comfort her.

"Maggie we all make mistakes and your mother made a big one. Please don't judge her too badly," he said. "She was in a bad situation and tried to make the best of it."

"She was always a drunk, she was that way when my pa was alive, she's only worse now," cried Maggie.

The group gathered on the dock before boarding the steamship *The Get Way*. Captain James Hart explained the details of the ship and a few of the rules regarding it. There would be no meals provided to any passengers. Passengers still had time to buy food at the general store two blocks away. There would be water for drinking only, nothing else. No alcohol was allowed on the ship.

"Everyone will stay in their small assigned cabins while the ship is in motion," Hart said. "When we slow you can move around. The women will be housed together and the men will be housed together. No exceptions."

Some of the passengers left the dock for provisions, but the Mountain group was well supplied.

The group began to board the ship when Captain Hart said to Sarah, "Sarah my dear, is that you?"

"It is indeed me, Jimmy, how in the hell are you?" asked Sarah.

"Sarah, are you going with us to Albany?" Hart responded.

"Yes I am, and it's good to see you again," said Sarah.

Hart grabbed Sarah's hand and asked her to come to his cabin with him. William stepped in front of Hart and asked him what was the purpose of Sarah going to his cabin. Hart said that they were old friends and he wanted to talk to her.

"William, Jimmy is a very close old friend of mine and I want to talk to him too," said Sarah. "There is no problem, I think you are getting overprotective."

As they walked away from the group hand in hand, Sarah never said anything to Maggie as she left.

When Sarah and Hart reached his cabin he asked her how she got away from Oscar and Desmond. Sarah told him the story and said she was now free to do whatever she wanted.

"One thing is for sure, I'll not be going to Whisk-con-sin with this group, maybe just as far as Albany," said Sarah.

Captain Hart replied, "Sarah, you know you broke my heart when you wouldn't let me buy you from the Delaneys. We could have had a nice life together."

"Jimmy, you know I wanted to go with you, but I knew the Delaneys were just playing with you. They would have kept your money, as well as me, and slit your throat to boot," she said.

"Well now we have a chance to be together. I have a small house in Albany, far away from Five Points," Hart said. "I travel down river and back up once a week. I work only five days and then I have two off. We could have a nice time together Sarah, my dear. What do you think?"

Sarah thought for a moment and said, "Jimmy I have a daughter. She is the young girl in our group. Would you be willing to take her too? She's been through some hard times."

"I'd rather not have the kid, but if that's what it takes to get you, then alright," said Hart.

Sarah jumped into his arms and dragged him to the cot in the corner. When they were finished, Hart dressed and poured both of them large glasses of brandy.

"You'll be staying in my cabin for the trip, you better tell your young one," said Hart.

Sarah agreed. She knew by staying with Hart she would get enough brandy every day to take care of her thirst.

Sarah dressed after two glasses of brandy and stumbled below to the girls' cabin. She informed Maggie in slurred words that Captain Hart had offered her a fine place to stay during the trip, but Maggie would have to stay below with the other girls. She told Maggie that she intended to live with Hart as soon as they arrived in Albany.

She stuttered, "Jimmmy has also agreed to let you come along with me to live in Albany, sort of a package deal. Ain't that nice of him? We'll be a family again."

Maggie was fuming, as she tried to control her anger.

Before Maggie could say anything, Molly spoke up, "Sarah, just how well do you know this man? Haven't you had enough hard times in your life to jump into what could be another bad situation? Also, Maggie is not ready for what you are suggesting. She needs time to heal from her past, don't you understand?"

"No, I don't understand. I've known Jimmy for two years. He came to the pub every other week to see me. He even asked if he could buy me from the Delaneys, but I wouldn't allow it. This is my chance for happiness and Maggie will not spoil it for me," Sarah growled.

Maggie calmly said, "You go with your Jimmy, I will travel to Whisk-con-sin with the Mountains, if they'll have me. If not, I'll go alone. I would not want to spoil your chance for happiness. I've come to the conclusion that you're not mother material. You are just a drunken whore. Stay in Albany, but don't ever try and find me and stay away from me on this ship."

Maggie turned her back on her mother and looked out the porthole. Sarah left and went to Hart's quarters without any more words. That was the last conversation Maggie would ever have with her mother.

The three days aboard the ship were mainly uneventful. The ship did get caught in shallow water a few times and the men had to tie ropes to it and go ashore and pull it to deeper water. They arrived in Albany late on a Sunday afternoon. Hart informed all the passengers that wanted to continue through the Erie Canal that they could find steerage near the dock areas. William and Molly approached Sarah and asked her if she was going to try and make amends with Maggie.

"Why would I? She called me a drunken whore," said Sarah. "I don't want her; if she stays here I will only make her life miserable. Will you take her with you?"

Molly handed Sarah a bag of gold coins and said, "Here is your share of Delaney's money, $2500 in gold, just as William promised. Maggie will get the rest. She will remain with us and we will take care of her."

"My family and I wish you the best of luck, you deserve some happiness and I hope Captain Hart provides that for you," said William.

The Mountain family, including its newest member, Maggie O'Grady, walked away, eager to get onto the next leg of their journey. Sarah was all smiles with her new-found wealth, her new husband, and finally rid of the daughter she never wanted.

CHAPTER 21

The Erie Canal

THE MOUNTAINS REACHED THE DOCK AREA after dark and found a suitable place to sleep for the night. It was colder than when they left New York City and the chill in the air required them to bring out their blankets. If they could not find passage immediately, they would be forced to seek shelter in a hotel. They preferred to sleep outdoors to save the money, but the cold air was a problem, especially for the ladies. Maggie was happy; she had found people that were concerned for her well-being. Molly and Emilia treated her as if she were their little sister. They cut and combed her hair and promised that she would also get clothing when they found a suitable woman's shop. They explained woman issues to her about her body and what to expect when she got a little older. She already knew what men and women did to make babies. She learned that from some very dirty men that she'd wanted to forget. Maggie was still a little girl at heart, even through all her adult experiences. She was quick to laugh and found everything the boys said to be very amusing. She was doing well under the circumstances, and the girls worked hard to comfort her when she had flashbacks. The flashbacks came mostly at night in the form of nightmares, and the girls assured her it was all right to scream out. They would be there for her.

The next day they found a boat that would leave up the canal to Buffalo in three days. They booked passage for the seven of them with Molly negotiating the fee at four cents a mile. The trip to Buffalo was 363 miles for a total cost of $15.00 per person; that included food. The total for the family was $105 in gold. They found the Hotel Albany a short distance away and it appeared to be a respectable place to stay. They rented three rooms, two for the guys and one for the ladies for a total of $3.00 a day. The rooms were not fancy, but were comfortable. The hotel had a restaurant on the main floor where the family would meet for the evening meal. The rest of the time they ate the food they carried outdoors. Emilia and S.C. would be in charge of supplies for their next trip up the Erie Canal. They would buy food, beverages, and additional clothing for the girls. The boys felt they had ample clothing. Patrick and Molly supplied the funds and explained the amount of the budget set aside for supplies. Everyone followed the budget to the letter as it was important to save as much as possible for land purchases.

After hearing so much talk about buying land in Whisk-con-sin, Maggie asked William if she could ask him a few questions about her future.

Once outside the hotel Maggie said, "William, do I have any gold to buy land too?"

The question surprised him; he hadn't given it any thought. He always assumed Maggie would live with S.C. and Emilia or Patrick and Molly and share their homes and land. In other words, become their child.

William said to her, "Do you want to buy some land with your gold?"

"Yes, but with you. I want you to be my pa and I want a home with you," said Maggie. "I want to be in a family, but not without you."

"But Maggie," William exclaimed, "I'm not sure if I'll even stay in Whisk-con-sin. I'm hoping that my friend Anne will come there, but if she doesn't, I'll likely move on. If I move on, that would not be a good life for you."

Maggie did not shed a tear or get emotional, she just said, "I go where you go, you are my father now."

"Maggie my dear," said William, "this is not the time to make decisions like that, let's wait until we get to Whisk-con-sin, can we?"

She just smiled and said, "We can wait, but my mind is made up, I go where you go and no place else."

William had mixed emotions about what Maggie had said. First and foremost, he was proud she thought so highly of him. He enjoyed the thought of having her as a daughter. He always liked women with strong personalities and Maggie not only had a strong personality, she was a strong willed little girl. His concern was about Anne. If Anne did arrive in Whisk-con-sin, would she still want him, and if she did, would she want an adopted daughter with a strong will like herself and a ready-made family? He knew if Maggie insisted on only staying with him, he could not abandon her. He had developed a strong bond with her and was proud of the way she accepted her situation in life. She seemed well adjusted and happy even after her mother had deserted her.

"I guess I now have a daughter," William said to himself. "Maybe she's God's blessing to me from my own ma." The thought made him happy.

After spending three days in Albany the family was happy to get underway to the City of Buffalo, which was situated on Lake Erie. The boat they boarded was called a Packet Boat, and was 70 feet long and 14 feet wide. All packet boats featured the same accommodations: a lounge, dining room, a sleeping room with only a curtain separating the men from the women, and a kitchen. The boat was pulled by horses or mules and traveled at approximately four miles per hour. The boats floated in the water and the horses and mules walked beside the canal on the dirt towpath. Ropes were tied to the boat and then to the mule or horses. The boat would go only as fast as the horses or mules could walk. The sleeping conditions were horrible. The cabins were cramped, hot and stuffy. During the day the family spent most of their time above board on the roof, where it was considerably cooler. They were careful when approaching bridges, as the headroom was small and most times they had to leave the roof or lay flat on their stomachs to clear the bridges. Many times the family could actually disembark the boat where they could and walk along the canal path before re-boarding at a different location sometimes by jumping from a roof or bridge. Traveling at four miles an hour, the trip would take twelve days if they were lucky.

The trip was a restful one and everyone seemed happy to be starting a new chapter in their lives. The warm days and the sun had a lot to do with their change in dispositions. Mark asked William if he would leave the boat and walk on shore with him for a while. Mark opened up to William and said that he felt left out of the family and particularly with him. S.C. and Patrick seldom talked to him anymore and William had ignored him since the Five Points problems.

"Did I do something to offend you or make you mad at me?" Mark asked. "If I did, please tell me what I did. I've tried to stay out of everyone's way and keep to myself, but it is making me very unhappy. Maggie is the only one that wants me around."

"Of course, we all hate you, you selfish prick!" William said. "You are such a sourpuss no one can stand having you around. We all wanted to leave you in Five Points, but little Maggie begged us to take you."

Mark was stunned and almost began to cry, when William burst into laughter.

"You dumb shit, you're our cousin, we love you," William said. "I apologize if you felt I was ignoring you, or if anyone else was for that matter. Mark, we've had so many things happen to us in the last two weeks, no one has taken time to even realize you felt left out. I am so sorry. It will never happen again. I know my brothers are in love and only have time for their future wives. I have a plan for us, but it includes Maggie."

"Mark, we have enough gold for the family to buy 2,000 acres of land, 500 acres for each of us. According to Patrick that would cost the family a total of $5,000 in gold. We have much more than that. In addition, Patrick said there will be enough left over to buy tools, wagons, horses, wood for houses and a few cattle," William explained. "Also, Maggie has enough to buy an additional 500 acres of land that you and I will help farm for her. I suggest you and I pool our money and buy property together. If the Flynn girls show up and they still want us, we can all live together," William added.

Mark smiled and said he liked the idea, but he thought Maggie would live with Molly or Emilia.

William assured him that Maggie would stay with him as long as she wanted or until she found a suitable mate. That was what she wanted. Mark was elated they had this conversation. He felt like he belonged again.

William shared his plan with the rest of the family while on the rooftop of the ship. They were very excited about the proposal and agreed that building houses, clearing and plowing 2,000 acres of land would be a monumental task. They felt that with all of them working at it, including the women, they could complete the task in maybe five years' time. Patrick said after the land purchases the family would still have well over $5,000 in gold left to live on and that would last them several years. In addition, if they could get something of a cash crop growing in two years they would begin to have a revenue stream. One house would be built that they could all live in the first year. The rest of the homes would be built the next year. All would begin vegetable gardens immediately to supply them with much needed food for the winter. Just talking about their futures made them excited to get to Whisk-con-sin.

A few days into the trip, Mark encountered the boats' Captain Joseph Donahue.

"Sir, I was wondering if you would know anything about a territory called Whisk-con-sin and how my family and I would get there after arriving in Buffalo," asked Mark.

"Mark, please just call me Joe, this is only a slow moving piece of shit rowboat, pulled along by a few mules or horses, I don't demand that much respect," said Captain Donahue. "So, you're headed for Wisconsin? That's a nice place to begin your life here in America. I've been there and you'll be pleasantly surprised. There are stands of trees as far as the eyes can see. It's has beautiful rolling hills, plenty of water and nice warm summers. Winters are a bitch. It will be the coldest place you've ever seen. You get warm clothes and build a home with a fireplace. You store as much dry wood as you can for the long winter to heat that home. Buy shovels and store food for you and your livestock. Also get yourself a dog, they're good for informing you if intruders, such as Indians are coming."

"After we arrive in Buffalo," Joe continued, "you'll need to book passage on a steamship on Lake Erie, which will take you through to

Lake Michigan and on to the Village of Milwaukee. That trip is about 1,000 miles, but it will take less time than the trip you're on now. I told you to go to Milwaukee because that's where you will find the Federal Land Office. You can buy any property available for around $2.50 an acre. From there you'll need wagons and horses to cart you where your land will be. There are few roads and a wagon trip will take a long time no matter where you're headed."

"Joe, that's a lot to remember and to digest. Would you mind repeating what you have just told me to the rest of my family?" Mark asked.

"I'd be glad to," said Joe, "keep in mind I was born in that area, so I know the perils of their winters."

Joe did as Mark had asked. He told the same story to the other members of the Mountain family.

"Thank you Joe, this has been very helpful. We didn't realize the severity of their winters. We must be prepared," said William.

"We're still going aren't we? I can take the cold," said Maggie. "I'd rather be cold than hot."

"Maggie, you've never been this cold before, believe me," said Joe. "Now there are many good things to offset the winters. The winters are bad, but it's a time for the family to also relax and have fun. The hard labor is done for the year and if you prepare correctly the winter months are a time to rest. As you all know there are always daily chores to be done on a farm, but not the planting, tilling, weeding, clearing and preparing for the next winter. It's just a cycle, as in life."

"Maggie we're still going and the sooner the better," said William. "If we get to Milwaukee within the next month, it will only be May when we get to Washington County, plenty of time to get to work. Joe, when does winter arrive?"

Joe responded, "It gets cold at the end of October, early November, but the snow begins to fly normally at the end of November and the beginning of December. Spring begins in late March, early April. It gets warmer in May for sure."

The remaining trip on the packet boat was uneventful and slow going. The weather held up and it was sunny every day. The nights were hot and sticky and no one slept very well. Part of their listlessness was the anticipation of getting to their new home. Maggie was extremely nervous and excited all the time. She could hardly control herself and talked incessantly. She spent most of her time with Molly and Emilia asking questions, acting like a little sister. The girls loved her and both wanted to take her into their homes when they married. They both offered to adopt her as their daughter, but Maggie sternly refused. William was going to be her father and that was that. There were no hard feelings, but the girls thought they would be better prepared than William to take care of a twelve-year-old, inquisitive young girl. They would just wait and see how William handled his new duties.

The boat landed at the docks on Lake Erie just outside the City of Buffalo, New York. The next step was finding a steamship to take the family to Lake Michigan and on to Milwaukee. Patrick and Molly searched for the booking office of the ship lines. The steerage was expensive at $30 apiece for each traveler, which included food and lodging. The trip would take about ten days but they would end up in Chicago for a few days before the ship departed to the Village of Milwaukee. They had heard about how big Chicago was and were interested in seeing a big city. They hoped it was not like Five Points.

"Within two weeks we'll be in Milwaukee buying our land," said William.

They all smiled at him.

CHAPTER 22

The Feehan Family

THE FAMILY BOARDED THE STEAMSHIP ON April 15, 1842, full of anticipation and happiness. They knew there would be obstacles in their way, but this new beginning was a blessing for all of them.

The steamship was named the *Lady Love* and its captain was an older gentleman named George Feehan. George was from Northern Ireland and had been in America for twenty-plus years. He had worked on steamships all that time. He took a liking to the Mountain family right away because they reminded him of his own family back in Ireland. He was at least sixty-five years of age and had white hair under the cap he always wore. He smoked tobacco rolled in paper continuously.

After the ship had completed its daily journey, George would gather the Mountain family together in the small bar area for a few beers. George never got drunk, but he did get a bit tipsy. He laughed and smiled all of the time. He would tease Maggie about her non-existent boyfriends and Molly and Emilia about corralling Patrick and S.C. into marrying them. He joked with Mark and William and asked if they liked boys or girls. He shocked them both. Everyone laughed but Mark and William.

"We have girlfriends that we intend to marry," William said.

"You two buffoons can't take a joke, can you?" George laughed. "You boys must lighten up a bit and enjoy life and not be so damn serious."

The group waited patiently every night just to spend time with George. He was the highlight of their day. One night George asked the family if they were going to stay in Chicago for any length of time.

"I think we'll be there about two or three days," said Molly. "We have to wait for transportation to Milwaukee."

"Then it's settled, you'll be staying with me and my wife Bernadette, or Bernie, as I call her," said George.

"George, we can't stay with you, what will your wife say? We have enough money to stay in a hotel and not bother you," said Molly, surprised by his offer.

"It's not about money, it's about friendship," said George. "Don't you worry about my Bernie; she loves company as much as I do. We have a big house and lots of food. There are young children for Maggie to play with next door and maybe we'll find a wife or two for the single boys."

It was settled, they would be staying with the Feehans, but they would need to bring food and George's beverage of choice—beer.

"Would you two be interested in marrying your women when we get to Chicago?" George said when he found S.C. and Patrick alone on deck. "We have a Catholic church about a hundred yards from our house, with a full time Jesuit priest, Father Burns. He's very close to Bernie and I and would not hesitate to marry you. Think about it, discuss it with the girls and let me know. You may not see a priest again for a long while."

S.C. told Patrick that he and Emilia had already thought about asking George, as the ship's captain, to marry them before they docked in Chicago. Having a priest available to perform the wedding was more than they could have hoped for. Patrick excused himself and said he had to talk to Molly.

Molly and Maggie were together on the port side of the ship. Patrick asked Maggie if she could leave the two of them alone for a while as he had something to discuss with Molly. Maggie grudgingly left, leaving Molly and Patrick alone.

Patrick blushingly said, "My dear Molly, I am not the type of person that shows his emotions very well, in fact, I'm downright poor at it. With that being said, Molly, I love you so much and I couldn't stand it if I were not with you. Will you please marry me? I know I have many faults..."

Molly interrupted him, "Say no more, God only knows how much I love you. Yes, I will marry you!"

Patrick was smiling ear to ear as he told her of George's offer to have the priest marry them in Chicago.

"It will be a double wedding with S.C. and Emilia, if you don't mind," said Patrick.

Molly wrapped her arms around him and said, "This is the nicest surprise I've ever had, just think, a priest will marry us."

The ship docked in the Port of Chicago and George Feehan led them to his house six short blocks away. At the door George's wife Bernadette greeted them. She was about sixty-five years of age and short in stature, about four foot ten inches. She had white short hair and a continual smile on her face. George introduced her to the Mountain family.

"It is always nice to have company visit. We're so alone here in Chicago, with no family and only a few friends," said Bernie.

Molly said they hoped that they were not going to be an inconvenience for them and they would try and stay out of their way.

"We don't want you to stay out of our way. We want to enjoy your company. George never brings anyone to our home unless he wants to spend time with them," said Bernie. "This will be a wonderful opportunity for us and hopefully for all of you as well."

Maggie was very curious and took off to examine the entire house. Bernie followed her and showed her to her room. She would share the room with Emilia and Molly, but each would have their own beds. After seeing her room Maggie ran outside to explore the neighborhood. She found two kids about her age and asked them their names. The boy was Philip and the girl was Julie and they were twins. The two girls hit it off immediately, but Philip was not in the mood for any girl talk. He left to find his friends.

Julie was a year younger than Maggie and said she went to school. Maggie asked her to explain what a school was. Julie said she attended a school next to the church and the teacher was a nun. Maggie was confused.

"What is a nun and what is a school?" Maggie asked.

"My school is a place where I learn things, like reading and writing. My teacher is a nun, she's like a priest, only a woman. She wears what is called a habit, a uniform that is black and white. She prays a lot and teaches us how to pray too," Julie explained.

Maggie had never heard of anything like that. She had been taught to count and to add and subtract by one of Delaney's whores, but nothing else.

"Could I go to your school?" she asked Julie.

Julie said she'd run and ask the nun if it would be all right. Maggie thanked her and ran back to the Feehans' to tell the family that she may go to a school. Maggie explained to Molly, Emilia and Patrick about what Julie had said about the school. All them had been home-schooled and knew the basics of education. They apologized to Maggie and said it hadn't occurred to them that she would need an education or would want one for that matter. The girls said that they would immediately begin giving her lessons as soon as they left Chicago. In the mean time, they encouraged her to go to the school if possible.

For the next two days Maggie attended school with Julie and Philip. There were eleven children in the one room schoolhouse that was attached to the church. Sister Mary Jean was the nun that taught the children. She was a wonderful young woman with a loving personality and could relate to all the children. She placed Maggie with the younger children and began to teach her to read. Maggie knew some words and caught on quickly, but Sister said she would need much practice. When school was out for the day Maggie would run back to the Feehans' all excited to tell everyone that would listen about her day. At night the girls worked with her and promised that when they arrived in Whisk-con-sin they would try and find her a school.

After Mass on Sunday the Feehans and the Mountain family gathered for the double wedding. Bernie had washed and pressed all of the girls' dresses and bought some flowers from the market for them to carry. Maggie was the maid of honor for both Emilia and Molly. William was Patrick's best man and Mark was S.C.'s. The priest, a Jesuit from Milwaukee named Father Burns, officiated at the ceremony. It was the best wedding they had ever attended, since none of the Mountains had ever attended a wedding before. They returned to the Feehans', including Father Burns, for a wonderful dinner served with George's favorite beverage—beer.

Bernie told Maggie she would sleep with her tonight and Mark and William would sleep in their living room. Maggie questioned why she would not sleep in the room she shared with the other girls.

"When men and women get married they share a bed together," Bernie tried to explain. "It would not be appropriate for you to sleep in the same room."

Maggie smiled and said, "They're going to make a baby, aren't they? You're right, I don't want to watch that. It doesn't even sound like fun. I mean, doing it. Ugh."

The newlyweds retired early to their separate bedrooms while the rest of the Mountain men, Father Burns and George spent several hours reminiscing and drinking more beer than they could handle. At midnight, Bernie came into the living room and told the men they were making too much noise and they were all going to bed immediately.

George followed Bernie and said to her, "You just want play honeymoon with me tonight, don't you?"

Bernie responded loud so the boys including Father could all hear, "You old fart, try as you might in your drunken stupor, that little thing will hide like a frightened turtle."

Everyone laughed, including the priest. Father Burns said his goodbyes and wished the Mountains good luck on their travels which would begin tomorrow morning.

The family met in the kitchen at 9 o'clock to have breakfast and say their goodbyes. George, Mark and William were all hung over and were very quiet. S.C. asked if the boys celebrated a little too much?

George responded, "You can never celebrate a little too much. It's not every day friends and relatives get married. It's a time for great joy. I for one believe it's my duty to overindulge, get sick, and get hung over to support my friends in their new journey in life. Now that I've done all that, you can all get the hell out of here so I can sleep the rest of the day in peace."

Everyone laughed, cried and hugged one another and said their goodbyes and thank-yous, for they knew it would be the last time they saw each other. It was a good day, but also a sad day for the now almost complete Mountain family.

CHAPTER 23

Land Barrons

ON THE STEAMSHIP TO MILWAUKEE, MAGGIE asked a simple unanswered question of the family: "I am the only person in this family without the last name of Mountain. When do I get that?"

"Today! You are officially Maggie Mountain and are my daughter today," said William. "Welcome to our family, we are proud to have you as its newest family member, as well as Emilia Mountain and Molly Mountain."

The trip to the Village of Milwaukee took over three hours, longer than expected. The steamship developed engine trouble and had to be repaired on the water. It was a nice day, May 1st, and the sun was shining. The family spent most of the time on deck discussing what they would do first in Milwaukee. Molly and Patrick both agreed that William, Mark and S.C. should go to the land office and see what was needed to secure the land. In the meantime, Molly, Patrick, Emilia and Maggie would find the much needed supplies. All agreed, except little Maggie. Maggie was bound and determined to go to the land office and buy her land too.

"I want to do this by myself, if they'll let me. I want to own something all by myself," Maggie said. "William, I will put your name on it along with me, but I want to buy it myself."

"Maggie, if it's that important to you, please come along with us," said William.

At the United States Land Office maps of different counties in the territory and plots of land for sale were displayed. William spoke to an agent and specified that he wanted to purchase land in what was called Washington County, close to the Town of Erin in the southeastern part of the territory. The agent, David Smith said he knew the area well. Many Irish immigrants had purchased land in that community in the last two years. He said that since the land values around the town of Milwaukee had soared in recent years the land in the southeastern area was beginning to be in demand. With the increased demand for land in that area, prices had risen to $2.50 per acre from $1.25 per acre in the last two years. There was, however, still plenty of land for sale.

William said his family was interested in purchasing 2,500 acres of land and they had the cash with them to pay for it. Smith said he would draw up the legal deeds for the property and all the official owners must be present to sign for the property. Smith showed them a map locating exactly where their land was. He said there were small lakes on the property as well as stands of trees as far as the eye could see. "You'll all have your work cut out for you," he said. "Clearing the land will be a monumental task." They paid the $6250 in gold coins, received their receipt and were told to come back in two days to sign the deeds.

They walked out amazed at what just happened. Their dream had just come true. They were free Irishman and were landowners of 2,500 acres, more than what Lord Charles Webb owned in all of Killeagh, Ireland. However, if they could have foreseen their futures that day, they would never have been able to predict how daunting the task of clearing 2,500 acres of raw land would be.

William, Mark, S.C. and Maggie went to the general store to meet the rest of the family and tell them about their land purchases. William said they bought 2,500 acres for a cost of $6,250 that included 500 acres for Maggie. The group smiled and asked when they could leave.

"In two days we sign the deeds and we can leave. The land agent suggested both husband and wife sign the deeds on their designated properties," William explained. "Mark and I will sign both our names on our 1,000 acres together and I will sign along with Maggie on her property. If anything happens to me, Maggie will get her own property and half of mine, Mark gets the other half. Maggie will also inherit any coins I have left, just in case something happens to me. I want her always taken care of."

The purchases at the store were the largest in recent history. Lucky for the family the store was well stocked. They purchased tools, three covered wagons, food, warm clothing for all, work clothes for all, new leather boots, brimmed hats, books for Maggie, and all the other personal necessities for the ladies. They also purchased furniture and several beds for the first house. They had gotten used to beds while staying in hotels and at the Feehans'. Now they all refused to go on without that luxury. The storekeeper told them that there would be ample sawmills near their homesteads to purchase lumber. They might also supply their own raw trees to the mills and just pay to have them milled. He told them they can purchase cows, bulls, sheep and pigs in the town of Erin.

After leaving the store they loaded the wagons with their new goods, hitched up the horses and rode a mile or so out of the small town of Milwaukee to a place by the lake to camp for the night. It was still light when they finally settled in with a small fire and sleeping gear in place. The girls prepared a meal of beef jerky, potatoes and fresh vegetables. They were tired and after eating the meager meal they fell fast asleep.

They spent the next two days camping by the lake and Mark and William showed Maggie the finer points of fishing. They had purchased a thin line for the poles they made from tree branches. They also bought different sized metal hooks at the store and an item called a bobber. The so-called bobber was made out of cork, with a stick through the middle of it and was attached to the fishing line. The bobber floated in the water and when it bobbed it signaled to the fisherman that a fish was biting and taking the bait. They caught several fish, but the boys didn't have any idea what species they were. They found that they were very good to eat. What a great little invention this bobber was. They could hardly wait to show it to Anne and Margaret. After mentioning Anne and Margaret and the fishing, the boys became a little sad and depressed. Maggie snapped them out of it right away when she caught a very large fish that Mark estimated to weigh over five pounds. They would all feast on Maggie's catch.

The family packed up and left the campsite for the land office. In front, they tied the horses to fence posts, left them unattended and went in. Milwaukee was clearly not anything like Five Points. The people treated each other with respect and no one carried weapons, at least in sight of one another. The boys thought that in a frontier community, the penalty for lawlessness was dealt with in a harsh and severe manner, maybe even death.

They signed the appropriate documents and Mr. Smith said he would file them with the Wisconsin Territory. They kept a copy for themselves and thanked him for his help. Smith also gave them a map to use to get them to their properties. Smith said that the route they should take would get them to their destination in three to four days. He said the trip was about 35 to 45 miles long and they'd be traveling west by northwest. There was a road, but it was narrow and full of large potholes.

CHAPTER 24

The Trip to Erin Township

THE FAMILY SET OUT AT NOON on May 5, 1842 for their new life. The trip was a wonderful experience for all of them. The road was narrow and full of potholes, but the scenery was breathtaking. Lush forests, rolling hills, abundant freshwater lakes, waterfalls and an assortment of different wildlife were seen at every bend in the road.

"This is truly the land of milk and honey," said William. "Just as Anne's pa, Patrick Flynn, said it was."

The trip was taking longer than expected with spring rains slowing the wagons down to a slow crawl. The wagons were also weighed down with supplies and the horses were having a difficult time maintaining their footing on the muddy, slippery slopes.

The family stopped frequently to rest and water the horses. They found an open area, large enough to accommodate the three wagons, the horses and the family. They decided that this would be an excellent place to camp for the night. There was a waterfall that emptied into a small pond. The water was fresh, cold and appeared good for drinking.

William started a fire after Maggie gathered the needed twigs and dry branches. The older girls began to prepare the meal while the men sat and watched. Maggie told William she would try her luck fishing in the pond.

"Be careful and don't go too far away. We'll be eating soon," William told her.

"You're acting like my Pa now and I like that," said Maggie. "I think I'll call you Pa or Dad now, if you don't mind."

William just smiled and said, "Whatever your little heart desires."

CHAPTER 25

The Kidnapping

AS THE FAMILY WAS ENJOYING THEIR rest, Maggie had wandered further and further away than expected. The lake was much larger than anyone could imagine and its shoreline meandered in and out of the dense forest. Maggie was completely out of sight when William realized he couldn't see or hear her. He jumped to his feet and yelled her name out in a very loud voice. He got no response. He walked quickly around the pond in the direction Maggie had taken yelling her name, still no response.

William was panicking and running at a very fast pace, when he found her fishing pole lying beside the lake with three small dead fish. He continued screaming her name, but got no response. After slowing his panicked mind down, he surveyed the area where the pole was and found several moccasin footprints. Maggie's small prints were there too, but there were also several larger sized prints, that William assumed were made by Indians.

William could see the route where they had taken her. There was a small path cut through the trees and it appeared there were several men involved in the kidnapping. William raced back to the camp and retrieved his knives from his wagon. All the family members were on their feet asking, "Where is Maggie?"

William said in a distressed voice, "Some bad people have taken her. I'm going to find her and they will pay dearly. You all stay here."

The boys volunteered to come along, but William would have none of it.

"Stay here and protect our women and supplies. I'll take two pistols with me and you keep the other four loaded and don't be afraid to use them. This country is getting worse than Ireland."

"William, remember what George Feehan warned us about the renegade Indians?" Mark said. "They were members of either the Pottawatomie or the Menominee tribes. They wanted to rid the area of the hated white man and had captured many white women and sold them to the fur trappers or to the other Indian tribes as slaves. Be careful, they are dangerous men."

William just nodded and said, "What a fool I was to let her go off by herself. They were likely watching us for many miles, just waiting for a chance to take her or someone else. I must leave now. If we're not back in two days leave without us. I'll find you. Be careful, and don't trust anyone."

William had attached his knives to the usual spots, one on his back just behind his head, one on his right forearm, one attached to his right leg and the bowie knife in back just above his buttock. He carried the loaded flintlock pistols in both hands and made sure the powder was kept dry. He was armed, dangerous and raging with anger. He would kill them all and show them no mercy.

Less than a half day ahead was a band of savage Indians, who were dragging a very frightened little white girl along with a rawhide rope wrapped tightly around her neck. Her hands were also bound tightly together with rawhide rope. She was made to keep up and if not she was dragged by her neck. They found great delight in slapping her face and kicking her. Her knees were scraped and bloody, as well as her elbows. She refused to cry out and told them her father would find her and would kill all of them. The only one that spoke English was the leader Gray Hawk and he laughed and kicked her in the face.

"You'll be dead or be an Indian squaw before he even knows you're gone," said Gray Hawk. "Do as we say and we won't damage you too badly for your next owner."

The kick in the face broke Maggie's nose and she was bleeding profusely, but she didn't cry. Tears rolled down her face as the pain was almost unbearable. The Indians laughed and mocked her. She couldn't understand what they were saying, but knew she was in trouble. At first she was sure William would find her, but now she wasn't as sure. A great deal of time had passed and they were deep in the forest. She knew William was a hunter, but this land was so vast and the forest was so thick she now had her doubts. She thought she would surely die in Five Points, but never expected to die in Whisk-con-sin.

William followed the moccasin trail with little problem. His main concern was that he knew Maggie was being dragged along. He found the place in the trees where Gray Hawk had broken her nose. There was blood everywhere and he assumed it was Maggie's. His temper raged. He was able to move quickly through the forest, but realized he was not in the physical condition he had been in when he left Ireland. His breathing was labored and he tired easily. He kept going as fast as he could, constantly reminding himself of Maggie's dilemma and the urgency to save her from a fate that would be likely worse than death.

William trudged along after dark, hoping he would find them sometime during the night. He felt the darkness would even things out a bit. From the amount of moccasin tracks, he assumed there were about six of them, more than enough to satisfy his hunger for revenge. In the distance he spotted a raging fire and the aroma of meat being cooked on the open flames. The Indians were clearly not concerned about white men attempting retrieve a child.

"How wrong they are, they will suffer greatly and I will show them no mercy," William thought. "They will all die violently tonight."

William checked the pistols first and made sure the powder was dry and cocked both of them. His knives were in place and he waited patiently for the Indians to turn in for the night. They were a confident bunch; they had not even posted a sentry to alarm them is case of an ambush. William waited until the fire was burning low and the Indians were close to sleeping.

He walked slowly into their midst and fired shots into the first two renegade heads he saw. He calmly dropped the pistols and reached for the knife behind his head and buried it into an onrushing Indian's chest. He then pulled out the bowie knife from back of his waistband and lunged it into the heart of the older, slow moving man that had remained on the ground. William had lost count of how many there were and turned his head quickly back and forth in all directions. He saw the Indian with the bow and arrow too late, as the arrow struck him in the back left shoulder and stuck out through his front shoulder. The Indian dropped the bow and charged William. William slid the knife from its forearm sheath and threw it side arm in the direction of the man sprinting toward him. It hit him in the stomach and stopped him in his tracks.

William did not see Maggie or any other Indians. He thought there were six and he had killed or wounded five. He heard Maggie scream from the forest. He grabbed the end of the arrow that was protruding from his front shoulder and snapped off the arrowhead. He then reached around his back with his right hand pulled the arrow out through the opening where it entered his shoulder. The pain was excruciating, but his adrenalin was pumping and he could only think of Maggie. He reached for the knife that was strapped to his leg and ran hunched over in the direction her voice was last heard. When he reached Maggie, the Indian Gray Hawk, had his right arm around her chest and a knife in his left hand pressed hard against her throat, as he leaned against a large oak tree.

He had a big grin on his face and laughingly said to William, "You whites are all cowards. You never fight your enemies face to face, only in darkness, when you can't be seen. Well, what are you going to do now? You come any closer and your little girl will die in front of you. I know you white men will never let that happen. You would rather I kill her when I have her alone than when you watching."

"I'm a coward?" William responded. "You and your dead friends take women and defenseless children! You're not men. Real men would never do such a thing. Let her go and face me alone, you red-faced mongrel."

Gray Hawk pressed the knife hard against Maggie's throat causing a trickle of blood to run down her neck. He opened his mouth wide as he yawned, like William was boring him. He was just beginning to say something when a razor sharp knife flew from William's hand and lodged in his mouth. Only the knife handle was exposed, the rest of the knife was embedded in his mouth. His eyes bulged out, and he began to choke as blood flowed out of his mouth and nose down his shirt. As he was falling, Maggie pushed his weakened hand away from her throat and ran away. Gray Hawk dropped to his knees as he tried in vain to pull the knife from his mouth.

William taunted him as he was dying, "You're crying like a little baby, can't you at least die like a man?"

William reached for the knife and yanked it from his mouth and grabbed his hair and cut off the scalp. Gray Hawk tried to scream from the pain, but was only able to let out a small moan.

William was weak too, but his intent was on inflecting as much pain as possible on the dying man.

"That's enough, William, no more, please," Maggie begged.

William lowered his knife, but reared back and kicked the Indian in the face. Gray Hawk died an hour later, by himself in the woods, without any scalp and a broken nose.

William was bleeding to death. Maggie covered his wound with part of her dress.

"You better not die and leave me alone," Maggie told him. "I would never give up, and you better not either. We're walking back to our camp, do you understand?"

William smiled and said, "I'm not leaving you, but let's get my knives and make sure they're all dead before we leave."

When they reached the Indians' campsite one of the renegades was still alive. It was one of the Indians that William had shot first in the head. He had a large wound and it appeared he wouldn't last long.

"I'll leave him be and let him die in peace," William said. They retrieved his knives and pistols and moved on.

The walk back took many hours. Maggie realized she couldn't support William's weight any longer and would have to leave him and run ahead and get help. William didn't even realize she had left; he was in an unconscious state. William woke for a moment and saw birds flying way above him. He could also see treetops swaying slowly in the breeze. He had a burning sensation throughout his entire body, but he was in a peaceful state and he was sure he had died. He awoke again when it was dark and he was cold, as cold as he'd ever been. He realized he was covered with blankets, but that did not stop him from shaking uncontrollably. He tried to move around a bit, but couldn't. He had no strength. There was a fire somewhere close and he enjoyed the heat it gave off. He tried to talk but the words escaped him, as he dove back into a deep coma.

William woke again, but this time he was not sure if he was dead or not. He recognized Molly sitting by his side.

He said in a weak voice, "Molly my dear, please tell me you're not dead."

"William, why would you think I might be dead," Molly responded. "I've been right here beside you for five days now. I'd never leave you while you're in this state."

"Molly, what happened to little Maggie? Did she die? I tried to save her," William said. Molly tearfully held William's hand.

"Maggie is alive and well, you did save her. She has some scrapes and bruises and a broken nose," Molly told him. " I set the nose and she will be just as beautiful as before."

Molly said, "I've kept Maggie away from you because she got so emotional whenever she saw you. That little girl carried you almost all the way back here. When she couldn't carry you any further, she ran back here and got the boys to come and get you. You saved her life and she returned the favor, she saved yours. You're both just as tough as nails."

Maggie heard the good news that William had come out of his coma. She slowly crept into the wagon where William was sleeping. He woke and smiled at her. Maggie began to cry and leaned over, hugged him and laid her head on his good shoulder. She wept so much she couldn't talk, she just stuttered. William held her tight and kept saying over and over again how much he loved her. William finally was able to look into her little face and realized both her eyes were black and blue and almost swollen shut. Her nose was swollen and was also black and blue. Her throat would have a scar where it was sliced and her knees and elbows had raw scabs on them that were trying to heal.

He laughingly said, "I hope I don't look as bad as you do."

Maggie said laughingly in return, "You always looked worse than me, you old fart."

The rest of the family, one by one, came by for short visits. Molly would not let anyone stay too long. William needed his rest and by God, he would get it.

Luckily the family had bought enough supplies to last for several weeks, as it appeared William would not be able to travel for quite a while. A week after William came out of his coma, he informed the group he was ready to travel. He promised he would lay in the wagon and would not attempt any hard labor. Molly had the last word on the decision and she agreed to begin their trek to their new home. The excitement was back, but everyone - including Maggie - knew this was still dangerous a territory and caution would be practiced at all times. No more wandering away.

William's wound was healing well, but he was worried that he might lose the use of his arm as Desmond Delaney had. Molly assured him that with the proper exercise he would not lose the use of the arm. She would work with him right away strengthening and exercising the arm.

Maggie was afraid of walking alone, so someone was always with her. She had learned to read quite well and was very inquisitive about what she read. She asked difficult questions that most of the family members couldn't answer. They needed to get her into a school as soon as they got to the town of Erin.

The family reached the Township of Erin in Washington County, the Territory of Wisconsin, on May 22, 1842. The town of Erin that greeted them was a very small community of about twenty people. There was a general store, a blacksmith, two saloons, a small hotel, and a cobbler and tailor. There was a sawmill nearby in the Town of Mequon. The town was small but was growing. At the general store the owner, William Fitzgerald said the land was selling quickly and every day more settlers like the Mountains were arriving. They asked about their property and showed him the deed and the coordinates.

"First, call me Fitz. You folks bought some good tracts of land," said Fitzgerald. "The Little Oconomowoc River meanders through the property and there are small ponds and lakes throughout. There's plenty of water but full of trees to cut and haul. There are wonderful places to build homes in that rolling countryside. In a couple of years, you will all have nice farms to call home."

Fitzgerald showed them to the cow path called a road that would lead them to their property. He also warned them there was an unwanted squatter on their property and he was determined in making a home there for his family. He'd been there for over two years and was a surly fellow. His wife was nice, an Indian women with three kids. They were very poor and with no other place to go. The Mountains told Fitz they would address that problem when they got there.

"If you have a problem, we can fetch the County Sheriff to help you," Fitz told them. "It will take a couple of days for him to get here, but the problem will be solved."

The three wagons trudged along the cow path towards their new land. It was an exciting time. They agreed to find a spot to camp out by the river and maybe it would be warm enough to bathe. The walk took two hours to get to the squatters' place. S.C. and Mark went to the door of the shack and knocked at the door. It abruptly opened and a tall black man came out with long rifle in hand.

"You'se be trespassin' here and you don't never belong here neither," said the man.

S.C. was livid and said, "That's where you're wrong, we do belong here. It's our property and it's paid for in full. Now, I suggest that you are the people that are trespassing. Would that be a fair statement?"

"We'se ain't movin', we'se got no place to go," the man said.

"We have no desire to uproot your family, but this is our land and we paid a handsome price for it," Patrick said. "Now, we probably don't need all of it, so we can sell you this bit you're living on now at a fair price. We paid $2.50 an acre for it and that's the price we'll charge you, what do you say?"

"I say you could charge me one penny and I couldn't pay it. We done got no money," the man said.

The man's wife came out followed by three children all below the age of ten. They were dirty and very poor.

"Please let us stay, we have no place to go," the woman said. "We'll work for our keep and we'll not cause you any trouble, will we Lewis?"

Lewis said with a lowered head, "We'se not gonna cause no trouble, that for sure."

Molly stepped in and said, "I can only speak for my husband and I, but you can stay and we'll work something out later. We've been in the same situation as you are in now, so we understand."

The entire family introduced themselves and asked their names.

"We'se is the Lewis family, I got no last name. This here is me wife Fanny and the little ones is Jacob, Davis and Emma," said Lewis. The children were polite and all said hello in low voices.

The Mountains told the Lewis family they would camp by the river and asked them to come by in the morning and they would share breakfast with them. They politely accepted their offer.

The Lewis family arrived promptly at 8:00 am. Molly, Emilia and Maggie had prepared oatmeal with raisins and served the last of the fresh fruit they had left. The Lewis family was hungry. The children were drawn to Maggie, who was reading a book. They asked her to read out loud, but she refused.

"When I get better at reading, I'll read out loud to you and will teach you all to read," Maggie told the children.

They asked Maggie about her injuries and Maggie responded, "I fell out of the wagon." The Lewis children stayed close to Maggie as the older folks talked about the property problems.

The Lewis family had not seen William before as he had been fast asleep in the wagon. William staggered close to the fire and introduced himself. William said to Lewis, "First and foremost, know this—this land belongs to us and I won't begin to tell you the hardships we endured getting it. I'm sure you have had many hardships yourself. We're prepared to offer you a deal so you can own some of this little corner you are currently squatting on.

"I ain't no good at deals, I been done fucked by so many of you'se whites, I don't make no deals," Lewis said.

Fanny interrupted him and said, "Don't be so bullheaded, that does us no good. Listen to what these folks has to say."

Lewis agreed to listen.

Molly stood up and said, "We are prepared..."

Lewis interrupted her. "I don't make no deals with no woman."

Molly saw stars. She said, "You are a stupid, goddamn fool, then. I represent our family in all of our financial matters, along with my husband Patrick. You can just pack all your shit up today and get the hell off our property. If you refuse the sheriff will be summoned, you dumb ass."

Lewis backed up a bit and said, "We ain't going no where."

William stepped forward with knife in hand and said, "Now this bullshit talk is over. I've killed many men getting here to this property and I will not have the likes of you disrespect any of my family. Do you see my hand? It holds a knife. This knife has never shown any mercy to the men it killed. I suggest you leave now. If you don't, you will die here and now in front of your wife and children. Do you understand?"

Lewis' eyes were wide open as he looked at William's knife.

"Yes's sir, I wills make a deal with you'se," Lewis said.

"No, you will not, the only fucking deal will be made with Molly and no one else. If that does not suit you, you know your options," said William.

Fanny stepped in and said, "Please Lewis, don't do this. These people are willing to offer us a place to stay, don't be stubborn."

"I guess you'se not giving me no choice, what's your deal."

"I don't know why I'm still offering this to you," Molly said. "I guess I just feel sorry for your wife and kids, not you. My family will allow you stay on your current homestead under the following conditions; after your chores at home are completed for the day, you will spend at least four hours a day working with our men on their farming. That will include helping with our planting and harvest. Also, clearing the fields. You will help in the construction of our homes, corral and privies. In return, our family will help you with clearing additional acreage for your farm. We'll help with the construction of a new home for you and will provide the lumber and the rest of the materials. We'll help you with planting and harvest. If you do all that we require, you will own 100 acres of our land after five years. Free and clear with your name on the deed. That's the deal!"

Lewis and Fanny just stood there with their mouths open.

Fanny said, "Why are you doing this for us? The way Lewis talked to you, I thought we'd be gone today."

"We were treated with kindness and respect in New York by an entire Negro community," Molly explained. "We stayed with a Negro family named Pratt and helped him build his home. Eldon Pratt only asked if we would return some kindness to someone else in need. We thought helping you folks would fulfill our promise to him."

"Maybe I'se had you all figured wrong," said Lewis. "I'se sorry and Fanny and me would be happy to takes the offer. I'se also like to say I'se sorry to you Molly, it won't never happen again."

They shook hands and said let's get to work.

The ladies of the Mountain family insisted the boys build a privy first. S.C. and Mark, accompanied by Lewis, headed for the sawmill in Mequon with two wagons and purchased enough lumber for the privy and to begin work on the first house. They chose a building site on a hill just above the river nestled in the middle of several oak and maple trees. The site was perfect, with wonderful views of the river and the surrounding hills and forest. All agreed the first home and land would belong to Molly and Patrick.

The boys dug the holes for the privy and for the basement of the new house. They took what they had learned from Eldon Pratt and put the experience to good use in building the first home. Fortunately, there were many small and large boulders around the property, as well as in the river. Many trees were felled in order to capture all the important views and for much needed lumber. The boys took loads of oak, fir, pine and maple trees to the sawmill to have cut and milled into lumber for the new houses. Areas were cleared close to the homestead for gardens to produce much needed food for the winter.

The family agreed that clearing the fields would begin when the work was completed on the house, maybe in the late fall or early spring. Lewis was there every day and worked much more than was ever requested in his contract. His wife Fanny and the children were also around every day to help out. After the day's work was complete, the Lewis family and the Mountains would have dinner together. After dinner, Molly, Emilia, Maggie and the Lewis children, Jacob, Davis and Emma, would gather for the daily lessons. Molly and Emilia took the position of the teachers, but Maggie was a quick learner and soon she could be teaching the Lewis children. After a few weeks of lessons Fanny and Lewis sat in on the instructions. Lewis and Fanny could not read or write, but Fanny was much more literate and articulate than Lewis.

William's wounds were healing nicely, and he was able to help out on small projects. He threw his knives relentlessly every day. There were many targets since the area was filled with trees. He knew he'd be required to hunt again and wanted to be in good physical shape to do so. He threw with his left hand more than his right, as it was the much needed therapy for his wounded shoulder. It was getting stronger. Although he liked Fanny and the children, he did not warm up to Lewis. The attitude that Lewis had showed to Molly was more than William could or would tolerate in a man. Lewis stayed clear of William. William frightened him and after watching him throw his knives, he now knew William meant business when he threatened him.

"Yup, he be a man not to be trifled with. He be dangerous," Lewis said to Fanny.

Fanny responded, "He's a very nice man, and he was the one that put together their offer to us. You just made him mad with your stubbornness. He does not like anyone talking poorly to the women in his family. I like him."

Lewis said, "You'se like everyone and I'se don't trust 'em. We stay clear of that boy."

CHAPTER 26

The Hunters

WILLIAM TOLD MARK LATE ONE AFTERNOON that he was going off to hunt and would likely be gone for several days. He asked Mark not to tell the rest of the family about his leaving until later, as he feared they would try and talk him out of going. He told Mark he wanted to see the rest of their property and also see more of the entire landscape. William packed while the family was eating supper and quietly left.

It was July 2nd and the weather was warm. William immediately realized he was not in very good physical shape and this hunt could help him rejuvenate his body. It was almost dark when William decided to camp on a hill by a small lake. Although it was very warm, by camping at a little higher elevation there was a cool breeze in the air. He was very comfortable. His thoughts, as always, were of Anne Flynn. He missed her immensely and he wondered where she might be. He wondered if her family left Ireland and if they still intended on coming to Erin. He wondered if they had survived the six weeks at sea, if they had to go through Five Points, and if she and her family survived that. He thought the chances of him ever seeing her were slim at best. He knew he'd never forget her. The days he spent with her were the best days of his life. He fell fast asleep, exhausted by the first leg of his journey.

The next morning William awoke to the birds chirping and the sun shining. He was well rested and very hungry. He had taken along just some fruit and some jerky, expecting to kill enough game to take care of his hunger. Near the water was a pair of geese with little chicks. William remembered the geese at the lough in Fermoy where he met

Anne. He always wished he would have killed one, just to see if he liked the taste. He would not kill these—they had too many babies to take care of. William strolled through the forest seeing more wildlife than he had seen in his entire life. The stands of trees seemed endless. The lakes and streams were abundant. This was as Anne's father Patrick said, "The land of milk and honey."

William walked most of the day and did not encounter another human being. He killed a very large rabbit at about two o'clock in the afternoon and gutted and skinned it on the spot. He started a fire and roasted the rabbit on a wooden skewer. He slow-cooked the rabbit and took his time eating it. His stomach was full and he was tired and soon fell fast asleep.

When he woke it was nighttime. He must have slept for more than four hours. He was well rested and made up his mind to keep traveling by moonlight. As he walked he could hear the animals of the night hunting and being hunted. It reminded him of Five Points. As he wandered aimlessly he felt someone or something watching him.

He grabbed the handle of his bowie knife and carried it in his right hand. As he continued to walk he was sure something was following him. He decided he would stop by a large oak tree and wait out whatever or whoever was hunting him. William stood silently by the tree in a crouched position for more than an hour. Crouching there brought back memories of his past and the skills he had used hunting game in Ireland. He was where he loved to be, alone in a forest, tracking and waiting for elusive game.

CHAPTER 27

Fox -The Indian Chief

WILLIAM HEARD SOME RUSTLING OF LEAVES behind him and he was sure whatever had been tracking him would soon show its face.

He remained quiet and sat motionless for several minutes when someone said, "Don't be alarmed, I mean you no harm."

William jumped to his feet and said, "Show yourself or you will pay the consequences."

Slowly a figure appeared through the darkened shadows. It appeared to William the man was about his weight, but was much taller. As he approached, William could see the man was dressed in the skin of an animal. He wore trousers made of the same skin and a jacket that was open and showed the man's bare chest. He carried a bow and had several arrows in a small quiver attached to his shoulder and a knife in a sheath attached to his waist. He had coal black hair and his skin was much darker than William's, but not as dark as Lewis.

"I've been tracking you most of the day," said the man. "I saw you were a hunter and I was curious how you brought down that rabbit."

"Come closer, so I can see you," William said.

The two stopped about three feet apart and the man extended his hand to William to shake. William shook his hand as he said, "My name is William Mountain, and I'm from Ireland."

The man said, "I am called Fox. I am from the Menominee tribe and of the Thunderers clan. I was raised here on this land when it all belonged to my tribe. Your government has asked us many times to give up our lands and relocate to a Reservation. We do relocate as they request, but we come right back. The dumb bastards."

"You do not sound like other Indians I've come across," William said. "You speak very good English."

"My tribe was taught by the Jesuit priests," Fox said. "We have two religions, the Jesuit's Catholic religion and our own. To satisfy the priests, I always told them I believed as they do, but I don't. It was easier to lie."

William smiled and said, "I'm Catholic, but I've only seen one priest in my life, at my brothers' weddings."

The two sat down and began to ask each other questions. Fox wanted to know where Ireland was. William tried to explain, but as intelligent as Fox was, it was hard to comprehend a land so far away. Fox asked how he and his family got to this Territory. William explained the canals and the ships on the Great Lakes and how long it took them to get here. He told Fox about his run-in with Grey Hawk and his friends. Fox knew of Grey Hawk and said he was a dangerous man.

"Not anymore," William said. "I killed him and his friends. They kidnapped my daughter and I found them and killed the entire bunch."

Fox was impressed and asked, "How did you kill? I see no rifle, and killing them would not be an easy task."

"I had two flintlock pistols and I used both. I then used my knives on the rest," said William. "When I cornered Grey Hawk he had a hold on my daughter with a knife to her neck. He said if I didn't let him go he would kill her. He was so bored with me that he opened his mouth wide and yawned. That's when I threw my knife into his open mouth and he choked on the blade. Killing him was easy. He was a bad man that harmed my daughter, and I show no mercy to the likes of him."

Fox asked William if they could build a fire and talk for a while. William agreed and the two gathered up kindling and larger pieces of wood. Soon they had a roaring fire. William liked Fox immediately. Fox, although uncertain whether William could have killed Grey Hawk and his men alone, also liked William. Fox told William his tribe of about twenty-five, of which he was their leader or chief, were camped only a few miles away. He said he would take William to his camp in the morning to meet his family. William agreed and thought it might be encouraging to see the good side of these natives.

"Do members of your tribe speak English, as you do?" asked William.

"Many do. We were all taught by the Jesuits," said Fox. "My children and my wife all speak very good English."

Fox was intrigued by William's use of knives as weapons.

"How did you get to using knives as your weapons and how did you get so accurate with them?" Fox asked.

William smiled and said, "Fox, where I came from my people were not allowed to own guns. I had nothing to protect myself with and I needed something. My grandfather gave me my first knife and I worked for years learning how to use it. It took a long time but I eventually became an expert at using them. I became the hunter for my family and supplied all the wild game for them."

"We're similar in many ways. Your government would not let us have any weapons, especially firearms," said Fox. "My father, when I was young, taught me to use the bow and arrow. I also became the main hunter for my tribe and I still am."

The two talked well into the night and finally both agreed to turn in. Tomorrow would be another day to get to know each other better.

As the sun began to rise both men were awake and ready for the hike to meet the Fox family and friends. Fox was correct; the camp was only a few miles away. The camp was busy with children playing and the women working preparing food. When Fox came into sight with a white man following him, everyone stopped what they were doing and looked at William in silence. They had seen many white men before, and they were concerned that William might be an agent for the government commissioned to bring them back to the reservation. Fox took William to his teepee and introduced him to his wife Bena and to his daughter Chewoa and son Huritt. They all looked confused by the white man.

"William is a hunter, like me, and I want him to teach all our men how to use the knife as he does," Fox said. "William is from a long ways away and is now living here near us with his family."

William spoke directly to Bena, "It has been a pleasure meeting your husband and the rest of you. The last Indians I met were not so nice. I hope I am not interrupting your family."

Bena just laughed and said, "My people are not used to Fox bringing home a white man. That would normally signal trouble for us. I hope that's not your intention. We're a peaceful people."

"Please do not think I'm here to cause you any trouble," William assured her. "I live close by and was just exploring the area when I met your husband. We became friends, nothing more."

Bena smiled and said, "We'll see."

William knew she was skeptical of him and what his intentions were, but he hoped she would eventually grow to trust him. He also thought once she met the women of his family she would feel more comfortable around him.

Fox gathered the men around the several trees close to the campsite. William was to teach them how to correctly hold and throw a knife. He was surprised by the homemade knives the Indians had. Some were made of bone and flint stone but most had hand-tooled knives made by a blacksmith. William showed the group his bowie knife and they all admired its workmanship. As they gazed at the knife, William suddenly reared back and threw it into a tree about twenty feet away. They all stood in amazement at the feat.

"Now all of you do as William instructs you to do and maybe we can use this new tool for hunting," Fox told them.

William explained the first rule in knife hunting. "Don't throw the knife at anything in the water, or in a high tree, near rocks, or any place where you will be unable to retrieve it."

The men all laughed and Fox said, "We take it you speak from experience."

William smiled sheepishly and nodded his head up and down to indicate yes, I have. William showed them his skills at throwing with either hand or both at once. He explained the correct way to hold the knives before throwing. It took several hours, but they at least got the right idea of what he was trying to teach them.

At last he said, "You are all very capable hunters, I know that by watching you. You must keep in mind it has taken me almost a lifetime to perfect my throwing techniques, so expect it to also take you a long time."

After showing his new friends the art of throwing a knife, Fox asked William if he'd like to spend some time learning the bow and arrow.

William apologized and said, "I'd like to watch you, but I never intend to use one so I'd prefer not to. Please understand, I don't mean to disrespect you, it's just that I have no interest in it."

Fox laughed out loud and said, "I don't blame you one bit. I never intend to use the knife like you do."

William, Fox, and the rest of the family ate lunch and talked about the many issues the Indians faced trying to find a suitable place to live.

"Our people have always moved around, never living in one place too long. We lived in places like we are in now for the summer and moved to different areas as the seasons changed," said Fox. "My people hunted in many different forests and fished many lakes and rivers, never staying too long to ensure that we don't deplete the wildlife. We revere the wildlife and we protect it, taking only what is necessary for us to live."

"I have the same feelings. I take only what is necessary to support my family," said William. "Now let's you and I hunt for a deer. I killed only one in my life and I couldn't believe what a beautiful animal it was. My family needs food now and my goal on this trip was to find a deer. I have twelve mouths to feed, including the Lewis family, and I need to bring home a deer."

"As soon as the sun sets you and I will find a few deer," Fox said.

William thanked Bena for the meal and said his goodbyes to the children and told them all that he wanted them to come and visit his family. Fox said he would bring his family that way in a few weeks. The two of them then left for the hunt.

CHAPTER 28

The Hunt

THE TWO NEW FRIENDS WALKED SEVERAL miles in a light drizzle as darkness fell. Fox told William he preferred to stake out a place and wait for the deer to come to him. He had many places where he had taken deer in the past and they were approaching one of those places now. Fox positioned William across the clearing from him. He told him to get close to a tree and try and blend in. William had hunted like this many times before, but acted like it was a new thing and did as Fox had instructed. William was good at this. He loved the forest and the solitude of it. He leaned against the tree with a knife in his right hand; he was ready to take down a deer.

William and Fox sat quietly for many hours. They made no contact with one another, not even eye contact; they just appeared to be part of the scenery. Fox heard the noise first. He did not move. William sensed something different was happening around him, but did not know what it was. He stood still. After a few minutes a herd of deer walked into the clearing with their heads down, all content and enjoying the foliage the forest provided them. The doe were the first into the clearing, followed by several fawns. Behind them all was a huge buck. He was cautious, much more cautious than the doe were. He was several feet from William, with his head finally down feeding like the rest, when William, with a lightening quick release, fired his knife directly into the bucks' heart. The impact of the knife made the buck jump and try and run, but a second later William threw his other knife. This one punctured the buck's lung as he toppled over in front of William. A

167

second later a doe fell to the ground not ten feet away. A few seconds later another doe also fell to the ground and the herd scattered.

Fox came across the clearing and said, "William, I would never have believed it if someone told me he saw a man kill a large buck with only a knife. No one will believe me when I tell them what I saw you do today. I'll never forget this moment."

"Fox, you brought down two in a matter of seconds with a bow and arrow, and that's almost impossible," William said. "That is a moment I'll never forget as well."

The two men shook hands and both agreed they would be proud to hunt with one another anytime. Fox told William to start with gutting the doe and he would go and get the tribe to help with the butchering.

Fox returned with Bena and several of the women. They shooed William away and took over the job of gutting and cleaning the deer.

"We waste nothing. Everything will be eaten and the hides will be cleaned, stretched and tanned," Fox told William. "If there's anything you do not want we will take it."

William said he would be glad to share his kill with the tribe. Fox said he was not expected to share his kill, only give the tribe the part he may not want such as the heart, liver and kidneys. William said he would likely just take as much as he could carry and the tribe could take what was left.

Within two hours the women had the three deer butchered and the buck packed for William to take home. There was too much deer for one man to carry and William knew it. He told Fox that he would have to unpack much of the meat, as it was too much for him to carry.

"We all knew you could not carry that buck alone," Fox said. "The women packed it for two of us to carry. I'm going with you."

William said to Fox and the remainder of the tribe, "I can never thank you enough for your hospitality and friendship. If you ever need anything from me or my family, just ask."

The deer meat was wrapped in tanned hides and the two hunters slung them over their shoulders for the long walk back to the Mountain homestead. The walk took several hours, sapping their strength while carrying their heavy load through the very rough terrain. They stopped frequently to rest and to gather their strength. While resting, William asked Fox where he and his tribe planned to live in the future.

Fox explained, "We have been a nomadic people for hundreds, maybe thousands of years. We're not the type of people that can live on a small reservation, like your government wants us to. We will continue to wander and hunt until we are all gone. They will send us back to the reservation as soon as they find us again, we will just leave again. We cannot be farmers like you, we need open space to hunt."

"If you or your people ever need a place to stay, you will always be welcome at the Mountain homesteads," William said.

Fox smiled at William and asked him if he realized that Indians were not normally accepted guests of white men.

"We are hated by the whites and they are afraid of us. There are many stories of how we have killed settlers and raped their women," Fox said. "That has happened by the likes of Grey Hawk, but not by the majority of Indians that occupied this land for hundreds of years. We are a peaceful people."

"I know you are, and like I said, you will always be welcome at the Mountain homesteads," William said.

The two arrived at the Mountain campsite around five o'clock and were tired and hungry. Fox was introduced to all the family members except Maggie; she was nowhere to be found. William looked everywhere for her when suddenly she appeared with one of the flintlock pistols. She had been hiding in the wagon, very fearful of the Indian her father had just brought home.

William told Maggie quietly, "Please put the gun down. This man will not harm you, he is my friend."

Maggie shook her head "no," and aimed the pistol in Fox's direction.

William was getting irate and said in a loud voice, "Maggie, damn it, put that pistol down! I won't say it again. This man had nothing to do with Grey Hawk, he is my friend."

Maggie slowly pointed the weapon toward the ground and William took it from her. He hugged her gently and said, "Everything is alright, you just have to get to know Fox. He will not harm you. He has his own children and they will come to visit us soon."

Maggie began to cry and William just held her until it passed. She bravely walked over to Fox and held out her hand and said, "Mr. Fox, I'm sorry I acted the way I did, you just scared me. I wouldn't have shot you. I could never do anything like that."

"My people are often afraid of white men too," Fox told her. "Their first reaction is to shoot and ask questions later. I am not offended, I only hope you will get over your fear of me and other Indians. We are not like Grey Hawk. He was never one of our tribe. He was always a renegade."

Fox showed the family the deer meat and said much of this should be smoked and made into jerky.

He smiled at Fanny and said, "Fanny here will show you women how to smoke and dry this meat, but first here are some steaks that you should cook for tonight's meal. I am leaving so Fanny will show you the best way to cook the steaks too."

Lewis stayed well away from Fox. He knew Fox and the tribe did not approve of their marriage.

Fox said goodbye to the family and told William, "I'll be back in a week or so with my family. If you need to hunt just come and get me and we'll hunt together."

William said, "I think we have enough to last us, but we will look forward to seeing you in a week."

The Mountain family decided tonight would be a feast and a celebration in honor of their new beginning. Molly and Emilia had gone with Patrick and S.C. to the general store and purchased a much-needed wood burning cook stove and supplies that included raspberries, strawberries and blueberries. The girls' plan was to bake bread, and make pies to go along with the deer steaks. It was a real feast.

CHAPTER 29

Chewoa

THE FIRST HOUSE HAD BEEN FRAMED in and the basement was being used as a bedroom for the bachelors, Mark and William. The married couples used the framed-in bedrooms and Maggie slept in the soon-to-be living room. The stove was placed in the would-be kitchen and a stovepipe was inserted. The family gathered outside the house and ate their feast. The Lewis family was also invited to the feast. William brought out a jug of honey mead S.C. had purchased at the store to celebrate their new homestead. They were all enjoying the after dinner refreshments and deserts, when a haggard Fox stumbled in the area carrying his very injured daughter, Chewoa. Fox appeared not to be injured, but was almost hysterical. Molly took Chewoa out of her father's hands and ran into the house with her, followed by Emilia.

"What the hell happened to Chewoa and where is the rest of your family?" William asked Fox.

Fox sat down with tears in his eyes and said, "I was not there and I just came upon what had happened when I got to my village. Bena and Huritt were both dead and many more of the people in my village. I believe the government soldiers evidently came to take my tribe back to the reservation. Many of our warriors must have defied the soldiers. A battle ensued and the soldiers killed many of our men, women and children. Chewoa said her mother had her and Huritt stand behind her. An officer whom Chewoa said was in charge, shot Bena and used his sword on my son. He then had another soldier shoot Chewoa. She has a bad wound in her upper leg. She said she played dead after being

171

shot, but was still kicked in the stomach by the officer trying to verify that she was indeed dead. Before the officer killed Bena he screamed her, 'Where is your renegade husband? We are here to end this bullshit exodus from our reservations. It ends today! We will hunt Fox down and will hang him in the public square in Milwaukee.'"

"William, I have no other choice than to leave Chewoa with you and your family," said Fox. "I must leave and go north out of the reach of your government. Please take care of Chewoa, please try and get her medical attention and save her life. Tell her I'll come back someday for her, but it may be a long time from now. Will you take her and treat her well?"

William shook Fox's hand said, "We will treat her as one of us, rest assured. Are you sure you wouldn't want Fanny Lewis to take the child? She is of Indian blood."

"No, I want her with you, not Lewis. I don't trust that man. Fanny is a good woman, but he has much to prove to me before I'd leave my child with him," Fox said. "Please explain that to her, not him. If anyone comes looking for me, just tell them you've never seen me. Thank you for your help. I will never forget what you are doing for me."

Fox left the Mountain camp that day for Canada and was never seen or heard of again. Unexpectedly, eleven-year-old Chewoa became part of the Patrick and Molly Mountain family that day.

Chewoa was severely injured, and at first Molly did not think she would survive. The child was weak and frightened and had lost a lot of blood, but was comforted by little Maggie, who never left her bedside. It took several weeks of convalescing but Chewoa finally made her first steps on her injured leg. The entire family was there for the event. She smiled and walked very slowly around the front of the house, steadied by Maggie holding on to her arm. Maggie and Chewoa had developed a close friendship and were inseparable. They did everything together, including their reading and writing lessons. The girls slept close to one another to comfort their inner demons. Maggie still remembered her kidnapping, but living with Chewoa made her to begin to lose her fear of Indians. Chewoa, on the other hand, had a hard time adjusting to being around white men. Even though she was treated like she was a family member, she was still hesitant speaking to the men. She had no issues with the women and loved both of them. Maggie had told her what her father William had endured getting her back from Grey Hawk.

"My father is not like the soldiers that killed your family, he will always protect us from any harm," Maggie said.

As the weeks passed, Chewoa became more talkative and felt more like she belonged. Molly was now acting as her mother and treated her as such. Molly gave her chores to do daily, but Chewoa was used to chores and actually had more free time than ever before. Maggie and Chewoa were allowed to roam all over the property, but William insisted they stay within shouting distance.

Lewis told William that the blacksmith in Erin had a litter of puppies he wanted to get rid of. William thought that would be a wonderful gift for the young girls. It would also provide some peace of mind for him and the other family members when the girls wandered off.

William hitched up the horses to the wagons and loaded the girls aboard. They loved to go into the village and into the store. William always bought them candy and occasionally some new clothes if necessary. Their first stop was the blacksmith's shop. Mr. McIntyre was the proprietor. William had done business with McIntyre many times before and was comfortable asking about the puppies. McIntyre said he had two males and they could have both if they liked. The girls each selected a puppy and then they were off to the general store.

Molly had secretly told William she was pregnant and was likely due in five months' time. She asked if he saw a larger dress to buy it for her. If not she and Patrick would go to town later in the week.

CHAPTER 30

The Flynn Girls in Wisconsin

THE GIRLS LEFT THE PUPPIES IN the back bed of the wagon where they fell fast asleep. They then followed William into the store. There were many people in the store, more than William had ever seen before. The store owner, Mr. Fitzgerald, welcomed William and the girls and asked if they had seen the new puppies.

The girls responded in unison, "We both got the puppies that were left."

"My dad named one of them after a horse he had on the farm in Ireland—his name is Ned and we named the other Cy," Maggie said.

"That's wonderful girls," Fitz said. "Come over here and pick out a piece of candy to celebrate this good news."

As William watched the girls laughingly picking out the candy they wanted, his hunting instincts sensed someone watching him. He slowly looked around and saw a beautiful woman looking in his direction. At first he didn't recognize her; she had on a store-bought bonnet and what looked like a new dress. It was Anne Flynn!

William was stunned as she turned her back on him and continued to talk to the young man she was with.

William approached her and said, "Anne Flynn, is that you?"

Anne turned and in a chilled voice said, "Yes, I am Anne Flynn, who are you?"

William stood there looking at her for a moment when Maggie strolled up and said, "Dad, don't forget to look for a dress for Molly."

He nodded his head to Maggie and looked back at Anne and said, "Anne, it's William Mountain, don't you remember me?"

She looked him up and down and in a sarcastic way said, "I once knew a William Mountain, but I was told he was killed in an uprising in the town of Killeagh in Ireland. You can't possibly be the same William I knew."

"Anne, stop pretending you don't recognize me, you know it's me," William said.

"Oh, you do look a little bit like a William I once knew. If you are William it looks as though you're married now with a daughter. Where is your wife?" she asked.

Maggie was standing next to William with her hand resting on his arm when she said, "William adopted me and he is my mother and father, so to speak. Are you the Anne from Fermoy?"

"My name is Anne and yes, I am from Fermoy. Just who are you?" Anne responded.

My name is Maggie Mountain and I was born in Fermoy too and came to America with my parents, who both are now dead."

"I'm sorry to hear that Maggie, it must have been hard for you," said Anne.

Anne then introduced the young man standing beside her, "This is my beau Jared Wynn. He is from New York City here in America. We met while we were passing through."

A clearly shaken William shook Jared's hand and said, "Congratulations Jared, you have found a fine woman in Anne Flynn."

"Anne, is your sister Margaret here with you and the rest of your family?" William asked.

"Yes, my father, brother and Margaret and I are living with my uncle south of town until we build our house," said Anne.

"Where is your land?" William asked.

Anne said curtly, "We bought a small modest parcel of land just south of my uncle's place. Just 80 acres, but we've been told it's good land. We're happy with it—it's better than Ireland."

Chewoa came up to Maggie eating her candy and asked what was going on. Maggie introduced Chewoa to Anne and Jared, but William said nothing. Anne asked Chewoa how she knew Maggie.

Chewoa said, "I live with the Mountain family."

Anne was confused and said, "Do the Mountains take in anyone that needs a home?"

William joined in, "It's a long story, so one day when we have more time I'll explain it to you. We must be getting back now, please excuse us."

William was stunned and hurt. They parted ways with Anne and her beau and left the store. The girls got in the back of the wagon with the puppies and William drove the team back to their homestead in silence. When they arrived Maggie and Chewoa ran to Molly and told her what happened at the store.

Mark was listening in and excitedly said, "The Flynn family is finally here? Where are they? Is Margaret with them?"

"Anne said Margaret is with them and they're living south of town with an uncle," Maggie said.

Mark went immediately to William and said, "Let's go and see them together, I can't wait."

"Anne has a beau and she was very indifferent towards me. She said she had heard I was dead,"said William. "I can't go with you, Mark, but you should go and find out how Margaret feels about you."

Mark hitched up the team and headed off to find Margaret. Hearing the story from the girls, Molly found William outside, close to the house. He stood with his arms folded on his chest, saying nothing as Molly approached.

"William, I'm sure you are upset, but you need to talk to Anne alone," Molly said.

"Oh Molly, my dear, this is not what I expected," William said. "She thought I was dead. I think she also thought I was married when Maggie called me dad. Would you and Patrick mind looking after Maggie for a few days, I need to have some time to myself in the forest."

"William, take as much time as you need, we'll keep an eye on Maggie. Please don't stew over this, you need to talk to her," Molly encouraged him.

"I'll only be gone a day or so. I want to go to Chewoa's village and see if there is anything I can find that she might want," William said.

As William was walking away Molly grabbed his arm and made him stop. She hugged him and said, "I know this will work out. I know it will."

William packed his hunting and camping gear and placed them in his backpack and left for the Indian village.

Mark reached the Flynn temporary home late in the afternoon. As he approached the house from the rugged road, he saw Margaret running down the path to meet him. He stopped the team and jumped off the wagon. He ran to her and she jumped into her arms. She cried and cried and could not stop. Mark held her tight and was as happy as he'd ever been.

"I love you Margaret darling, I love you," Mark said over and over again.

She responded with a bit of the same, and added, "Let's get married right away!"

Mark agreed and said, "As soon as possible."

After their embrace Margaret grabbed his hand and said, "Come in the house, you need to meet my aunt and uncle and their children."

Mark took the reins and led the horses into the yard. He and Margaret went inside. In the kitchen he saw the smiling Anne and gave her a hug. Their father, Patrick, also gave Mark a big hug and young Patrick extended his hand to shake. Uncle Raymond and Aunt June were next and were happy to meet Mark. They both said they had heard enough about him to last a lifetime. They all laughed. Next were the children, Bonnie and Josephine. They were ten and twelve years old. Mark commented to June that her children are about the same ages as the Mountain children and they should come out to the homestead and meet the family.

"Where did you get the children? I didn't know any of you were old enough to have twelve-year-old children," Anne asked.

"I'll try and explain," said Mark. "William first found our adopted sister Molly at the Webb compound outside of Killeagh. She was being kept there against her will..." Mark stopped and said, "Maybe the children should go outside."

The children followed their parents' request and went outside to play.

"William went to Webb's compound for retribution for what they did to our family and our entire community," Mark continued. "They killed almost everyone except William, S.C., Patrick and me. William found Molly there and she and some other young women escaped with him, but not before William took care of Dante Wright and many of Webb's men. He set the entire compound ablaze and left. That's where we got Molly. Molly is now married to our brother Patrick and she is pregnant with their first child. Emilia joined us in Five Points in New York. She is now married to our brother S.C. I won't go into details, but William saved Maggie from a fate worse than death. She was abandoned by her mother and wanted William to take on the responsibility of being her father, which he did. We got Chewoa recently when soldiers attacked her village. They killed her family and left her for dead. She will be living with Molly and Patrick. That's how we extended our family. Our family was able to purchase over 2,000 acres of land here. William was the only reason were are all still alive and the reason we have the land. He was nearly killed, but Molly brought him back both times."

The Flynns were spellbound by Mark's story.

"Is William alright now?" Anne asked.

"Not after seeing you in Erin today," Mark said. "Molly and William are very close and when he has a problem he spills his guts out to her. Molly agreed with him that a few days away might be good for him, so he left."

"I nearly forgot, we also have the Lewis family with us most days. They were squatters on our property and we made a deal with them that allowed them to stay. We gave them a small piece of our land. The mother, Fanny and the three children are becoming a real part of our family. Now the father Lewis, he's a different story. We just don't trust him, but we allow him to stay." Mark finished.

Anne walked away after Mark's summary. She felt terrible. Her family had heard the story of the carnage that took place around the village of Killeagh. Her brother Patrick recanted the story that was told to him in Fermoy about the Webb compound. The story told was that a single man with only a few knives had killed many of Lord Webb's men. The story went on to say that he burned the entire compound to the ground and Webb only survived because he had left for Dublin that day to report the uprising. Martial law was declared and all Irishmen in the area were to be confined to their houses under penalty of death. That's when the Flynn family left for Dublin to go to America. Anne had heard in Dublin before they boarded the ship that a William Mountain was captured, given twenty lashes and was then hung until he died. She mourned him and was in a depressed state for months. She felt her life had slipped away.

Anne had met Jared in New York as they were waiting for transportation to travel up the Hudson River. He was nice to her and very handsome, but also very cocky, not the type of person that Anne was normally attracted to. She was still mourning William's death and was not ready for a new suitor. She told Jared her feelings, but he did not relent. He originally was going to Chicago to live with his wealthy family, but after meeting Anne he was going to follow her to the ends of the earth, if necessary. He professed his love to her and she rejected him. He said he would not give up and followed her to Erin.

Jared was staying in the little hotel in town and was waiting for an answer to his proposal. He had received a jolt of confidence today when Anne declared him her beau. He was certain she had finally given in and would accept his proposal for marriage. He could finally leave this hell-hole and get back to Chicago where his family was waiting for him. He knew Anne would reject their moving to Chicago, but after marriage she would have no choice but to do as he says. He was excited for the first time since he got here. He would talk to her tomorrow and convince her they should get married. He was a happy man as he headed toward the pub to celebrate his success.

William walked several miles and came across the campsite that Fox had called his home. There were skeletons everywhere, picked cleaned by the carnivores of the forest. As William walked through the ruins it brought tears to his eyes. He sat in the midst of the carnage and thought, when will this brutality ever end? He walked around the campsite trying to determine which of the corpses were Chewoa's mother and brother. He couldn't find them for sure and decided to bury the remains of those dressed in Indian garb. After gathering bones he buried them and for the first time in his life he said a prayer. He asked God for His forgiveness for all the people he had killed. He knew he was no better than the soldiers that slaughtered these women and children. He regretted all the killings, except Dante Wright. He deserved what he got and so did Webb, although he did not kill Webb. God would have to take care of him.

William was sad about the day's events but he had to do something about them. Molly was right; he needed to talk to Anne alone. The decision was made—he was going home to try and talk to Anne.

It took William several hours to get back home and there was Maggie waiting patiently for him.

"I'm sorry I didn't tell you I was leaving, but I've not been feeling well since seeing Anne Flynn," he apologized.

"I know you're upset," said Maggie. "Molly told me so. I'm sure you can work it out. I liked her and she would make me a good mother. Don't mess this up, please."

William just smiled as the two of them walked toward the house.

Mark was returning home and was all smiles as he jumped off the wagon and ran to William.

"I saw Margaret and she still loves me and still wants to marry me, can you believe that?"

William shook his hand and offered his congratulations. The rest of the family heard the commotion and came out to offer congratulations too. Mark was ecstatic and couldn't shut up. William was irritated and a bit jealous of him. He left the commotion and went to the corral to get the horses unleashed from the wagon. He had to get his mind off Anne.

Two days later on Sunday morning, a wagon carrying Margaret and Anne and their father Patrick Flynn, came down the dirt path to the Mountain property. Chewoa saw them first and rushed to tell the family someone was coming. The family gathered in front of the house as the wagon came to a stop. As the Flynns climbed down, Mark ran to greet them. Margaret and Mark embraced and after that they all came forward for introductions. One by one, the Mountain clan was introduced and exchanged small talk. Anne was very quiet, saying very little. She just smiled. William and Molly had been in the house and were late coming out. Molly introduced herself first to Margaret and said she was very happy to meet her. Patrick was next, followed by Anne. All the Flynns were stunned by Molly's beauty and Anne's mind raced with thoughts of William and Molly together.

Anne asked boldly, "Just who are you married to, Molly?"

"Why, I'm married to Patrick Mountain," Molly responded.

"For some reason I thought you were married to someone else," Anne said.

William said hello to Patrick and Margaret and asked them how difficult their trip to Erin was.

"It was a bitch, but we survived," Patrick said.

William asked if they went through Five Points in New York.

"Yes." Patrick explained that they had heard that Five Points was the most dangerous place in America, but they had no problems there. The gangs were fighting one another over territories and pubs and they were too busy to harass new immigrants.

Molly and Anne were engrossed in a conversation about Maggie and Chewoa. Anne was curious and wanted more background on the girls.

Molly said, "Anne, there is a story about both our girls, but William was the one who rescued them. He also rescued me and Emilia. Please ask him about the details. While you're discussing things with him, please be truthful and tell him you still love him. I can tell how you feel by just looking into your eyes."

Anne smiled at Molly and said, "You have good intuitions when it comes to me. That is exactly how I feel. I came here today to tell him just that. I hope he's not too upset with me for the way I treated him at the store."

Molly hugged Anne and said, "He'll get over it, and it will be nice having you as part of the family."

Anne strolled over to where William was standing and said, "Hello, William." She took him by the hand and guided him away from the others.

Once they were out of sight, Anne said, "William, I had heard you were dead, that you were whipped and then hung. We heard many conflicting stories while waiting for our ship to leave Dublin. We were told you killed many men and burned an important Lord's compound to the ground. They said you killed women and children too. I never knew what to believe, but I thought you were surely dead. Seeing you at the store confused and stunned me. I didn't know how to react. On top of it all you had a daughter with you. I was sure you were married and didn't wait for me."

William tried to get a word in, but much to his dismay, Anne would not let him speak. She said, "You keep quiet until I've finished. I cried myself to sleep every night on that ship and all I ever thought of was you. I knew my life would never be the same. I don't care what you have done in your past to get here but now that you're here, you are mine. I love you so much, you will never know how much and I'm here today to tell you that. If you still love me and I hope you do, I promise I will never leave you."

William blurted, "Can I talk now?"

She nodded her head as she wiped the tears from her eyes and said, "Yes, you may speak now, but I'd better like what you're going to say."

"What about your beau back in Erin? Will he not be upset?" William asked her.

"I don't know and I don't care. He's a stuffy ass," Anne said.

He slowly approached Anne and hugged and kissed her until she had to make him stop.

"We have a lot of catching up to do. First, are you still willing to marry me and if so, when? My uncle's house is very cramped?" Anne said.

William laughed at her comments and said, "We'll get married whenever you want. You can move in here until we marry. There is room."

Anne questioned William's motives. "Just how will you explain that to my father? I don't think that would be very ladylike and I certainly would not propose that to him, would you?"

William laughed and said sheepishly, "Do you think I'm insane? Why don't we get married at the same time that Mark and Margaret do, it will be a double wedding?"

The Flynns left for home all very excited, except for Anne. She had to stop and tell the stuffy ass Jared Wynn that she wouldn't be marrying him. That conversation went as well as possible. Jared used a few non-complementary words to describe his feelings toward Anne and left in a huff.

The Mountain men and the Flynn women were married on October 15, 1842 by the Justice of the Peace for the Wisconsin Territory. They were married in the general store with all family members present. The Flynn girls had new dresses and the Mountain men wore new britches and shirts. They all cleaned up very nicely. S.C. was Mark's best man and Patrick was William's. Maggie was the maid of honor for Anne and Aunt June was Margaret's. The wedding party, along with family and friends, celebrated at one of the pubs in town. Everyone was quite tipsy when they left for home. Mark and Margaret's home was completed with help from the two Patrick Flynns and all the Mountain men as well as Lewis. William and Anne's was almost complete, but livable.

After the weddings the family began in earnest working their farms. William, Anne and Maggie's home was completed in late December, just ahead of a major snow storm that dropped almost two feet of snow on the family farms. Luckily, the family had enough food and wood stored for the winter.

William told Anne, "It's a time to relax and make a baby."

Chewoa and Maggie had approached William before the weddings and asked if he would teach them how to throw a knife.

William was surprised by the question and asked, "Why in the world would you two want to learn how to use a knife?"

"To protect ourselves from the likes of Grey Hawk, that's why," Chewoa responded.

William told both of the young ladies, "I'm here to protect you. That is my job and that is also the job of all the Mountain men."

Chewoa and Maggie were adamant about learning how to defend themselves. Realizing that the girls would not give up and there was ample time to commit to their training, William reluctantly agreed.

William started out showing the girls the correct way to hold the knives, how to sharpen them, the use of the sheath and the care of storing them. The girls grew tired of the basics of knife care and wanted to get right to throwing. William told both of them that would be the last thing on his list. He wanted them to be prepared, but understand that this could be a dangerous weapon and could be used to kill a person. It was not a toy or plaything.

After a week of fumbling while drawing the knives out of their sheaves, the girls finally got the hang of it. Chewoa immediately understood how to grip the knife, but Maggie was a bit slower. Chewoa also had her own knife, given to her by her father when she was ten years old. She had used it only as a tool for cooking or cleaning wild game, not as a weapon. That would change. Chewoa was bound and determined to learn the art of throwing this knife. No longer would she have to rely on someone else to protect her. She had her father's sense of survival and his ingenuity.

The girls worked on their skills every day, whether it snowed or was freezing cold. If the conditions were poor they would move inside to the cellar to hone their skills. Chewoa quickly became an expert in hitting her targets. Maggie was a bit slower to learn, but was very determined to learn this skill. William had given Maggie one of his knives; he felt there was no reason to carry anymore than one knife while working on his farm. There was still a fear in William's mind of reprisals from the folks back in Ireland. But regretfully, it was slowly diminishing.

After several months of practice the girls were ready for a hunt. William took the girls into the forest and explained the art of hunting as he knew it. Chewoa however, had learned from the best, her father. She knew how to stalk game and to hide her scent. She was patient, like

William, and could lay in wait for hours for a rabbit or squirrel to come into sight. Maggie did not have the patience that Chewoa had, but loved to be in the forest with her dad and her best friend.

William watched Chewoa in amazement at her throwing skills. He thought she must have inherited her father's skills. She could throw a knife with such force that she killed a small doe after many try's. She could hit a bird in flight and even killed a goose by a pond. Even William had never attempted that. William assured her that throwing a knife at a human being was a completely different skill, but if anyone ever threatened Chewoa or Maggie, he knew Chewoa would have the courage to protect both of them. He was not so sure Maggie had the killer instinct that Chewoa appeared to possess.

Molly and Anne were a bit worried that the girls were spending too much time with the knives and not enough time with schoolwork and chores. William insisted that the winter was for leisure and spring would come soon enough and the girls' workload would increase. In the meantime, he said, let them have fun.

Chewoa was relentless in her pursuit of perfection in the art of throwing knives. William had bought both girls new knives while on a trip to the town of Erin. He also bought both of them new sharpening stones and spent several hours instructing them on how to keep the blades razor sharp. Both girls could now throw with either hand with deft accuracy. Maggie was not quite as athletic or strong as Chewoa, but had no problems hitting the targets William set up for them.

William emotionally stressed to both the girls, "Your new skills are for hunting, nothing else. I don't expect you'll ever need those skills for anything else, but I'm happy to have someone to hunt with."

Spring was a welcome event for the Mountain clan, having come surprisingly early in late March. The Mountain men were able to till their fields and plant their seeds in mid-April. Lewis helped, as expected, and the men returned his effort and helped him. The Mountain family was only farming about 300 of the 2,000 acres they eventually expected to have under plow. It would take several years to get up to capacity, but the family was very happy with their current progress. Property values had soared in the last year as more immigrants poured into the area. Land was selling at approximately $3.50 an acre and was expected to reach a high price of around $5.00 an acre within a few years. The town of Erin was also booming, with more stores and businesses opening monthly. There were so many new faces in town and the surrounding area that the Mountain family realized they knew very few of their neighbors.

After the seeds were planted, the boys worked mainly on cutting trees and clearing the land of the stumps. The job was labor-intense and backbreaking. The trees had a good purpose though; they would provide heat for all the family's houses next winter. The women planted vegetable gardens close to their houses. All helped one another getting the gardens tilled and planted. Rabbits were welcomed intruders by the women. Maggie and Chewoa had accepted the job of killing as many of them as possible for the evening meals.

Sunday was a day for rest. The family got together for a homemade religious service with S.C. officiating. Prayers were said as a group and all took time to thank the Lord for all his blessings. The family members agreed the biggest blessing of all was getting them safely to Wisconsin Territory. Thank the good Lord. Life here was wonderful. William, however, couldn't completely agree with them. He still feared that Lord Webb, with his wealth and influence, could find them with little trouble here in America. William, regretfully, had good intuitions.

CHAPTER 31

Kilkenny, Ireland

WILLIAM HAD GIVEN THE THREE GIRLS he set free from Lord Charles Webb's compound back in Killeagh, Ireland some simple instructions before they parted ways: use the back roads to travel, and do not let anyone know what happened at the estate that day. William regretted that he had said his name and the town he was from to those girls; he also remembered that he agreed to take Molly along with him to Americay in front of them. He knew the threat these girls represented to him if Lord Webb ever got his hands on them. As he settled into family life in Whisk-con-sin, however, he didn't realize at the time how great the threat was.

After William and Molly headed south toward the Cove of Cork, the three girls headed north, as planned, in the direction of Belfast, on the workhorses William had confiscated from the Webb estate. The girls, Katie, Bonnie and Marie were all elated about their escape from a potential lifetime of misery. They were excited about their futures and about all the coins that William had given them to start their new lives. They did not stay off the main roads and travel at night, however, as William had instructed them to do. He also told them to make up a story of where they were from and where they were going. In addition, they were to make up a story of how they acquired their coins. In their jubilant mood, the girls had done none of what they were told.

After traveling for a few days, but still in southern Ireland, the three girls were stopped by James Browne, a constable from the Town of Kilkenny. Constable Browne wanted to know where the three young girls in rags got the expensive workhorses. The girls had not prepared themselves for the questioning and the experienced constable knew how to confuse them. He questioned each of the girls alone and they all came up with different stories. Before Browne locked them all up, he found their coins during the body search. That led to more questions that the girls were unable to answer.

The girls were beaten by the constable and some of his men and were threatened with a whipping at the local town post. The girls broke down and told Browne they had escaped from the Webb compound where they had acquired the coins. The constable had heard rumors about Webb's compound being burnt to the ground. He instructed one of his men ride to the Township of Killeagh to retrieve Webb's representatives to aid in the questioning. He also figured there would be a handsome reward for information about how the fire was started and who was responsible. Browne knew the girls were not smart enough or strong enough to pull off a theft like that without help.

Browne's man rode straight to the Township of Killeagh and out to Lord Charles Webb's burned out compound. He was searched and tied up until the new overseer could question him. Webb's men had been severely reprimanded for their lackadaisical effort in guarding the compound the night of the fire. The new overseer was named Ed Conley, a hardened man with a criminal background. He was well suited as Webb's right hand man. Conley was a tall and muscular man of forty-four years. He was unattractive, actually very ugly, with a pocked face, large nose and protruding ears. He once killed a man that joked, "You were so ugly when you were a kid your parents had to hang pork chops on your ears to get the dog to play with you."

Conley approached Browne's man with a menacing look on his ugly face.

"What the fuck is so important that you're interrupting us with all the cleanup we have to do here?" Conley asked.

The man said, "My boss is Constable Browne from the Township of Kilkenny. He's apprehended three young women that supposedly escaped from this compound the night it was burned. They were riding on horses they say they stole from Lord Webb. Constable Browne thought Lord Webb might be offering a reward for information on who burned it down. He thinks he has that information."

"Lord Webb will be gone for several months and won't return until we've rebuilt the compound. Tell Browne to hang onto the women until Lord Webb gets back and then we'll pay him a visit," Conley told him.

The man answered, "Do you want us to hold them indefinitely then?"

"Yes that is exactly what I want," Conley responded. "We may not get there for several months, but Lord Webb will pay all the expenses and will also pay Constable Browne a handsome reward."

Lord Charles Webb and Ed Conley and three bodyguards arrived six months later. Webb was in a rage. He rushed in the cell and dragged Bonnie out by her hair. Bonnie was the young woman that Dante Wright had raped in the upstairs bedroom. After killing Wright, William burned down the barracks that housed some of Wright's men, with Bonnie's help. Webb slapped her across the face four times as hard as he could while Conley held her. Her face immediately turned bright red and her nose began to bleed profusely.

"Who burned my estate? Who burned my estate?" Webb kept saying over and over again.

Bonnie was crying so hard she couldn't answer. Conley went back into the cell and dragged out Katie. He held her with her arms behind her back as Webb began slapping her.

"Who burned my estate? Who burned my estate?" Webb questioned her. He finally said, "Bring in that last whore, I'll kill her first and then the other two."

Katie screamed, "I know who did it, I know who did it, if you promise not to kill us, I'll tell you."

"I'll promise you all that I will not kill any of you, as long as you tell me who burned down my goddamn estate and where I can find that person," Webb said.

Katie said slowly, "I think he called himself William Mountain, from the town of Killeagh. He and the pretty young girl named Molly McCarthy said they were going to go to Americay. William was meeting his cousin and two brothers at the Cove of Cork. He gave us the coins for what he said we endured and to help us find a new life in Belfast. That's all he said to us. It's the truth. Now, can we go?"

"Thank you for your honesty," Webb said. "I said I wouldn't kill any of you and I won't. But constable Browne here will have you shipped to Australia to our famous penal colony, where you can live out the rest of your lives. That will be your punishment for stealing from me. I hope you enjoy it— most women don't." The girls looked at Webb with horror in their eyes. They had heard of atrocities committed by the guards and the inmates there. The men had a very hard life there, but the women had it harder. There would be no return. It was a death sentence.

Webb looked back at Browne and said, "Take care of these women and make sure they're not harmed. Get them shipped out as soon as possible. You keep the horses, as well as all the coins you found."

"Lord Webb, won't you need one of these girls to identify this Mountain fellow?" Browne asked.

"I don't need to identify him, he'll be with Molly McCarthy and we all know what she looks like. She's beautiful and she's going to be my woman. I guarantee the Mountain fellow will not let her out of his sight. We find her and we'll find him," Webb said.

Webb continued, "Now I have another proposal for you. I need your services immediately. You take my overseer Ed Conley and as many men as you can muster up and go to Cork. See if the Mountain boy is still in Ireland and if he is, my man Conley here will kill him, but not before he suffers greatly. Find that girl, Molly McCarthy and bring her back to Killeagh. You'll all receive a large reward. Remember the girl is not to be abused in anyway. I'll be back at my estate, return her to me there. In the meantime lock up these three until you get back."

It took several days to find enough men to agree to go to Cork and find the one man that burned down Webb's compound. Most of the prospective deputies wanted no part in hunting down someone with the skills to kill so many and turn a fort such as Webb's into ashes. That man was someone to be feared.

With much prodding, Browne finally found a suitable number of men to accompany them to Cork in search of Molly McCarthy and the killer William Mountain. It took five days to reach the Cove of

Cork. The men searched the pubs, stores and booking agents looking for William Mountain to no avail. They decided they would refine their search and use a description of Molly instead. Immediately, people remembered the beautiful Molly. The pub owner where William and Molly ate remembered her, as well as the booking agent. He didn't remember the Mountain boys, but who could forget her. The boys had registered under the last name of Donahue, William's mothers' maiden name, just in case someone would try to follow them. Browne found out they had taken a sailing ship called *Schuylkill* to the Port of New York that left seven months before. The agent said the trip would likely take six weeks to reach New York. Browne was perplexed and unsure what to do next. He dispersed his men and he and Conley headed to Killeagh to explain to Webb what they had found out. He was sure Webb would be upset and hoped he would not take out his frustrations on him.

When they entered Webb's compound the place had a rancid odor. The smell of smoke was still coming from the burned foundations. The fowl odor of decaying animals and humans was almost gone. The stone foundations remained standing and carpenters had been working non-stop for months trying to rebuild the compound. Webb had set up his headquarters in the only building left standing, the first barracks where William had slayed six men while they slept. Webb had a small office on the first floor and met Browne and Conley there. Browne explained the difficulty of trying to find William Mountain. He told them they refined their search using a description of Molly instead of William and everyone remembered her. He gave him the name of the ship and said they were going to the Port of New York. Webb stolidly smiled and thanked him for his service and said a reward would be forthcoming. Browne was told he could return home, which he did.

Webb had Conley rounded up several of his bodyguards and headed immediately for Dublin. His plan was to see an Englishman by the name of Rodger Young, who was a man with a criminal past and who could get things done, for a price. Webb needed professionals for this job not some local small town constable. A member of the English Parliament, who wanted no part in Webb's plan, arranged a meeting with Young.

Rodger Young was a man of about fifty years of age, with a full head of blond hair, a short man, all of five foot six with a very muscular body. He appeared to be an intelligent man as he spoke articulately about his credentials. Rodger was born in London and came to Dublin twenty or so years before. He was contracted to hunt down a few Irish rebels for some important Englishmen stationed in Dublin. He did his job and was rewarded handsomely with land and gold. He remained in Dublin and set up a covert business doing special "projects" for wealthy people, projects which could or would end in someone's death if the customer requested it. Young was always paid in advance for his efforts and stood by his motto: "No job is too big, or too dangerous, to be completed in the allotted time. If not satisfied with the results, all funds will be returned." Young reminded all potential customers that no one had ever asked for their money to be returned.

Webb explained to Young that his business had to be conducted in America and it could be very dangerous. He would need to take several assassins with him and that the cost would be no object. He wanted William Mountain to die an agonizing death. If there were family members that helped Mountain, then he wanted them killed too. He wanted a young woman by the name of Molly McCarthy returned to him unharmed, if possible. Webb would give him as many details as he had, but Young would have to do the detective work to find out where they went in America.

Young didn't say anything for quite some time. In his mind he thought that this job could earn him enough to retire very comfortably and live a life of leisure. He had never undertaken a job with these requirements. Travel to an unknown country, in search of a man and woman that no one could identify would be difficult task, but doable.

"Lord Webb, I'm honored that you feel that I am qualified for such a difficult assignment," Young said. "I'm confident I can complete this task, but I will tell you in no uncertain terms that it will be costly. I'll need a minimum of six full time experienced mercenaries to travel with me. In addition, I may need to hire more after we arrive at our destination in America. Travel expenses will be high and there will be bribes to be paid. I could not even give you estimate of costs of venture like this."

"Cost is not important! I want this Mountain boy to suffer for what he did to my estate," Webb said. "I want the girl back here so she will also suffer for aiding in his escape. Now, I'm prepared to extend to you fifty thousand pounds in advance for your services. There will be another fifty thousand pounds waiting for you when you return with the girl and show me proof that Mountain is dead. I realize this job may take a year or longer, so I am also prepared to pay your six mercenaries a total of twenty thousand pounds for their work, but their expenses will come out of the first fifty thousand pounds that I pay you in advance. That's my first and final offer, if you succeed you will be a rich man. If you fail, you'll still be well compensated for your efforts. I need an answer now."

Rodger Young thought this could be the job of a lifetime and he would be a fool not to accept. What an adventure this would be. It would be relaxing, as well as stimulating and what could be more enjoyable than hunting down an Irish farmer.

Young extended his hand to Webb and said, "I'd be happy to accept this assignment. The terms are agreeable and I believe we can be ready to leave within two months. We'll take a ship that leaves Dublin harbor and head for America as soon as possible."

They shook hands and Webb gave Young instructions for where he could pick up his retainer and expense money.

Because of his line of work, Young had known and hired many mercenaries throughout the years. He had no problem rounding up some very talented killers who would be happy to do a job for two thousand pounds and get a chance to see America. Young had no plan to pay these thugs the twenty thousand pounds Webb had set aside for them. They'd get what Young decided to give them. Expenses were a different story, however. Good accommodations for the men would be essential to their happiness. Good horses and guns would be a priority as well.

Six men reported to the pier in Dublin on May 16, 1842 for the trip across the Atlantic. Jack Gregory, also called One-Eyed Jack, for obvious reasons, was noted for his use of knives in close combat. Adam Price was a drifter and an expert with a sword and short saber. Peter Clark was an expert in hand-to-hand combat and well versed in the use of all weapons. Harold Morgan was an expert with a whip and an excellent sharpshooter with a pistol. Reid Harris was also a sharpshooter, and Travis Collins was an expert in killing with any weapon.

Before the men boarded the sailing ship called *The Othello*, Young gathered them all together and handed each of them a new handgun. The handgun was called a Colt revolver. It would hold six bullets and could fire all six within seconds. Young had paid a high price for this new technology to make sure his men were properly armed. They were all impressed. They dropped their flintlock pistols in the trash. This new weapon would change their jobs for the better. In addition to the guns, Young wanted all his associates well dressed and presentable. He took them to a local haberdashery to get them dressed properly. Young explained to the men that he would provide the funds, but it was mandatory to upgrade their wardrobes. He wanted a uniformed look, with matching linen Dusters overcoats and broad brimmed hats. The men were outfitted with cotton shirts, ties, vest, coat, and riding breeches. When they were fitted with the new clothing, Young was happy with the look, although the men were not. They appeared as gentlemen, which ran against their grain.

Rodger Young knew this would be a very long trip. They were leaving in the middle of May and Mountain and the woman would have almost a one-year head start on them. He also realized that trying to find them if they left New York would be very difficult. The search in New York could take another two or three months and if they left the city, it could take over a year. Now Young was concerned that this job could take two to three years. That length of time would take a drastic cut into his profits. He wondered if he hadn't thought this job through properly. He didn't take into account the vastness of the country they were going to. He thought he would have to offer incentives to his men to get the job completed within two years. He also worried how this group of mercenaries would get along with one another during this extended manhunt. He would know more about his men after a few weeks aboard a cramped ship. If they didn't kill one another on the ship, they might make it. He was worried, however; he knew he would have little control over them. Money was the only thing that could control men like this.

Before leaving port, *The Othello* ship's captain, Peter Duffy, decided to address all the passengers on board about the perils that lay ahead for them. They were leaving early in the year, he explained, and the weather would be unpredictable. The likelihood of a slow trip was strong, and it was quite possible that they might encounter many storms. He also warned them to be prepared for seasickness because of rough seas.

Young and his men found an area below the ship's deck where they could have some privacy, albeit in very cramped quarters. Young had told his men not to talk to anyone about their mission. The last thing he needed was to have the law inquiring about his kidnapping and murdering plans.

After leaving port, *The Othello* was overcome by foul weather almost immediately, and it did not let up for the entire voyage. Seasickness and typhoid infected almost all of the passengers and most of the crew. Young lost two men to typhoid, One-Eyed Jack and Adam Price. Their bodies were buried at sea with twenty-five other passengers that all perished within days of one another. All told, seventy five passengers died of related illnesses out of the two hundred and eighty that boarded the ship in Dublin. Young's two men were buried in their new clothing, but without their new weapons. Young had confiscated those.

CHAPTER 32

Assassins in America

THE TRIP, WHICH DID NOT BEGIN until May 16, 1842, ended at the Port of New York on July 15, 1842, nine weeks after departure from Dublin. The many storms, high winds and rough seas threw the ship off-course daily. The passengers and crew were haggard and in surly moods when they docked. Young and his men had lost extreme amounts of weight and were in a weakened state. Young knew it would take a few weeks of rest and food for the men to gain their strength back. This delay was costly for Young, but the only saving grace was he was not going to replace the two men he lost at sea. He would complete the job with the four of them or hire cheap labor along the way.

Young's group of mercenaries found lodging at a hotel called The Points, located in Five Points, New York. They immediately went to the Beef and Brew Saloon for dinner and libations. They ordered beef, potatoes, bread and lots of beer. Young allowed no whiskey until their job was completed. The men spent two weeks recovering from the trip. They had regained some of their weight loss, but not all. Young told them it was time to work. The men spread out in Five Points and asked questions to a reluctant audience. People in the Points knew to keep their mouths shut. Young was upset; more than three weeks had passed and they knew no more than they did when they started.

Young set out without his men and entered a pub that was called the Cellar Dwellers. Young had heard the person to speak to was Cory Lambert, the boss of the Paradise Squirrels gang. The two sat at a table in the back of the saloon. Lambert now owned the saloon, but the previous owner was a dead boss by the name of Desmond Delaney.

"What do you want?" Lambert asked Young.

Young answered, "I need information and since everyone around here is so tight-lipped, I thought I'd come to someone who would not be."

"Information in Five Points is expensive and everyone knows that only a few can sell it," Lambert said. "So what exactly do you want? I'll tell you the cost and help you if I can."

"I'm trying to locate an Irishman by the name of William Mountain and a beautiful woman that accompanied him to America named Molly McCarthy," Young explained. "You may not remember Mountain, but I hear the woman is something special to look at."

Lambert was stoic, but grinned slightly before he said, "I'll check with my associates and see if anyone remembers either of the two. Come back tomorrow around noon and I'll have an answer for you. In the meantime, know this: the cost for any information as to their whereabouts will cost you 2,000 pounds silver. If you want us to find them for you, it will be 10,000 pounds silver, dead or alive."

Although Young thought the cost was exorbitant, he knew he had limited options. "I will agree to your price for the information if you have some, but I will not need any other help. See you at noon tomorrow."

Lambert immediately put Chuck Foley, his second in command, in charge of scouring Five Points for information.

Foley set the information mill in motion by having his men check all the pubs in the Five Points Paradise Park area. Several men remembered a beautiful woman that was accosted last year in the park by Desmond Delaney. She was with a group of Irishman that they thought had just got off the ship from the homeland.

One of the men said, "Wasn't that the one they called the Knife Man? He was the man that took down Desmond Delaney."

Upon hearing that comment, Foley remembered William and the note that was left on Delaney, it was signed William Mountain from the Village of Killeagh, County Cork, Ireland. He also remembered that he and his men were paid well for their part in killing Delaney and his men.

He rushed back to the Cellar Dwellers and sought out Lambert. He explained what he had heard and the connection between Mountain and Delaney.

"This is very interesting," said Lambert. "Didn't Delaney post a reward for this Mountain fellow and the girl?"

"I believe you're correct, but I don't know what happened regarding it. Give me a week or so and I'll have this all figured out," Foley answered.

"I'll just stall my customer. If we can provide good information it will be worth the wait," Lambert replied.

Young arrived at the pub at exactly noon accompanied by one of his men, Reid Harris. Harris stood well behind Young as he and Lambert discussed the information. Young agreed to wait for a week if necessary and would return at noon the following Friday.

The men shook hands and Young smiled and said, "I assume it will be good news."

Lambert responded, "Yes, count on it, and bring the silver."

Chuck Foley knew he had limited time to acquire more information regarding the elusive William Mountain and his girlfriend Molly McCarthy. Foley and his men searched the saloons, pubs, brothels and whorehouses trying to reach as many of the Five Points criminals as possible. They found several that remembered Mountain, but only one that remembered the girl. He was a southerner, ex-soldier, ex-tracker, named Burt Shane. Shane remembered them well, as he walked with a limp because of a knife thrown by Mountain on a tenement house staircase just north of Five Points. He was tracking the woman to earn Desmond Delaney's reward for her whereabouts. Two of his friends died at Mountain's hand that day as well. He had heard that they left the Five Points area and went into Seneca Village, the Negro community. Someone located them but the Negroes would not give up their location. A while after Delaney's death, Shane heard that the crazy family left New York on a riverboat on the Hudson River.

Foley arrived at the docks on the Hudson River just before sunset and went to the booking agent's office. He and his men threatened the office manager with a knife and searched the booking manifest for the names of Mountain, McCarthy or Donahue around the end of February. The names Donahue and Campbell appeared on the manifest leaving on February 26, 1842. The steamship, *The Get Away*, was captained by Jimmy Hart. Foley knew Hart well. He was a regular customer at the pubs owned by Cory Lambert. This was all he needed. He returned immediately to Five Points and ran into the Cellar Dwellers with the good news. Lambert was elated. He knew he would soon be 2,000 pounds richer. Lambert asked Foley to find out where Young was staying and have him come over right away.

Young said he would be at the Cellar Dwellers within a half hour. He wanted all his men present and well armed in case Lambert planned on a double cross. Young and his men were packed and ready to travel. When Young reached the pub he was escorted to the back room where Lambert and his men were waiting. Young and his men, wearing matching dusters and wide brimmed hats, were impressive. Lambert liked the look and wished he had enough control of his men to match the look.

Lambert got right to the point and explained all he knew. Young was a little disappointed with the skimpy amount of information.

"This is good news, but where in the hell were they going?" Young asked.

Lambert shrugged and said, "All you need to do is find Jimmy Hart, the ship's captain, and you'll find their destination. In the meanwhile, I'll take the 2,000 pounds silver we agreed upon."

Young knew he couldn't start a confrontation in this saloon or any place in Five Points, at least not at this time. He knew better. They would eventually have to come back through Five Points to get back to Dublin.

He reluctantly paid for the information and told Lambert, "I hope someday you can repay me when you're looking for someone in Dublin. Thank you," he said sarcastically, "For your help."

Young and his men headed for the Hudson River in the hopes of finding Jimmy Hart. It took most of the day to find the booking agent that represented the steamboat that Hart captained. Young bought only one ticket for passage to Albany, fully expecting to interrogate Hart before the ship left the dock. Upon boarding the ship very early, Young immediately found Hart in the wheelhouse. He approached Hart in a lackadaisical manner, inquiring how a steam powered boat worked. After Hart took him below to show him the engine, Young pulled out his revolver and shoved it under his chin.

"If you want your head to remain on your shoulders, I suggest you answer all my questions truthfully," Young threatened. "I want to know everything you know about William Mountain and Molly McCarthy, do you understand!"

Hart was so petrified he wet himself. He said, "I met a fellow named William and a woman named Molly a while back right here on this boat. My woman introduced me to both of them, I'm not sure of their last names."

Young interrupted, "Where is your woman and where did she meet them?"

"She lives with me in Albany and I'm sure she could answer your questions," Hart said. "She's had a hard life, but things are going nicely for us now."

"My men and I are going to Albany with you, and if your woman cooperates with us, you and she will have a nice reward. If not, well, you don't want to know the if-not," Young said.

Young's men purchased tickets and boarded the ship immediately. The trip to Albany took three long days and the men were getting surly and began to act like caged lions ready to attack. Tempers flared and the rest of the passengers, as well as the crew stayed clear of Young and his men. Hart was frightened out of his mind and holed up in his cabin as much as possible. When the ship reached the docks at Albany, Young found Hart locked in his cabin. He kicked the door in and grabbed Hart by the arm and escorted him off the ship. Young, his four hired hands and Hart went directly to Hart's modest home a few short blocks away from the docks.

As the group approached Hart's house, the front door flung open and a very intoxicated Sarah O'Grady stepped out and slurred the words, "Welcome home Jimmmy darling, it looks like you brought us some company."

Hart rushed to the door and shoved Sarah into the house, followed by Young and his men.

"Goddammit Sarah, sober up and listen to what I have to say," Hart said angrily.

A blurry-eyed Sarah was stunned and quietly sat down and listened.

Hart began, "Sarah, these men are looking for William Mountain and Molly McCarthy. Do you remember where they were going? We need to give these men the answers to that question now! Do you hear me, now!"

Sarah smiled and said, "Jimmmy, slow down, of course I know where my daughter was going. She was going to Whisk-con-sin, wherever the fuck that is."

Young approached Sarah, grabbed her by the throat and lifted her off the chair. He slammed her head against the wall. The blow almost knocked her out, but she regained some sensibility.

Young shouted, "Listen you bitch, answer my questions. Is your fucking daughter named Molly? What is Whisk-con-sin and where is it? Who was traveling with them?"

Sarah sobered up and began to cry. She was trembling and crying harder and louder and was unable to speak.

Young grabbed her again by the throat and screamed, "Enough of the blabbering bullshit, stop crying now or I kill your man. If that doesn't sober you up I'll cut off all your fingers one by one. Now tell me what I want to know."

Sarah sobbed, "My daughter is Maggie not Molly. William Mountain is a killer and he is with his family, two brothers and a cousin. I don't remember their names, but Molly is with them. There was another girl too, Emilia, I think. My daughter didn't want to stay with Jimmy and me, so William said he'd take her to Whisk-con-sin. I don't know where Whisk-con-sin is, I only know that's where they were headed."

Young screamed again, "You let your fucking daughter go with a man you didn't even know, to a place you didn't know? Bullshit! Cut off her finger."

Travis Collins unsheathed his large bladed knife and grabbed Sarah's hand, placed it flat on the table and cut off her pinky finger like he was chopping celery. Sarah snapped out of her alcohol induced stupor immediately and began screaming in agony. Blood flowed all over the table and down to the floor as Collins prepared to cut another one off.

Sarah screamed, "Stop, that's all I know, please stop!"

Young said to Jimmy Hart, "If you want your girlfriend to live, she or you better tell me something, now!"

Jimmy said, "They had to be going up the Erie Canal to the Lake Erie. If they were going to Whisk-con-sin they had to go from Erie to another lake called Lake Michigan. From there I imagine they went to Chicago then onto Milwaukee, Wisconsin. That's all I know about traveling west."

Young and his men left Sarah and Jimmy in rough shape. Besides the finger, Young had Collins beat her with a closed fist until she passed out. Jimmy got less, his eye was blackened and his nose was broken, but he would survive. They told Jimmy if he told anyone about this confrontation, he and his girlfriend would die a horrible death. Jimmy was no fool, he knew these were dangerous men and no one but he and Sarah would know what happened there that day.

Young and his thugs left to find passage up the Erie Canal to Lake Erie. They had to ask several people on the docks just exactly where Whisk-con-sin was and was it another country. Folks on the docks all smiled and told them the same thing, America is a very large country and Wisconsin is just a small territory in it. They also explained the spelling and pronunciation. The men boarded a Packet Boat on the Erie Canal on September 3, 1842. The trip would take approximately fourteen days.

When they reached Buffalo they were told that all travel on the Great Lakes had been suspended due to bad weather. Several large storms had hit the lakes and four of the fleet of five steamships had sunk or been washed ashore. The management of the shipping company said that the earliest the fleet would be operational for travel would be again in the spring when the ice was off the lakes, maybe next March or April. In any event, they would not be traveling anytime soon.

Young thought about going back to New York, but the thought of running into Jimmy Hart made him think otherwise. They would just have find lodging here in Buffalo and wait until spring. This delay could last five costly months.

Young had not figured this type of cold winter weather into his planning. He and his men had never seen cold such as this. The temperature was hovering close to zero degrees and several feet of snow covered the ground. The men had to purchase new boots just to keep their feet from freezing. On top of the cold, Young had to provide food and shelter for his men, which was an expensive undertaking since the only lodging left was at a very high-end hotel. With so many travelers stranded the costs soared. Food costs were high, but the liquor bill was higher. Since they were not working, Young allowed the men to drink hard liquor. Tempers also rose as the cramped quarters led to fights almost daily. Fortunately no one was maimed or injured too severely.

Lake Erie opened for travel on May 3rd, after the harshest winter anyone could remember. Young and his men left on the first ship out of Buffalo onto Lake Erie and headed toward Lake Michigan. The ship's captain told Young that the city of Chicago was very large and he was sure the information he needed could be obtained there for the right price. Young and his men reached Chicago in ten days on May 13, 1843 in a heavy rainstorm. They found shelter at a hotel near the docks and remained there for two days until the storm subsided. Young couldn't believe the horrible weather in this country and wondered how the residents could possibly live in these conditions. It was either cold, snowing, raining or the wind was blowing. They had not experienced a calm day since they left Ireland. He could hardly wait to get out of this Godforsaken country. Finding Mountain and the woman could not come soon enough.

They went back to the docks looking for dockworkers or ship crews that might remember the Mountain family or the beautiful Molly McCarthy. While questioning several dock workers, one man remembered two beautiful Irish women a year or so back. They were accompanied by three or four men and were staying with a ship's captain named George Feehan. The man pointed out the Feehan home that was only a few short blocks from the docks. Young and his men were almost ecstatic as they headed down the street to Feehan's house.

Young banged on the front door and soon an elderly man answered. Young introduced himself to Mr. Feehan and asked if they could come in and ask him a few questions. Feehan looked the group over and thought they could only mean trouble.

"I'm sorry, but I'm due at the docks, my ship leaves port in fifteen minutes," Feehan said. "Walk with me and I'll try and be of some assistance. What are your questions?"

Young liked this George Feehan immediately and smiled and said, "That would be fine."

Young explained that he was looking for a family with the last name of Mountain from County Cork, Ireland. George nodded and said that he had in fact had met the family and liked all of them. Young said he had some business with a William Mountain and was trying to locate him. Feehan asked Young if he could divulge what business he had with Mountain. Young said he was hired to seek out the Mountain family to settle a debt back in Ireland.

"I'm sorry, but the Mountain family I met were as poor as church mice," Feehan laughed. "You'll have no chance of getting money out of that group. They barely had enough money for food. In fact, they were going to a small farming community in southern Illinois called Hoopeston, to work on a large farm. Sort of a sharecrop deal. They met the owner while in New York City and he offered them housing, food and a chance to own some land for their labor. I encouraged them to take it. They were walking, all of them, the four boys and the three girls. That's all I know."

Young was skeptical of what Feehan had just told him, but it did seem logical. He knew they were likely penniless and an offer to work for a chance to own some property seemed like something a poor Irishman would do. No different than sharecropping in Ireland.

Young said to Feehan, "Are you sure that was their destination?"

Feehan responded, "That's what I was told, but maybe they lied to throw off folks like you. I just don't know. If you're serious about finding them, I'd at least check Hoopeston, it's only a few days ride."

Young told Feehan he appreciated his honesty as well as the information. They exchanged a cordial goodbye. George Feehan knew he and Mrs. Feehan would be taking a long trip as soon as these men left town. He knew their type, they were killers and they would not be happy with the detour George had led them on. Yes, he and the Mrs. would be taking a long vacation, perhaps somewhere in Michigan.

Young and his group of mercenaries left Chicago and headed directly south to the little community of Hoopeston. First, they had to purchase horses, saddles, bridles and saddlebags. Young had carried thousands of dollars in silver coins with him to pay expenses and it was cumbersome. He decided he would purchase a packhorse as well to carry the silver and other gear.

The men left Chicago on May 20th and had expected to get to Hoopeston in two days of hard riding. They were wrong. It took five days, just as Feehan had expected. After arriving in the Hoopeston area, Young and his men split up and went farm-to-farm trying to locate the Mountain family. Obviously, they didn't find the Mountains, but they did get some information that they could use in their search. A landholder by the name of Peter Schenk, a German immigrant, gave the men some sound advice. He said if this family was going to Whisk-con-sin, they should begin their search in Village of Milwaukee, at the land office. If they had any money that's where they would go to buy land. The land records there would show exactly where their land purchase was. Young realized Feehan had tricked them, but they would catch up with that old man on their way back to New York. He would be sorry he was ever born.

Young and his men arrived back at the docks in Chicago at the end of May. They purchased the tickets for the trip to Milwaukee and left an hour later. The cost of the tickets was much more than Young wanted to pay, but he realized the additional cost of transporting their gear and horses was cheaper than buying new in Milwaukee. The trip took three hours and when the ship docked they immediately unloaded and went to the land office. Since it was a Sunday the office was closed. Young wondered if anything would ever go right on this trip. Nothing had so far.

Monday morning, the Young gang were the first ones in line at the land office, which was quite crowded. David Smith, the land office official, greeted them. After some small talk was exchanged, Young got right down to business. He said they were in America from Ireland to locate a William Mountain and his family.

Young said, "The Mountain family and I are related and they told me to come here to Whisk-con-sin where I could find opportunities to begin a new life. I need to know where they settled so I can contact them."

"Mountain is an unusual name, so I remember them well," Smith said. 'There were two women and a child with them. Both women were beautiful, but the one called Molly, she was the most beautiful I've ever seen. They bought large tracts of land in Washington County near the Town of Erin. A real nice family."

Young lied, "Yes, they are a wonderful family and Molly and I are to be married when I get there. Now, where is this place called Erin?"

Smith was taken aback by Young's comments about marriage to Molly. He became suspicious immediately since Molly and Patrick signed land documents declaring that they were married and were co-owners of some of the Mountain property. Smith realized these men were up to no good. Since the land office records were public domain, he had no choice but to show Young where Erin was. He did however, have the right not to give them the location of the Mountain properties. He showed the men a map of Washington County and sent the group several miles east of the Mountain farms. He thought Young and his men would be forced to ask for directions once they reached Erin and maybe the delay would tip off the Mountains that trouble was brewing.

The trip to Washington County took three days. Young and his men reached the town of Erin and went to a pub immediately. They ordered beer and some jerky. They were hungry and thirsty and wanted to get this trip over with. They asked the bartender if he knew the Mountain clan and he said he didn't. He said that there were so many new faces in town and more came in daily. He just couldn't keep track of folks.

They then went into the general store and ask a similar question of William Fitzgerald. Fitz didn't like the looks of these men and he was not about to share information with them.

"I've never heard of them. Are you family?" Fitz asked.

Young smiled and said, "Yes, my sister is Molly McCarthy and I want to surprise her."

Fitz responded, "I wish I could help, but we have so many new people around here I can't keep track of them."

Young realized they would have to find the Mountains on their own. He had drawn a map of the larger map that Smith had shown him at the land office. They decided to save time and split up. Young wasn't sure the information he received from Smith was correct. He saw a distinct change in his attitude after he said he and Molly were to be married. He knew he screwed up.

"The likelihood of the Mountains being east is remote," Young told his men. "Harris and I will go east and check the farms in that area, you three go west. If you find them, remember the girl Molly is not to be touched. As for the rest of the women, you can do whatever you like. I will also give the man or men who kills William Mountain a 500 pound bonus."

The mercenaries headed west. They didn't split up as Young had told them to. They wanted a small army together when they met this notorious Mountain fellow. If he had killed so many and was able to burn down an entire compound full of men and escape, he was a man to be reckoned with.

The men stopped at several farms along the way. No one was eager to give out information. Most people in this area had escaped persecution in their homeland and were not in any hurry to pass out information on anyone.

The men finally approached the Lewis homestead. They asked Lewis about the Mountains and he quickly responded without much thought, "Why, da Mountains lives just down dis road. They done got four houses and they done share da land."

The men thanked Lewis for the information and left.

"Lewis, what have you done?" Fanny said after the men rode off. "You must go and warn them. Those men are trouble and you of all people should have known that."

"I'se knows dat. Let dem rich bastards fend for themselves, I'se not help'n," Lewis said. "Maybe we be get'n some money for tell'n on dem."

"You bastard, Lewis!" Fanny was surprised at Lewis and his comments. "All they have done for us and you don't care. Well I do!"

Fanny took off on foot and ran through the woods straight as the crow flies to warn the Mountains. She was too late.

The mercenaries rode into the front yard of Patrick and Molly's home. Chewoa and Maggie saw them first and hid behind the outhouse. Patrick, S.C., Mark and William were all working in their fields either clearing or plowing new ground. Anne, Emilia, Margaret and Molly were having lunch together in the house after a morning of helping with the tilling and planting of Molly's vegetable garden. Molly heard the horses come into the yard and came out the front door followed by Anne.

Harold Morgan had assumed the leadership role of this gang. He looked over the two women and said with a smile, "You must be the famous Molly McCarthy. I'd know you anywhere."

Molly was taken back a bit, but said, "Yes, my name is Molly, but it's not McCarthy, it's Mountain."

Morgan said, "I don't give a shit what your last name is, all I know is you're coming with us back to Ireland. There's a man named Lord Webb that wants to see you and I believe he wants to see you naked at that."

The men were all armed with their new revolvers and had them drawn.

"Get everyone out of that house, now!" Morgan demanded.

Emilia and Margaret came out reluctantly after trying to hide.

"Is this all of you fuckin' Mountain whores?"

Molly said sarcastically, "Yes, this is all of us whores."

"Now, I will only ask you once, if I don't get the right answer, one of you will die where you stand, understand?" Morgan said with a smile. "Where is William Mountain?"

Anne spoke, "William is my husband and he is working on our farm, just south of here. What do you want with him?"

"I hope he shagged you good this morning, because that's the last shagging he'll ever do. He dies today, in fact within minutes," Morgan said. "Collins, you come with me and we'll leave Clark and the packhorse here to make sure the ladies don't get into any trouble. Trouble will be coming soon enough when we get back."

Morgan and Collins rode south to the field where William was working. Chewoa had climbed into a back window and took a flintlock pistol out of the cabinet drawer. She loaded it and climbed out the window while Morgan was talking. She met Maggie behind the outhouse and told her they must warn William. Upon reaching the woods the girls ran into Fanny Lewis. Fanny told the girls what Lewis had done and that she came there to warn the their family but it was too late.

"Go find our men and warn them," Chewoa told Fanny. "I don't know what they can do, but maybe something."

After the girls split up from Fanny they ran as fast as they could through the woods to the clearing that William was working in. William had a plow attached to team of two horses and was tilling a newly cleared twenty acres of land. Chewoa told Maggie to go around to the other stand of trees and wait as the assassins approached.

Morgan and Collins rode close to where William was working. Their guns were drawn and pointed at William. William appeared puzzled by their presence. He was about to say something when Morgan fired his revolver. The bullet struck William in the right side of his chest and he dropped to his knees and hunched forward.

The men, still on their horses laughed as Morgan said, "You aren't so tough now, are you. You're just a fucking farmer. Know this, you'll soon be dead while me and my men will be enjoying your wife and the rest of your ladies. And that little Molly, we were told hands off of her, but I will guarantee you all of us will have our way with her."

William was almost unconscious as he raised his head and said, "You don't know our women and you'll all be dead before this day ends. Count on it."

Out of the dark shadows of the trees on the right, a very confident Chewoa slowly walked directly toward the men. Behind her back she carried a loaded flintlock pistol.

Morgan smiled and said, "What do we have here?"

Chewoa was dressed in her traditional Indian clothing consisting of a deerskin shirt with small beading, as well as a deerskin skirt and moccasins. Her father Fox, a great hunter and chief, had told her as a child the fastest way to get a man off a horse was to kill the horse. Chewoa pulled the flintlock from behind her back and in one motion shot Morgan's horse pointblank in the heart. The horse reared up, fell on its side and crushed Morgan's right leg, as Morgan had remained in the saddle. The force of the hitting the ground made Morgan lose his weapon. He screamed in agony. Chewoa calmly pulled out the knife from its sheath from behind her head and threw it into Morgan's chest. He continued to scream louder and yelled for Collins to help him. As Collins pointed his gun a Chewoa, out of nowhere came a second knife that lodged into Collins back, between his shoulder blades. It was Maggie, and her aim was deadly. Unbeknownst to Maggie, Collins was the man that tortured her mother and cut off her pinky finger.

"Attend to your dad, I'll take care of these two," Chewoa said to Maggie.

Chewoa pulled a second knife out of its sheath that was in her waistband. She approached Morgan as he was screaming obscenities at her. Morgan was dying. Besides the knife wound he had a compound fracture of his right leg and was bleeding freely from where the bone had pierced through the skin. The knife was protruding from his chest and Morgan tried in vain to remove it. Chewoa, without the slightest bit of emotion, calmly jerked the knife out. She grabbed a hand full of his hair and scalped Morgan without blinking an eye. Maggie was astounded at what she had done.

"Chewoa, we are not like them," Maggie yelled.

William in his weakened state said to Maggie, "Keep quiet child. She is doing what her culture has taught her to do, nothing more."

Chewoa went on to Collins who was also dying, grabbed his hair and scalped him too. Both men died shortly afterward.

Chewoa was completely in charge. She ordered Maggie to cut up the hem of her skirt to make bandages for William.

"We need to stop the bleeding, now!" Chewoa said.

While Maggie was cutting up her skirt, Chewoa unhooked the team from the plow and brought one of the workhorses over to where William was laying.

"We need to get him on this horse and get him home so Molly can help him." Chewoa said.

The girls strained themselves getting William on the horse. Once on the horse, William leaned forward and rested and let the horse take him home.

"Walk him back slowly to the homestead, I'll run ahead," Chewoa told Maggie. "I have work to finish. Before you leave, William, can you see this gun?"

Chewoa held up the new revolvers she had taken off the dead men.

William looked at it and said, "It's new. I don't know how it works."

Chewoa went into the woods, pulled the hammer back and pulled the trigger. The gun exploded and a new cartridge was in the barrel chamber immediately. This was a good sign. She went back in the clearing and confiscated all the bullets from the holsters and saddlebags. She also found a large supply of silver coins; she'd get them later.

She ran back to her house, well ahead of William and Maggie. She had one of the pistols in her waistband next to her knife on her backside. She did not intend to use the pistol. As she approached the house, Clark had all the women siting on the ground. He was taunting them and was telling them all the horrific things he was going to do with them. Molly was upset, her new born son James, had been sleeping and it was time for him to eat. She was worried this ugly man might kill her child.

Chewoa walked slowly into the yard from the forest. Clark didn't see her right away, but all the Mountain women did. Clark turned abruptly, to see a smiling Chewoa starring him down.

Clark froze and said, "Who the hell are you? You're an Indian, what the hell do you want?"

Chewoa replied in a very calm voice, "Yes, I am an Indian, and I'm very proud of it. Why are you threatening these women?"

"It's none of your business, now get your ass out of here before I kill you too," Clark said.

Chewoa was enjoying the banter. It was like stalking a rabbit, so easy. She moved closer and asked Clark, "Have you ever seen a weapon like this before?"

She had removed the gun from her waistband and presented it to Clark.

He asked, "Where the hell did you get this?"

Chewoa smiled, stepped back a bit and said, "From some of your friends that were trying to kill my uncle. They're both dead."

A stunned Clark shouted, "What the hell are you talking about, did this Mountain fellow kill my friends?"

"No he didn't, but I did and I enjoyed it, likely as much as I'll enjoy killing you," Chewoa replied.

He turned and pointed his weapon at Chewoa. Before he could cock the hammer on the pistol, a knife flew from Chewoa's hand and embedded into his chest. She made a direct hit to his heart. He never saw it coming. Clark slumped forward and died in his saddle. After Chewoa had taken his feet out of the stirrups, she was able to flip him out of the saddle and onto the ground. She then retrieved her knife and promptly removed Clark's hair from his head, as the Mountain women watched in stunned silence. Molly and Anne rushed to Chewoa to see if she was harmed. She told them she and Maggie were unharmed, but William was badly injured. Molly ran towards the field William had been working in and found Maggie guiding the workhorse down the path. One look at William and Molly knew William was in grave danger.

Fanny found the rest of the Mountain men and after they heard the gunfire they came running. They carried William into the house while Molly prepared to remove the bullet from his chest. Molly had removed bullets from men before, but not from a chest wound. Chewoa told Patrick she was sure there were more men after William. She handed the new weapons to S.C., who in turn gave one to cousin Mark.

"We need to be prepared if others come looking for William," Patrick said.

After a few hours Rodger Young and Reid Harris knew they were on a wild goose chase. The Mountain family clearly did not live in this direction from Erin. They turned back and were certain by now the other men had found the Mountain farms. Young's main hope was that his men had left the lovely Molly alone. They had been without a woman for several months now and nothing they did would surprise him. If they had already abused her, he would have to fabricate a story for Lord Webb. This far away from Ireland anything could happen. Young thought, "I am almost done with this shitty job that has taken so much of my time, as well as so much of my money." His retirement seemed only a remote possibility now.

Chewoa told S.C., Mark and Patrick to take the three new revolvers and look them over. She said they were easy to fire and were very accurate at least at close range. The boys wondered how she knew that. They would ask her questions later.

Maggie was in the house with the rest of the women and was very upset. Molly and Anne tried to calm her, but she wouldn't listen to them. She rambled on about William and about killing a man. Chewoa heard Maggie wailing and decided to quiet her. Chewoa approached her, grabbed her by the hand and escorted her out of the house.

Chewoa rested her hands on Maggie's shoulders and calmly said, "Stop your crying now! It does us no good! I'm sure there will be more of these men here any minute and I'll need your help. You killed a man; that's life. If you hadn't killed him, he would have killed your father, you and me. Pull yourself together. We're at war and you and I can help if we stay strong. You're a strong woman, Maggie! You showed me that today. Get yourself together."

Maggie moved her head up and down, indicating she was indeed ready. She dried away the tears and said, "I'm sorry to be such a baby. It will not happen again."

Fanny heard their exchange and smiled at Chewoa's courage, thinking it must be from her Indian blood. Maggie also impressed her; she thought she would also turn out to be a very strong woman.

Chewoa checked her knives and made sure the sheaths were tight. She asked Maggie to do the same, although Maggie carried only one knife. The Mountain men positioned themselves in the woods on both sides of Patrick's house. Each of the men had one of the new revolvers and a one-shot flintlock as a backup. If the intruders approached them from the road they'd be all right, but from behind would be a different story.

Young and Harris approached from the front, straight up the rutted dirt road. They saw Clark's horse and the packhorse, but not the others and that concerned them. As they rode close to the house, a young Indian girl came into view from the side of the house.

They halted their horses a few yards from the young girl and asked, "Where is the man that owns this horse, he is a friend of ours."

Chewoa sheepishly said, "I don't know, it was tied here when I got here."

"Who owns this property?" Young asked. "Is it William Mountain and Molly McCarthy?"

Chewoa calmly said, "Why no, it belongs to me and my people, we are the Menominee tribe and we don't like white intruders. You and your friend are white and you're intruding on our property."

Young turned and smiled at Harris, who smiled right back. Young turned back to face Chewoa. In less time than it would take to blink an eye, Chewoa launched a knife into Rodger Young's throat with such force he fell sideways off his horse. As Harris reached for his revolver a volley of shots echoed through the air. The Mountain men came from their hiding places and unloaded their pistols on Harris' carcass. He rolled off the saddle with his foot stuck in the stirrup as the horse reared up and ran down the road with Harris dragging behind. Young was trying to speak, but speaking was painful.

Chewoa walked over to him and said, "You are just like the men that killed my family and the members of my tribe. You will never kill anyone again. If I were you, I'd take this time to pray to your God for His mercy."

She flipped off his hat and much to his surprise, she grabbed a hold of his blond hair and removed it from his scalp. Blood flew everywhere and Young muttered in a whispered tone, "You are only a bunch of farmers, you cannot do this to us. We're trained professionals, this is no way to die."

S.C. walked up to where Young was laying, put a shell into the chamber of his pistol, and fired the round into Young's head. "Is this a better way, then?"

"Let's gather up all their weapons, horses and valuables," Mark said. "After that we'll bury these bodies deep in the woods. We must hurry in case there are more of them."

The family worked hard depositing the bodies. They took all their belongings into Patrick and Molly's house. The horses were put in the coral and the saddlebags and saddles were put in Patrick's cellar.

Molly had removed the slug from William's chest and bandaged him the best she could. S.C. asked her what his chances were and she replied, "Knowing William as I do, my guess is he will be up and around soon. His previous injuries were worse; he did not lose as much blood this time."

Fanny told all the Mountain family members she was sorry for what happened to William and it was her fault. She explained that Lewis, knowing these men were up to no good, told them where they could find the Mountain farms. "I tried to run and warn you all, but I was too late."

"I will never live a day with that man again," Fanny said. "I'm so ashamed this happened, but thank God it wasn't worse. Both those young girls could have been killed."

"What have we done to make him feel this way towards us?" S.C. asked.

"Nothing, you've all been very kind to us. But Lewis always remembered that confrontation he had with William and Molly and having to back down embarrassed him, she said. "His ego was bruised and he would not forget it. He had to get even."

"Go get the children and bring them back here. After you get back here we'll go have a talk with Lewis," S.C. told Fanny. "You may not ever see him again. Can you live with that?"

Fanny responded, "My children and I can live without him. I would have left him after this anyways. He has beaten and abused the children and me for the last time. Never again will I subject my children to a man like that."

After Fanny returned with her children in hand, S.C., Mark and Patrick headed to the Lewis homestead. Lewis was expecting the Mountain men and came out the front door and onto the porch armed with an old flintlock rifle.

"That be far enough, I'se knowed how to shoot and I'se don't care whose I'se be kill'n," Lewis said.

S.C. walked to the staircase of the porch with the revolver in his hand and said, "Lewis, you're not welcome on this property any longer. Now we will give you two choices; one, you can leave now and never come back and we will not harm you. Or two, you can die where you stand. It matters none to us. You have ten seconds to make a decision. Keep in mind we just buried five men today, one more will be no work at all."

"I'se be leaving, but I'se be taking the wife and the kids whit me," Lewis stammered.

S.C. quietly said, "You'll leave by yourself and with only the clothes on your back. Your wife wants no part of you. Don't come back; you're not welcome. If we see you around here again, we will shoot you down like a rabbit. Get off our property now!"

Lewis nodded and smiled. He then raised the old flintlock to his waist and pulled the trigger. The shot hit S.C. in the right thigh and knocked him to the ground. Mark and Patrick unloaded their new weapons into Lewis body. He died on his front porch without muttering a sound.

Mark and Patrick carried the wounded S.C. back to his house and Molly, Emilia and Anne came to tend to his injury. Margaret and Fanny and the children remained at Patrick's home. Mark returned to tell Fanny what had happened to Lewis. He asked her to step outside away from the children and then explained to her why they were forced to shoot him. She had heard the shots and had assumed the worst. She said she would tell the children and wondered if they could bury him immediately. Mark told her as soon as S.C. was patched up they would get him buried.

A week after the assault, the family members were still not at ease. They expected someone else from Ireland to show up at their doorstep at any moment. William was right. Webb had wide ranging tentacles.

The family had gone through the saddlebags and found thousands of dollars in silver coins. They a found note payable to a Rodger Young for fifty thousand pounds, signed by Lord Charles Webb, that appeared not to have been paid. There was also a receipt for an additional fifty thousand pounds that had been paid and another for twenty thousand pounds that also had been paid. The group informed William about the discovery of the notes. He was very upset by what they told him.

"Webb was willing to spend quite a fortune to find Molly and me. That is disturbing," said William. "Just think of the effort these men took to find us. It must have taken way over a year, perhaps two, to find us. I can tell you all this, we are not safe here. Fifty thousand pounds of notes were not cashed, meaning Webb has more resources to spend on finding us and will likely send more men. Provided he has not sent anyone yet, we have time to move on. We can sell our land, hopefully at a profit, and find a place further west to live. We cannot tell anyone of where we intend to move when we make that decision. I'm sorry I brought this upon us. It seems like everything that has happened to us is my fault. I could end all of this by going back to Ireland and have it out with Webb. He would be sorry he was ever born. Plus, it would catch him totally off guard. "

"William, you will not be going anywhere without all of us and we're not going back to Ireland," said Molly. "Anne would kill you first before she would let Webb do it. As you said, we can sell our farms and move. We've moved before and we can move again. We also will have more money than before when we add what was in those saddlebags."

Patrick interjected, "I agree with my dear wife. I'm not real crazy about waiting for the next assassins to come and to try and take my wife away. I say we find a buyer and get the hell out of here. I have Molly to worry about, but don't forget my little one, James."

The family, including Fanny, all voted to leave and move further west.

217

Patrick and Molly went into Erin the next week inquiring about potential buyers for their farms. William Fitzgerald at the general store told them that there were several wealthy and not so wealthy men looking to purchase farmland. He would make inquiries with them and would try and find qualified buyers. He said property in Washington County was trading somewhere between $3.50 to $4.00 per acre and there were many eager to pay the offered price.

Fitz suggested if the family wanted a quick sale, an offering price of $3.25 to $3.50 should get it sold quickly. Fitz asked the question that Molly dreaded, "Why in the world would you want to sell that wonderful property, after doing so much work to make it your home? Does this have something to do with the men that came looking for you last week? One fellow said he was your brother, was he?"

Molly answered, "Fitz, please don't think I'm being disrespectful, but we just do not want to share our reason for moving or where we are going. Please forgive us, but this is a personal matter."

"I've never had an issue with you folks, and I just want the best for you," Fitz told her. "Those men were trouble and I knew it. Whatever happened to them, happened, it is none of my business. I'll help you sell the property with no questions asked and at no cost to you."

Molly hugged Fitz and said, "Thanks you for your cooperation and your friendship."

Fitz had one more question. "What are Lewis and Fanny going to do? Are you giving them their land or will that be part of the sale?"

Molly cleared her throat, looked down and said, "Fanny and the children will be going with us. Lewis left them and we don't know where he went. Their property will be part of the sale."

"Enough said," Fitz replied.

Several months passed when Fitz showed up at the Mountains' homestead.

"I have some very good news for you. I have two buyers for your properties and they are willing to pay $3.65 an acre and an additional two thousand for the houses as they stand," Fitz said. "That would include Fanny's house as well. The total amount of the sale would be $11,125, which included the price for the houses."

The family offered Fitz $200 for brokering the sale, which he refused. The buyer agreed that payment for any crops sold this year would go to the Mountain family. In addition, the closing date would be April 1, 1844 and the family agreed they would vacate the property by that date. This would give William and S.C. time to recover from their injuries and time to prepare for their move.

After the family signed the sales agreement, Fitz sat them down and asked if they had considered a new destination. If not, he had a suggestion.

Since Molly was the designated spokesperson for the group, she said, "We have no idea where we're going yet, but if we knew we'd be reluctant to share that with you for your own good."

"I understand and thank you for that," Fitz said, "But I've heard that the Minnesota Territory is growing. I don't know much about it, but I've been told that there is rich farmland and it's cheap. The main problem as I see it will be the Indians. They're not real happy with the dirt farmers and they could likely be a problem. This is only a suggestion, but I think you should think about it."

They shook hands and thanked Fitz for the incredible job he did in brokering their property.

The Mountain family left their land in Washington County, Wisconsin for good on March 30, 1844. They left in five covered wagons with fifteen horses: eleven workhorses, and four of Rodger Young's riding horses. They left behind their furniture except beds and all their implements. They had enough food to last a month.

The travelers included Fanny, Jacob, Davis, and Emma Lewis; Mark and Margaret Mountain; Patrick, Molly, Chewoa and James Mountain; S.C. and Emilia Mountain; William, Anne, and Maggie Mountain, and William and Anne's unnamed, unborn baby. Also traveling with the family were their two dogs, Cy and Ned.

Their destination: unknown.

ACKNOWLEDGMENTS

I'D LIKE TO ACKNOWLEDGE SOME OF the folks who encouraged me to write this book. First, to my wife LaVonne, for putting up with a solid year of complaining that my writing was drivel. Without her encouragement this manuscript would never had been completed.

Second, to my three sons, Patrick, Mark, Scott, and my daughter-in-law Emilia Mountain for prodding me on to complete this book. Their enthusiasm always brightened my days.

I'd also like to thank Julie Barrett for her work on editing and formatting. She also worked diligently on proof-reading and getting the cover ready for printing. Her encouraging words helped eased my bruised ego. Also, to Julie Schrader at Minnesota Heritage Publishing for her help also with editing and formatting. Julie was the first to read the rough draft of my manuscript and encouraged me to complete it. Lastly, but clearly not least, thanks to my young Bulgarian friends Tisha and Nickolay Alexandrov. Tisha, an author herself, instructed me on how to begin the process of writing a book. I followed her instructions and the words just flowed.

www.ingramcontent.com/pod-product-compliance
Lightning Source LLC
Chambersburg PA
CBHW020312260626
47156CB00004B/1195